Modified Raptures

Jamie Spencer

Printed in the United States of America
ISBN 978-0-9983809-7-1

Contents

STAGE ONE: Shelley and Astrid

Yes. She'd as good as assured him of it nine hours ago. And yes, sure enough: there she was. That cascade of auburn hair. (No cornrows threading through it, true; no longer caged by that crimson baseball cap, granted.) It was true that he hadn't glimpsed those broad, bare and elegant shoulders. But her slender and finely-muscled build were now strumming a major chord or two. So was that warm but mischievous smile.

Scott Preston was in his third year as an English graduate student, his second as a Teaching Assistant. He'd been trying lately to climb out of a funk he'd been in for half a dead year. It'd been six empty months since his boyfriend, Visiting Professor Gavin Kuiper, had taken off—literally. It was true. His "Gav" was up there ("out there" is more cosmically accurate) on a planetary way-station, in perpetual stilled motion. Doing what? Educating. Educating whom? A parade of assorted technicians, botanists, astrobiologists—all of them prospective Martian settlers, pioneer

1

colonists. Up there, out there? What difference? Successive waves of them were racing in that same perpetual hover.

"Well, it serves you right," Scott sighed, repeating his usual murmur, "*Your* suggestion. *Your* dumb clever idea."

"Ground Hog Day" is the term Americans apply to what astronomers call the annual winter "crossing day," the day when the tilt of our splendid azure globe reaches half-way to the Spring equinox from December's dark solstice. (Of course, folks in New South Wales celebrate it as the brilliant solstice.) In spite of those bleak six months, one part of Scott had started whispering lately that he'd mourned long enough. And he knew that the old Scott was now newer: personally more ebullient and more confident; professionally, a better teacher—more witty, more inclusive. And who deserved the thanks? Who'd helped "birth" him? Gavin.

But those sad and celebratory reflections were distracting him from that inviting view across the festive room. As he gazed, distinct memories of the alluring junior riffled through his mind's eye, a delightful Rolodex that began to shoulder those Kuiper memories aside. One was from that fiesta he and Gavin had organized—when was it? It was in fact nine months to the day (May Day). The sight evoked in turn a touch: her firm yet delicate hand grasping his floury one across a flaming grill. Then, next moment, she was hovering, her camera primed, in that bright red Cardinal hat one deck below them at Busch Stadium. And yet one more: tennis shoelaces clicking, ankles bared, as she paced through the hot, deserted University lounge.

And, now, here she was again. Live. And way more vividly alive than those recollections. At rest, she perched on his department chair's hearth: her still firm, still dainty hands elevating a Spode saucer of rich, bluish cream; a quaint jade pendant nestling on that firm, bare chest. The sight held him, stirred him, arrested him. As his feet stopped short, so did time.

That singular instant harbored infinite and novel possibilities.

Excavating Shelley

Now. Shelley. Though barely twenty, she'd been acquiring some impressive depths. Exploring each level is like prizing open an orange, releasing a complex mist—aromatic, but with delicate sour threads.

But first a more pedestrian question waves a hand. It wants to know what has brought her there. Such gatherings were meant for the university's English faculty and its grad students. But Scott that very morning had let loose an innovation which the department greeted enthusiastically. (One which time, in its turn, would make a tradition). Why not welcome any current sophomores who might be contemplating English as a major? A great notion, sure. But wait. That first question still begs for an answer. Why was Shell there? She was none of these: neither faculty nor grad student; a junior, not a sophomore. Plus, she'd already declared herself a History major.

Still, a morning email invitation from Scott, pretty much out of the blue, had intrigued her. *She* had memories of her own. Of *his* hand across a flaming grill; of *him* (along with, of course, her wonderful "lit perfessor" Gavin) a hundred feet above her at that Cardinal game; his and her shared moment in that muggy Holmes Lounge. So she'd been intrigued enough to respond.

But (characteristically, he was discovering) she'd responded on her own terms. "I believe I'd like that. If I get there, I'll find you." Since her arrival half an hour before, she'd been exploring the stately home (she particularly admired the balcony's mahogany balustrades) and surveying the milling folks with a calm smile. But what she'd been lavishing her closest attention on were the two elegant dishes she'd spent the afternoon preparing. And on one of them in particular. Now and again she'd return to the festive table and cadge a small sample, to test the cream's evolving flavors. On her third "again," a new item there intrigued her. At first inspection it seemed simply green spinach, but she knew she smelled chickpeas and a whiff of, what? Was that curry? Name and ingredients eluded her, but her curiosity was piqued. She adjourned to the hearth with a sample.

That rich dish and that glorious but homey fire were so seductive, however, that they were driving her to carve wormholes into her past. Deeper and darker but illuminating.

* * * * *

The one she was revisiting as Scott swung into range was a prolonged instant of ecstatic anxiety from nearly three years before. An overly conscientious reader might want to create a timeline for this growing array of caught instants. *Don't*. On *that* still vivid evening, in warm, breezy, early May, she'd also been waiting. Waiting for her Astrid to arrive for a dinner with her family.

And, on *that* expectant night, in turn, other memories were cascading. (Just when we think we have caught her, we recognize a timely warning: any new moment holds at its heart multiple previous moments. So, while memory may be disorderly, its jumble can yield perspectives that are both ever-receding and eye-opening.) A riffling cascade of memories, some sweet, some bitter, began to flow. These were *new* old memories, she realized—scarcely recalled, never examined before, flowing and mingling in scarcely an instant. To unspool them demands time.

*****

First, a warm sun flooding through a dusty room; windows in funny, squat shapes letting in the summer sun, dust motes swirling. The sun cast gentle searchlights as she fiddled with a trunk lid. Then she was hitting it with a blue plastic hammer. Soon she stands at the center of a slow galaxy of genial dust; some radiant creature barely visible beneath her through a golden haze; someone draped in blue; someone who smelled wonderful.

A voice called her, wafting up. "Oh Shell. On my *belle*. Come *down* my wonderful girl." Then came a long silence when she would giggle to herself, limbs frozen in hilarious expectation.

And then a face coming up, yes *up,* through the floor, cooing: "Cocoa! Come snuggle." …

… But a shiver swallowed both voice and aroma. A wooden thunderclap. *"There's nothing for us up here."* Her dad's trembling voice as he lumbered down, down, down from overhead. "She's gone, sweet baby. Trunks packed away and locked. Your wonderful mom.... But we have to move on, baby."

Tears hung in her eyes, but he took her hand between his. They reeked of the attic's dusty molecules. He slapped them on his legs, to rid himself of their grains and aroma. Then he flung the stairs upward until—amazing, scary—they disappeared into the ceiling. Gone too. All that remained was a cold, white, forbidding expanse, as the young girl huddled below. She retained for years to come that blank ceiling, that reverberating report: Aromas, dust, radiance all sucked in an instant into a diminishing black hole. …

… Next a loud metal clang. As she gazed from some high window, a mammoth truck standing outside, maw open, tailpipe breathing out thick vapors. Arms lifting boxes up and out of dad's room. Boxes full of her stuff stacked by the door. He closed her bedroom door tight, then took her hand as he led her for one last time along the hallway, then down the stairs that led down from that room of hers, down and out from that cold white place. To "Our new home, baby." …

… A green-lined street with lush saplings—just her height, it seemed. A long, long street ran absolutely straight and even, ran to the door of a wide, one-story, brick house. As they walked up the brick path, the bright windows hung before her, right at eye level. A tiny rise on her toes, with her calves barely lifted, let her face the glowing brass knob that seemed to grow from the door.

The two of them walked into the central hall. What would grow in time for the teen-age Shelley into a comfy ranch home was, to her four-year-old self, vast. No stairs leading up. No basement. Nor an attic: no "there" to go "up" to. But still enormous. Whether she turned right or left, all she could see was room after room multiplying in the distance. It was like her head's mop of short curls in those mirrors at her dad's barber's, repeating before and behind her endlessly.

The room she picked for her own was a snug one. It was just past the room that was the heart of the house—the spacious, spicy welcoming kitchen. She found those aromas faint, but still they beckoned. There in the kitchen nook's windows hung "her" new curtains, sheers that captured sunlight from the sky beyond and released it in festive strips.

From day one, she loved the nook. It's where she housed a growing passel of her coloring books. In that paradise she could read, draw and inhale at will. Her eyes danced from book to book, from table to stove, from spicy cupboard to an array of hanging, jostling pots.

These old sights and sounds and smells, like a subterranean stream frozen for years deep down, were now flooding through her as she stood by the front door, transfixed, awaiting her Astrid, (like those mirrors at the barber's) as she sat on that warm and inspiring hearth by the fire, awaiting Scott. "What's doing all this?" she'd thought to herself back then. "Graduation? Turning 18? No. It's my sweet Astrid. Opening me up." She'd hugged herself with delight and impatience.

"God, girl will you hurry!? Dad's going to love her. We *all* will."

Astrid

Astrid Perot was not Shell's first crush. Far from it. But she *was* the first crush that grew into genuine, loving, burbling affection. And a woman's first love says a lot about her, more often than a man's. (Men's attractions are often more spontaneous and usually more frequent. They can also prove less discriminating.) Her choice not only captured the Shell of that moment; it firmly predicted her character, tastes, and appetites— her journey of discovery.

Astrid, a Hosmer Academy alumna, was a college sophomore at Antire College. She was devoting her spring semester to that Ohio college's "Work the World" program. (Committed to public service, the progressive college encouraged its undergraduates to explore possible careers *during* their undergraduate years.) She chose to do her experiment at her old high school.

A multi-talented, many-lettered star of Hosmer's track program, she'd set records for speed (dashes), endurance (the mile), and a combination of speed, strength and coordination (hurdles). She knew she had strong skills to offer and now she wanted to see whether she could spread them, share them. (Her optimism was soon confirmed in spades.) She'd initiated the placement procedure from campus the prior September; had assembled, polished and broadcast a resume; had made calls. She'd come to campus for an interview on the Columbus Day weekend. So, now, three months later, here she was—back home in an intense, one-semester transit, eager to assist what she called her "younger sisters" (and, well, okay—any talented younger "brothers") in their running, dashing, hurdling, vaulting life.

The day Shell first noticed, first *really* noticed her, the track season was three weeks old. That chilly and drizzly Friday made that year's vernal equinox, Spring's debut, decidedly unimpressive. On that last day before Spring break, the coaches had decided, comfortably indoors, to put the time to good use by giving the squad some vital pointers. Half-way through the three o'clock "chalk talk," Coach Winter yielded the floor to Astrid.

Her firm voice, her obvious expertise, and her self-evident familiarity with both track's tough demands and Hosmer's intricate social customs, won her instant respect. Then too there was her firm, slender body with its graceful curves, and a fall of stunning gold hair, features that had drawn the guys' instant (and, yes, spontaneous) attention. Their gazes would start with her face, move to her hair, and then, a good many, slide down for a fuller appreciation of the complete woman. As she stood that day at ease in the center of the room, with her hair bunched in a tight pony-tail, the gazing was even more concentrated.

And not just by the guys. It's true that Shell had seen the coach / alumna / woman at practices; and, yes, she'd "listened up" when Astrid, making her rounds on the rare mild days, would spend her attentive two minutes with each member of the various women's squads—relay, dash, mile. What had first impressed Shell was the coach's professional expertise: on her own initiative Astrid had bought a videotape camera—to record, assess, and then review each runner's performance one-to-one. Shell respected such close attention; she found it both concerned and objective, devoted but professional.

She'd also noticed the calm voice and the air that seemed to glow around the woman, even on dark, blustery early March days. But Shell did not as a rule retain impressions: her revolving enthusiasms kept her at a continual but unfocused simmer. So that Friday she was hearing and seeing the woman up close, garbed now in her loose tee-shirt and snug shorts, not the baggy cold-weather sweatpants and hooded sweat-shirt worn outdoors. Shell hadn't picked up on how lithe, slender, and well-put-together she was. Nor on how deep were her hazel eyes. That day it was all registering, and it beckoned her close attention.

A young woman of normal, though maybe more than usually catholic tastes, Shell typically found hot studs hot, women only rarely. She appreciated good-looking women, naturally, but they rarely aroused her. She'd begun dating guys her sophomore year and, a quick learner, soon grew adventurous in her sexual explorations. She found she enjoyed giving and receiving equally. And frequent compliments from two or three fellows assured her that she had an exceptionally daring and considerate tongue. That talent held great promise for a swath of future partners.

Her sudden attraction to Astrid was unusual, but Shell took it, as she took most new things, in stride. As the coach delivered her remarks, her body, sensuous and tightly muscled, swayed gently—one hand now resting on a hip, now darting out to illustrate key points in a vibrant alto voice, directions about pacing, timing, breathing. Within two minutes, Shell was more than appreciating her.

"So here's the deal. This is primarily for you 'LDs'…. Long distance people? You fellows—sorry, guys: *men*" (her careful split-second pause won an appreciative laugh) "when you dial your honeys ("sweetie-pies", "babes", whatever), you try to use those monthly cell-phone minutes with care, right? I see a few nods. You *pace* yourself? Same for you ladies, am I right? When it's your dime—sorry, it's a phrase my grandpa used—when you phone your favorite man on campus or he's here and you're on vacation on Padre Island? And, oh yes, I almost forgot Jeff" … she paused to point to the team's self-proclaimed "stud" and (to be fair) emerging athlete. He displayed a wide range of gifts (shot-put

13

and 400 meter) and, as he never failed to point out, he managed to land a new woman, and from a different school every week or so. "You too, Jeff. *Your* favorite man. Right?"

The room got it. A trickle of fake-soprano laughter grew into a boisterous torrent. Jeff balled his fist and thumbed his nose at her but sported a broad grin.

She resumed with a straight face. "Now listen up! Breath's like money; if you use it up all at once in an event, you won't get it back. No time to recover. So, all of you: you gotta keep that big picture, your total air supply, in view. *Every* time.

"It's called pacing. Now. Sprinters. You go in bursts. I know. You should. But for you "distance" folks. We don't want '*slow* and steady' like for our friend the tortoise. No. But 'steady' we *do* want. No need to fly out of those blocks in a blur. Timing. *Timing* is the key.

Astrid's developing pedagogical principle was, whenever possible, to call on young women, in the newly-coordinated school program. (Hosmer had been all-girls for its first century.)

"Now. Is Jean here? My miler?"

Jean's eyes glance at her, then she looks down.

"I hear they call you 'Roadrunner'?" (A popular cartoon of the day about a lightning fast bird.)

14

A smile revives Jean's face. She lifts her eyes into a firm stare. "That's right, ma'am. Roadrunner."

The room exhaled a quieter laugh. Shelley, standing near Jean, nudged her with an affectionate elbow.

"Well, Jean. And *all* of you, track's no cartoon. Don't treat it that way. You—even you, Jean—just can't keep it up. And relax, there's no Mr. Coyote chasing you." (Another raft of laughs.) "It's you versus *you*, remember...Oh and oh yeah, the name is Astrid. Not 'ma'am'. Got it?"

Jean saluted and mouthed the name. Astrid took a step toward her. "Now. Let's see a leg—"

Shell instinctively reached an arm out for Jean to grasp as she raised her leg first to a perfect 90 degrees, and then still more.

"—She's lucky. The DNA goddess has given the woman some gifts. Now, that leg. *Might* work for short bursts. But it's her shoulders that hold 'LD' promise: she's made for endurance." The guys may have glanced briefly at Jean, and one or two alit for an instant on Shelley, but soon enough they returned their full attention to Astrid. "Surprise, guys: We're not built all that different. So treat your gifts with respect. All of you."

"Say, Miss Perot," interrupted Coach Winters. "Astrid. Tell 'em about State. Three years ago. The mile. How you outfoxed those runners? Endurance plus brains."

"You won? You took it?" several voices near Shelley wanted to know.

"Did she?" Shelley whispered, half to herself.

"Sure did," Jean overheard and whispered back. "Her name's on that plaque in the Alumnae Room."

"Really? Never looked."

"You should go see. God she's neat."

Shell nodded and gazed.

"You're right, sir." Astrid saluted her boss and colleague. "Good. Jeff City. Late May. Hot. The men were in charge, so they scheduled the women's mile event for—what else, ladies?—four p.m. We're always last, right?"

The ladies breathed a chorus of "Oh, yeahs". Shell found herself nodding.

"Well, we all started off together at the gun, pretty firmly, pretty fast. But I knew—listen up here, folks. I knew I should—" she paused in good teacherly fashion. "Should *what,* fellas?"

A distressing silence. "Today's lesson?" She began to tap her foot.

"Okay, ladies. Fill the guys in. Should *what*?"

Soprano and alto notes of "pace" "pace" "pace" echoed through the room.

"Ah, yes. Our women rescue us. *Pace.* Believe me, Coach Winter saw to it I'd learned *that* lesson." She threw him a wink and put her hand to her heart. (The gesture gave Shell's heart a bonus thump.) "So when the others moved ahead, second circuit, it didn't faze me. Some bitch—I mean, some Pem-Day runner, and, oh yeah, then another"— she kept talking through the titter that was bubbling through the room—"they both went past me, muttering 'Loser'. 'Can't hack it?'

"Well, long story short: third lap now. I'm sixth, but closing in. Going steady, see? Pacing! They can't maintain their 'roadrunner' speed, see Jean? Half-way through the final lap I'm easing past 'em—just *three* of 'em ahead of me now. They're fading. Next I pass the one who was second, then the leader. I hear each of 'em gasp as I stride past, steady and firm. *Pacing."*

Each new stage of the tale wound the room tighter. "Took it by a half-second." Alto and soprano whoops matched baritone grunts ("Go, Hosmer!" "Coach Astrid!"). Shell simply stood and gazed, her usually busy eyes at a fixed stand-still.

"Cool name," she thought to herself. "Cool woman."

Spring Training

That night at dinner with Ben (dad); Averill (step-mom); her daughters, Ashley and Angie, (Shell affectionately called them her "sweet steps"), she enlivened the table with what would prove to be just her first tale of Astrid. "She's so neat. Fantastic athlete, tells great stories. They say she's an alum. Two years ahead of me, don't recall her. Wish I'd noticed!"

"Oh, you silly," piped up Ashley. "Ang' and me have some yearbooks. Dad-Ben gave em to us our first year in lower school. Bet she'd be in there, don't you think?" Shelley wasn't a collector of school traditions either, nor the annual printed accounts. When something appealed to her, she'd try it out but then it was as if something urged her to draw back. "Steer clear of that. Just keep yourself busy," she'd advise herself.

"So, Big Step—" Ashley took over from her younger sister. "Do some, what's dad Ben's word? Research?"

"Mouths of babes," she winked at her step-mom. Dinner over, she scooted down the corridor to paw through her stepsisters' shelves. She grabbed the yearbook from two years before and, sure enough, there she was. Astrid. She flipped another page. And *there.* Kept flipping. Oh, and *that's* a nice one—Astrid, sleeveless, her bare arms gleaming, hefting a glinting metal pole. Happening upon them in haphazard order made the series of delights even more amazing, and more and more intense.

Astrid's many awards and activities littered her senior page—Honor Society, Service Project, winner of the mile, team winners in the 800-meter relay, and honorable mention in two "non-distance" events: hurdles and pole vault. "What *can't* she do?" From those scattered snaps, Shelley began to compose a full-length feature—Astrid's face indistinct in a crowd of sophomores, then suddenly catching fire like a comet nearing the sun, junior year. Then, the senior blazed like a nova. "How could I have missed her?" It was as if the senior's image had skimmed off the sophomore's eyes like a svelte stone skittering off a pond.

* * * * * *

That first inspection ignited an explosion of vitality which kept radiating next day. On that first day of Spring Break, while many of her classmates were tanning on distant beaches, she recalled out of the blue a water-fall in Forest Park. She'd always shivered when she drove by it; the height put her off. But now a novel idea swept her up, unbidden. *Just* the place to build strength, develop some endurance. "*That*'ll impress her."

So Sunday, with sweatpants and only a thin Hosmer tee shirt, she drove to the Park, meandered through its winding lanes til she came upon the fall. She took up her position on the path at its foot, breathed deep, and charged up the incline. Shell proved a fallible disciple; failing to pace herself, she barely made it half-way up. Her initial drill lasted only fifteen minutes. But she returned later in the day and twice a day thereafter. By vacation's end her determination built her up to a full hour daily. Ten complete ascents. And after each one, she learned to pause at the top to survey, calmly and at length, the green expanse of Forest Park, and the glorious and noble Art Museum, and the wide reflecting pool just past it.

* * * * *

The first day after vacation, Shelley got out to the track early and undertook a deceptively leisurely run, hoping she might cross paths with her coach. No luck that afternoon, but she adopted the same strategy next day. Astrid was already at the first turn, striding purposefully. Shell poured some steam into the second lap of her mile. For those crucial moments, she abandoned pacing for a higher goal. She brought herself, yard by determined yard, into sync with Astrid. (An observer from the field house announcer's booth would have seen the two women's elliptical orbits sliding ever so gradually into conjunction.)

For five seconds, Shell paced with her in perfect tandem: two pairs of pumping legs, two pulsing heads of hair—one a gold cascade, the other a pulsing ear-lobe-length auburn. Shell darted her eyes over to her new partner. She matched her coach's strides and re-introduced herself. Even an intense crush wouldn't leave Ashella Jaspar too shy to stay mute.

"Hey, Astrid. Hi. Shell." The woman nodded but kept her gaze fixed on the horizon. "Thought first week back would be hurdles."

"Ten days off. Try stay in shape." Astrid ignored grammatical niceties.

Shelley was determined to impress, even if she had to do all the talking. "I'm *pacing*," she gasped. "See?"

Astrid gave a brief smile. "Brava! See you there…" and she shot ahead like a golden arrow. Shell, now nearly winded, toiled helplessly in her wake.

In those brief seconds of close eye contact, though, she'd devoured Astrid's dark irises and the hazel flecks that swam in them. The instant result? Charmed all over again. A whiff of blueberries tingled her nostrils. She felt a thin gush—maybe some of the quantum foam that, physicists insist, passes seamlessly through all matter and all minds.

* * * * *

21

The whiff—thoughtful and attentive readers will not be surprised—ignited a flashback. Another sliver of her past was rising, drawn into life by Astrid's gravity. With this one, though, she was long familiar. She often recollected it....

A float trip with her father and his then fiancée, Averill. Her mind's fuzzy eye saw that sun, a friendly orange giant, peeking over a range of emerald hills, and just about to gild some rustling poplars. They formed a green cascade that fell and lapped at the blue, whispering stream. Her toes felt again a thousand tiny but sweet nibbles.

She was already up, sitting cross-legged on a spit of soft sand mingled with gritty gravel. Her hands probed a deep, fire-blackened, metal pot. A calm smile lit her face as she got the bolt to accept the loose nut so she could re-affix the handle. (Shaking the pot which she'd filled with lentils the night before had loosened it.)

A musical sigh carried her to her next labor. (She had already stirred the embers of last night's fire. "Don't need dad. I can manage it.") The flames were starting to lap at the bottom of the tin coffee pot. As her hand hovered where the fire licked at the metal, she felt the sensations, and wondered—during the usual split second of attention she accorded most of her dizzy array of notions—what it would be like to be the coffee pot? To hold and dispense warming liquid for everyone? ("Silly; that's not real.

People aren't pots.") She had already lined up the metal canisters like obedient soldiers: of coffee for them—for her, of her invariable favorite, cocoa. Well, hmm, maybe she'd try some of the coffee in her cocoa. "Dad seems to like the coffee I fix him. Should I?" The water had no bubbles yet, so she turned to other things of the random moment.

Oh, right. Those blueberries. She had assigned herself the night before the dawn task of hunting down a quart or so of the plump fruits the recent June rains were hastening to perfection. Now she plunged into the four or five laden bushes she'd identified. Her hands were soon weaving into and out of the soft twigs in a blur: the rapidly filling metal bowl gave ample evidence of her success. Her hands saw to it that not one round blue atom plopped to the ground; a few even swooned in, stems attached.

Next came the more tedious task of picking those few stems from their berries: "Ten minutes. Then I can call them." She edged the rolling liquid toward the back of the grill, and the roil soon calmed to a gentle simmer. She turned to the batter she'd made and covered the night before. Into it went the blueberries. Next she dug again with her willow wand into the coals, stirring them. Then, unplanned as usual, she grew meditative. Her mind drifted from the bright azure overhead to … what? a ceiling slamming shut. She shuddered and banished the image.

That's when the side of her mouth felt a sudden hot jolt. "Ouch." She'd let that hot wand snuggle up to her mouth, hot ashes clinging, not the warm soup of pancake batter she thought she'd been stirring. She scuttled down to the end of the spit and splashed some water on the half-inch-long burn. Around her feet, as she scooped the cool liquid into her hand, boiled a miraculous sight—a concerned squadron of fish churning the liquid surface, nibbling at her toes.

Shell took the magical moment in stride. "Relax, fishies. I'm okay. Come back later. Pancakes for you. And blueberries!"

Unplanned Wonders

Three days later, after the close of Friday's practice, she saw Astrid flying around the track, her hair the usual honey-blond stream. Even that late, she was the object of perhaps six pairs of male eyes. A line of docile ants, *en route* to their lockers, they were being distracted into a series of dilatory epicycles. The "l. d. relay brotherhood" was taking its sweet male time and giving its many eyes a full regale.

Shelley also dawdled (extra sit-ups on the infield, white towel around her neck) long enough to see Astrid come in from that day's laps.

As she sat up at each "crunch" and feasted her eyes, Shelley could catch (like a stop-action camera) Astrid's hips' steady gyrations and her thighs' remarkable muscling. Her golden hair streamed against the thin but shimmering green of the April hills as she completed a final circuit. She then went on to her personal finale—attacking a set of hurdles, all with her usual liquid grace of motion.

Nearly. As she lifted off for the last hurdle and stretched like a gazelle, her extended leg grazed the wooden crossbar. It wobbled precariously as she completed a jiggled arc back to earth. A twinge creased her eyelids. Delicate crows-feet surfaced, then dissolved. She slowed to a limping adagio not ten feet away from Shell, who leapt from her twentieth crunch and hastened to her coach's side.

Her excitement at the wonderful close encounter up-ended the many thoughts she longed to convey. Genuine concern mastered the moment and shoved them aside. "Oh, hey. You okay?" She saw Astrid's left hand stretching down to trace a red welt rising behind her knee. "Is it bleeding?"

"Nope, nope. Just starting to bind up."

When Shelley's hand reached out to palpate the bruise, it was as if a huge, unbidden shelf of her mind were rising softly to the surface, absorbing and ordering the mingled world of green and blonde and skin and hurdles that danced and bunched before her eyes. And her toes began to itch.

"Wow, those hands of yours. Magical."

"Glad I was near-by. But I think what you need is a cold compress."

"Yeah, I agree. Good chance to put my new ice-maker to use. Oh, fuck."

"Fuck?"

"Damn."

"Okay, then, 'Damn.' Why?"

"I'm carless: a friend said he'd come get me, but he emailed me mid-morning. Called to Chicago."

Shell was touched by her candor and felt an idea stir. But womanly curiosity took precedence.

"Friend? Tall guy, stunning hair? And," she pretended to dab at some drool sliding down her chin, "dreamy green eyes?"

"Yes," Astrid laughed. "Tall, green-eyed Mark. It's Ashella, right?"

"Just on my driver's license." She stood taller. "Shell."

"Shell, then. Good. Well, sharp eyes and good memory Shell."

Shell patted the back of Astrid's hand. "Lucky you."

Shell was standing so close that her eyes gorged on Astrid's broad shoulders, and on the bronze triangle below them where steamy rivulets glistened. Then back to those hazel eyes. *Were* those flecks hazel? God.

She unwound the wet towel from her neck and offered it.

"Thanks." Astrid bowed her head, then began dabbing at her neck and chest, eyes closed.

"Yeah, lucky me to have Mark. But he goes and picks the day I had my sweet Mini's brakes fixed." She gave a sigh and did an extreme pout: "Poor me."

Shelley found her lips enchanting and her new idea acquired new life. But she prefaced it with a question. "So. You really *are* stranded?"

"Pitiful tale, huh? Lame. Stranded." She laughed at her melodrama and drew her lips into a new pout. "But no problem. Dad can fetch me, if I reach him by six."

"No. Wait." Shell gave words to the plan she'd begun to percolate. "I have a car. One idea. And, second, these hands." She wiggled her ten digits in Astrid's face. "My steps would tell you I'm good at massages. And, say. Number three: I have a secret recipe—a healing ointment for that bruise. It's true. So what say?"

She retrieved Astrid's towel to swab the rivulets that still gathered on the woman's collarbone.

Astrid found the smile enchanting, the towel calming, and the offer irresistible. "Well, I don't know why you'd need to massage steps or how they can talk to you, but yes: I will take the *ride*. With thanks."

"And ..." Shell quietly exulted, "hey. You can share more running tips. Earn those coach shekels."

"Tough bargain." She looked straight into Shelley's eyes. Shell used the towel again, this time to hold aside a curling tendril from Astrid's face. "Well, then. I'm in your hands."

"Glad you agree, but *I* should thank *you*. My parents took my 'steps' (those are my *step*-sisters) to the Ozarks, long week-end. I'm abandoned. *Me,* their track star. The truth, coach Astrid is this: I'm going home, alone, to a deserted house."

"Hmm. My pain's your gain?"

As they walked toward the gym, Shell knew for sure that *this* was a memory that would stick. And she was right. It will recur two years later in Forest Park, when Scott, as Gavin's co-host and the fiesta's chief chef, will first meet her, will grasp her firm hand in his floury one. (And a shared meal with some girl Lucy who'd introduced them). And it's blossoming yet again as she views him from her hearth perch on what at this stage passes for "now". Each time it all rushes back—the feel, the night, the aromas. So, yes, some memories are keepers. They will fountain endlessly, well at least from time to time. Maybe with minor modifications, bending to life and the moment, but yes, in truth, time and again.

By the time they'd reached the gym door—Shelley slowing to match the older girl's limp—they were becoming fast friends.

"So, up top? Ten minutes?"

"Ten it is." Astrid formed her bronzed hand into a mock-fist and gave her novice chauffeur's shoulder a pretend pound. Then she stumped down the hall to the coaches' locker room, her glowing hair soon eclipsed by the closing door.

Shelley shadow-boxed her fists with delight ("Yes!") and winked toward Astrid's departing figure. She walked on, jabbing her arms and nodding her head to some new tune she'd heard just that morning. Its beat had stuck with her all day, her fingers pulsing taps on any nearby desk, her feet making rhythmic shuffles on the handiest floor.

Road Trip Home

Shell managed to shower and change in a record five minutes. Then she paused and took stock. She never quite got it when her teachers would crack puns. But now suddenly she realized: "Changing room! Yeah. That's what it is. *I'm* changing. And *she's* making it happen!" She then chanced a further ten seconds to survey her hair, whose slow-motion cascade, since spring-break, had by now reached a good inch and a half below her earlobe. "Coming along nicely, hair. Keep at it."

* * * * *

Two minutes later, Astrid was leaning for support on Shell's opened car door. She gave her hefty, laden back-pack a flip over the seat, then carefully eased her now professionally dressed form onto the seat next to Shelley. Brake off, first gear, ignition. (Shell had inherited Ben's aging stick-shift, though he'd still borrow it on occasion.)

Once well off-campus, Shell plunged again into womanly chat.

31

"So. About this Mark. Spill."

"Ah! So no 'how's your poor leg, Coach?' Gossip first?"

Shell's sly wink.

"Well, okay then. But sorry, Shell, but it's not as wild as it sounds. We had a thing way back. I was about at your age, your stage. You a junior?"

"Nope," straightening her shoulders. "Senior." She couldn't resist adding, "You should do your homework, Coach."

"I should, I should. Senior, eh? So, come June, we'll be fellow alumnae. Neat." Astrid reached her hand out to cup Shelley's right hand, which was resting at three o'clock on the steering wheel.

"Gee, another 'step'!" Shelley was tickled. She slid her left hand along the wheel's circumference to sandwich Astrid's. "Cool."

"I'll let you drive ..." Astrid withdrew hers with a light tap ... "and resume my tale. It was the end of *my* junior year. He was—and, yes, he still is—a good five years older, and just back from college. My brother set us up for prom."

"That's way before my time." Shelley pulled a long face, lamenting her callow youth. Astrid found Shell's mope all the more delightful. "There, there, Cinderella. You'll get to the ball. *Some* day."

Shelley could maintain the morose look no longer; her irrepressible laughter took over.

"I like your faces, Shell." Astrid continued. "Now. Do you want the Mark skinny, or not?"

Shell raised her right hand and slid it down her face, erasing the lingering smile.

"Okay, then. Yes, I fell for the guy. It was a great summer fling. But then, my senior year and college planning; *you* should know! And for him job-hunting."

"No letters? No visits?"

"Oh, we kept things up with letters and email. *Tried* to. But we were heading into our own worlds—me, visiting Ohio; him, living in California. Separate futures. Lost touch. Then last month. Ran into him at the 'Fox and Hounds.' He's back too; didn't know *I* was back. So we've been, what's the word, 'hangin'?' He's still good company, and all my old classmates are still at college. So, I'm just about on my own. Sigh."

Astrid's eyes and mouth formed yet another perfect pout. Shelley melted again, her smile a poor effort to mask her growing attraction. A wordless nod was the best she could manage.

"So we do a movie. Rides to work. Lunch or drinks. Nothing more."

"*Nothing?* With *that* babe?" She was letting her attraction find sublimation via Mark. "That *hair*?"

"Hold it," Astrid narrowed her twinkling eyes. "What are you, eh? My chauffeur or gee, my voyeur?"

Shell relished Astrid's rebuke. "You think so? Hmm." She paused, eyes twinkling: "Nah, just a healthy imagination."

"Yeah, sure.*"* Astrid sounded doubtful. "Well, fine. Hug that imagination around *this*, chica. Okay, yes; we *do* do some, uh, reacquainting."

"I knew it. Stud like him? And, what the hell, have to be honest, Astrid. A babe like *you?*" Shelley impressed herself with her candor. "Had to be."

"'Babe'? Well, *he* clearly agrees. Still, half of me says, 'Self-discipline. Be the school coach, be an adult.' But the other half, the one I'm favoring these days, says, 'Live life, go for it.' It'll hint 'couch' or suggest 'Couch!' Or—like last week, when we broke into my condo pool after hours," (a sly whisper) "'Jacuzzi'."

"Now *that* sounds intriguing. Just how do you … in a—" (Astrid's smile spoke volumes) "Uh-oh. Never mind. I'm too innocent."

"You?"

Shelley repeated the conspiratorial smile.

"Okay, fine. So our senior is another woman of experience. Oh, well, truth is, we do keep it in perspective."

"So you're like, maybe, oh I don't know, like sex buddies?"

"Hmm, 'sex buddies?' Nice. Appropriately kinky. But seriously, we *do* have fond memories. And no other romantic commitments. In some non-incestuous way, it's like sex with family. Safe, careful raptures you might say."

"So, *he's* not why you're back here—independent woman like you."

"No, no. Here's the deal. Know that Cassini probe?"

Shell frowned and shrugged.

"The one to Saturn? *You* know. The planet?" She pointed through the roof. "Up in the heavens?"

Shell kept her eyes straight ahead. "'Up' gets me dizzy. I'm all down-to-earth. Running track, fixing food, my steps."

"Can't argue with those, but still, um, senior 'babe'—you might start to expand your views. Wherever you end up in

September, Shell, take some Astrophysics." She extended a firm digit again to tap one of Shell's hands on the wheel. "End of lecture."

"Lecture noted, coach." Shell bowed. "But seriously. Cassini? What's that? Spill!"

"Well, the shot uses cosmic physics. Gravity. Two swings by Venus, for momentum, then back past the earth, to slingshot across the solar system. That's St. Louis, for me. I'm using the home hearth for a second wind. Then I'll charge out again, full throttle. This track gig is a safe risky start."

"So, a cautious start for cosmic Astrid, eh?" Astrid nodded "Well, speaking selfishly, 'coach babe,' I'm tickled you did decide to start *here*."

Astrid smiled fully and her eyes sought Shelley's.

* * * * *

Shelley clicked on the radio and did a rapid tour of the dial, her fingers a blur. She tapped the up button to move past the "top 40" channel her receiver automatically chose. Classical sounds slid into hearing and she glanced quickly, digit poised, for Astrid's reaction. Astrid nodded but her eyes asked "Mind?" as she reached for the bank of controls. Shell nodded and withdrew her hand. Astrid dialed up the public radio station, where the news of the hour instantly grabbed her attention.

36

Shelley grimaced. "Oh, please, dad. More news shows? Damn, he always resets it there."

Astrid held up a silencing hand, "Ah but Shell, that wider view. The news. His world. Mine too. And yours, any day now." Shell wanted to please, so she assented with only a soft harrumph. Then Astrid sat back to focus on a report from DC. When it ended, "Damn. Senate still won't back voting rights. Bastards." Frown. Arms crossed. "Okay, enough. You're back in control, lady."

Astrid had rotated back and was smiling again into Shelley's face. She merely raised her eyebrows. Shell nodded, pushed again, and found a pulsing beat from an alternative station, its numerals unfamiliar. Astrid curled a forefinger around Shelley's and eased it off the controls. "That's great."

Soon two heads were nodding, four soles pulsing. (Well, three. Shell kept one safely on the accelerator.)

They drove on in comfortable silence for a mile or two, past a dark blue pond dazzling with cream-colored fowl. Then Astrid, eyes closed, hand absently massaging above her knee, murmured.

"Man, Shell, this is pleasant. Even if I am lame and abandoned, I feel lucky. It's so great to relax. Open up. Drop that damned 'macho' mask, especially around those guys we're stuck with now we're co-ed. I'm almost grateful for this bruise." Shell

37

basked in Astrid's convivial pleasure and candor. "Plus it's cool getting to know you like at warp speed. Like in one gulp."

"Oh yeah, *sure*." Shelley flooded the air with irony. "Warp speed? Easy for *you* to say. Been trying to get you to notice me for two months. Coach."

"No! You're serious?" Her eyes, like a compass needle seeking true north, flicked from the whizzing road to the dashboard, slid up to the senior's face, and came to rest once more in those eyes.

"Whoa." A sight approaching on their right distracted Shell from their special moment. "Wait. Take a gander at *that*."

A young fellow on a bike was struggling up the steep incline. His broad back glistened; a thin pair of cycling shorts rode up two tanned thighs toward his bare, slender waist. As the women approached, his effort had him standing on his pedals, biceps ballooning, shoulders swelling.

"Gander?" Astrid, still turned halfway to Shelley, made an effort to re-pivot. Shelley's right hand reached around Astrid's shoulder to pull her golden strands away from Astrid's right eye. "Let me help. Yes. Gander. at. *that*, ma'am."

Astrid's eyes grew wide. "Oh, *yes*. How old? Fifteen? Damn. Oh to be a sophomore again, and a new license to drive. *I'd* pull over." She fake-punched Shell's upper arm. "But *you* can. Go on. Indulge a senior privilege?"

They grimaced in sympathy for the lad's efforts as they slid past him near the hill's crest. Boy and machine were nearly motionless in suspense; he was pulling on the bars as if to levitate into space. Four eyes gazed and appraised. Shelley oscillated her neck, and her eyes took quick delicious sips, from road to young stud, road to stud again, but, third time charm, from stud, to road, to ... back to rest on Astrid. She helped herself to a long draft.

Astrid kept her gaze on the kid in the rear-view mirror: "So? Not going to pull over?"

"Nope. I have a better view."

First Night Salve

When they reached Shelley's, Astrid swung her knees off the seat and stood up—only to find her leg had stiffened. Shell was beside her in a flash, offering a shoulder. Astrid slid her slender but sinewy arm across it, a cat cadging a free ride inside.

In the living room, Shell tried to issue orders. "Now, dear coach Astrid ma'am. Just sit here and unwind. I'll get you iced and go start my compote. You sit. I'll shout when it starts bubbling."

"No, ma'am, no. I will not be coddled. I'll follow you. I want to observe this Ashella magic. Up close. Got a chair or something?"

"Got a stool," Shell admitted. (It's the one she'll lean on, awaiting Astrid, two weeks later.) And it's a vital stage-prop in the memory she'll spool as she awaits (yes, yes—back in the *real* now). "But it's not very comfortable. Look. *My* job's to start the compote. *Yours?* Relax. Relax, while I rustle up some food for us."

"Okay, okay. Here's a compromise. First, go get the ice, I'll sit here and apply it. Then, two, go get your pots bubbling.

Once it starts working (stage three), I'll stride in and observe as you go through your doctor and chef paces."

The twin titles inspired Shell to fetch, bag, bring in and apply the ice to Astrid's knee. She then (two) abandoned her and set to work. The sound of clattering metal soon piqued Astrid's curiosity. Sooner than Shell had planned, Astrid limped (three) toward the kitchen, plastic bag in hand, rounded the doorjamb, and beheld... well, it *had* to be Shelley. But she seemed to be floating, dreamlike, in rich billows of steam. Before her, one pot lifted its lid, releasing a rich aroma.

Astrid held out her drooping bag. "Free refill?"

"Just couldn't wait, eh?" Shell materialized. "Fine. Here. I found a cushion." She laid it on the stool's wood surface. "Now, dammit. Park yourself while I finish." She flipped the egg-timer, as Astrid reveled in the mild April breezes that were stirring the kitchen's yellow curtains to life. As if, Shell thought, they too were yearning for her guest's vibrant hair.

"Perfect."

Shell stepped toward her patient and hovered above her. "Hey, coach. Mind if I call you Astrid? We're off-campus. And about to be fellow-alums."

"Of course. Do you remember what I told Jean? Don't you guys *ever* listen?"

Shelley rose on her toes and, hands on hips, launched into her own lecture. "Ever *listen?* Listen to *this,* you. I remember that day word. for. word. It was March 21, fourteen days and an hour or so ago. Quote: 'And oh yeah, the name's Astrid. Not ma'am.' We don't *listen?* Ha."

"I'm glad one senior's got working ears. Wonderful."

"*Some* of 'em don't. Well, then. I put your policy to work and gladly obey, *Astrid.*"

"Say, I like to hear you say it ..." (Astrid with a calm smile) "... Shell."

"And *I* like saying it...." She paused to rehearse the two syllables. "'As-trid.'"

"You make it sound so musical."

* * * * *

Shell glowed her thanks, but stayed business-like: "Well, now, 'Astrid,' my recipe has just begun bubbling." She lowered her voice to imitate one of the more pompous and theatrical chemistry teachers. "Ladies, we are now just"—a full slide into a near-baritone—"on the verge of sublimation."

Astrid guffawed at Shell's dead-on imitation. Then her nose quivered. "Thought you said blueberries. So why do I smell *cocoa?*"

"Really?" A shadow passed across Shell's face. "Really!? I never noticed. But yeah …" she took a deep whiff of the swirling steam, "Sharp nose. Hmm. Say, we got us some new chemistry at work. Or maybe…" She paused, suspended above her guest and patient. "It's cosmic? Some passing star?"

Shell's palm had just formed a cup and reached for Astrid's chin when the phone rang.

"*Damn.*" She signaled Astrid to rise a few inches and then plumped the cushion on the stool as she sidled toward the phone. "'Lo? Jay man! You did? … *That much*?" She pointed toward Astrid's knee and signaled her to hold the pack tighter. "That's terrific, my man. Boy, wish I *could*…No. Well, truth is I'm tied up"— (she winked at Astrid, shoved the receiver between her jaw and collar-bone, and crossed her two wrists through the cord). "But hey: tackle the next chapter. Try me later." Her eyes alit on Astrid's. "Uh, no. Sorry, better try me tomorrow. Ciao, Jay man."

Astrid's eyes followed Shell's hands as she hung up the phone. "Now hold on. Shouldn't you follow up with him?"

"No, no, no. He's just my peer tutoring victim. Name's Jay Ross? A sophomore? Cute. Funny. Dad's a fancy English professor, but geometry throws him."

"And you of course are there to help."

"I am. I do. But I forgot. He always checks in Friday evenings." As she resumed her stirring, she looked over at Astrid. "Guess I'm distracted, huh?"

Astrid's smile was silent, calm and poised.

Shelley's eyes danced over to the pots. "Come on, pots. Speed it up." The sand grains had all slid into the timer's bottom half. She moved the pot from the flame, sniffed once, stirred twice: even richer aromatic plumes arose.

She approached Astrid's cooling knee and laid her cooler palm upon it. Then her finger traced its way around the red welt. "Now. We count to five, ladies" (that teacher again) "as it subsides into primal blue ooze." (Her melodious mezzo reappeared.) "That's *your* cue."

"Cue? For what?"

"To *count*. And you say *we* don't listen?"

Astrid gave a full-throated laugh and acquiesced. "Yes, ma'am, yes ma'am. One, two—"

"Too fast. Go slower. Ahem, *pace* yourself, coach."

"Okay, smart-ass." (pause) "Three … four…"

"Good. Good. That's it."

"…and five."

"And here we are." She tested the steaming compote with a dribble onto her wrist. "Like I used to do for Angie. I'd warm her baby food and read to Ashley while we waited."

"So, then: not just doctor and chef, but mother too?" (Shell giggled at the parade of titles but savored the praise.)

"All three." Shell blew on the mixture, sending vapors streamlining around the bowl, first warm, then cool, on the scar.

"Too hot?" She read her patient's face.

"No." Astrid laid her hand on Shelley's as it massaged. She looked up at her. "Still perfect."

Ounce by blue ounce, Shelley applied it with gentle firmness, dipping two taut, delicate fingers into the mix, then using her full hand to knead its warmth across the bruise.

"Truly magical, Shell," Astrid's eyes rolled. "Medicine you can *eat.*"

Shell elevated one warm and priestly hand over the outstretched joint, "Bless you, Ms. Knee." Then she arose and laid a cool palm on Astrid's forehead. "And *you*, young Astrid."

Shelley's azure eyes gazed into Astrid's hazel flecks. In each rich iris she found she was seeing a miniature motion picture, twin mirrors for those steamy plumes that kept fountaining behind them. She inspected more closely and saw those twin images part and found herself staring deep—no, *diving*—into those twin pools. The immersion lasted an eternal three seconds.

With a mammoth effort, she made herself suspend the spell. "Well, now. Hungry?"

"Getting there." Astrid held Shell's inquiring gaze. "*Something's* stirring."

Astrid now reached, without permission, for the bowl and dipped her finger in it, as if to lick it. "Hang on." Now she drenched her index finger with the creamy dregs and reached up to Shell, who was still bending above her. "Here." She applied the dripping digit to that small ancient scar beside Shell's mouth. Then she hooted and finger-painted the blue smear the length of Shell's lower lip.

Her smile subsided into a whisper. "Sauce for the gander." Shelley wanted to smile but simply let the scar absorb the gift. Before the massaging finger could withdraw, however, she grasped it between her thumb and index finger and slid it into her mouth. Soon enough, the digit emerged, every last azure molecule vacuumed.

They Keep Feasting

Shell blithely pried Astrid's extended digit loose from her lip. Then, bending above her, eyes closed, she kissed her. When she re-opened them, she found that she in turn had turned Astrid's ripe pink lips blue. Like the primal atom that became our azure universe, wondrous smudges began erupting everywhere.

One half of her brain was finding it all quite comic—their postures, the novelty of the situation, and, most of all, those fluctuant colors. But the temptations to laugh kept phasing in and out with affectionate arousal, moments that served to both thrill and sober. Each woman allowed a smile to play on her lips, each pulled gently on the other's nearest ear, each caressed the other's cheek.

It was Shell who nudged the sensuous silence. "You still haven't answered me, star-shine. *Are* you hungry?"

"I am, Shell, I am. But, frankly hon, not for your food." She pulled her host down next to her onto the stool's suddenly spacious narrow pad.

One part of Shelley realized that her cooking skills were being dissed in favor of other appetites. But, well, she handled the disappointment with effortless tact. She reached her hand behind Astrid's head for greater purchase, a productive tactic that earned her a French kiss of some duration (who was counting now?). "Wait, wait." She arose, breathless, and reached out both hands to levitate Astrid. She had her hook a finger into a loop on her shorts. "Grab ahold, hon. I know a better spot."

She stood her upright and wound an arm around her waist; they shuffled in a three-legged slide back to her dad's den.

"Lordee, Shell. I was starting to love that glorious stool. Are you *always* on the move?"

"Never much noticed." Shell paused and let the new insight whisper. "Guess it takes someone new to notice. Someone special."

* * * * *

As they settled into her dad's comfy couch, Shell issued an alert. "Now listen, dear Ms. A." She grinned as she spoke the line from a popular TV show about extra-terrestrials. "We are *not alone.*"

"Aliens *here*? Exciting!"

"Nope. Not aliens." Shell pivoted their two bodies toward the bubbling tank in the corner. "Our fish! Please come meet them. Care to feed 'em? Watch 'em nibble?"

"No offense, but no." Astrid now grabbed *Shell's* handiest belt-loop and pulled *her* back.

Shell sighed in mock disappointment and offered some piscine pity. "Sorry, old fish."

"Leave them to their watery universe, sweet." She applied her lips to the other's warm neck, which that still short fall of auburn hair was leaving exposed. (By June, time would help biology take the corrective steps.) "Rather nibble on *this*."

The leisurely but determined explorations their lips had begun their hands soon seconded. After a few minutes, though, Astrid's professional side arose.

"I'm curious, Shell." She freed herself a millimeter or so, and for a second or so, from the buff senior's soft lips and firm neck. "I have to wonder. You say you'd tried to get me to notice you. So, what brought me *here* tonight? Devious Jaspar plan?"

"Oh, sure." Shelley found irony delightful, whether given or gotten. "Of *course*. *I* sent Mark to Chicago. And *I* disabled your Mini." With each dollop of Shell's sarcasm Astrid's smile widened still further. "And then, sure, for my grand finale (something Ben

49

calls a PS duh resistance, something like that), *I* voodoo'd you on the hurdles. That's it. Massive conspiracy."

"Okay. But earlier you said I was *dense*. What was that? Spill."

In reply, Shelley rotated Astrid to face her, the senior preparing to lecture her erstwhile mentor. Shell's past usually sank quickly from view, but lately she was so enjoying each day's novel encounters that she found they kept fountaining. She'd re-spool them whenever the impulse arose. Why the change? Well, who else? Shell leaned sideways to whisper into the golden cascade that curtained the woman's nearest ear. "Fact is, I *have* been hoping for this." She rotated the woman's face again. "Since your chalk talk. Then, a week ago Tuesday, you kicked me into hyper-drive."

"Me? Tuesday? What'd I do?"

"Damn, lady." She appealed to the fish, gesturing with her thumb toward Astrid. "They forget so soon." Shell then hid her wounded vanity behind her sheer delight in recounting her pursuit. "Okay. I'm your historian. Tuesday? That's when I *stayed late.* I saw you *chugging* around the track." She italicized each accusation with pointed but sensuous ascending pokes, first at Astrid's exposed collar bone, then her larynx, then her chin. "And then I so cleverly *let* you catch up with me."

Acceding to Shell's (not wholly accurate) version of events, Astrid captured Shelley's third poke and her lips took possession of the offending digit. "And tha- wheh-" she unshipped the finger but kept it caged in her soft and authoritative fist. "That's when we had maybe a nanosecond of chat. It rings a bell." When Shell extended her one available middle finger, Astrid's face lit up. "You didn't have *this* in mind, did you?"

Shelley's calm smirk spoke volumes.

"*Such* an angelic slut."

The smirk became a smile which inspired Astrid to initiate another round of kisses, before sinking back to nestle in Shell's arms. "Probably why I find you enchanting."

"Truly?"

"Yes I do! So many ways. And in just two hours? I love talking to you; love our jokes; how we crave guys on bikes. And seriously, Shell-angel: you're so *caring*. I had no idea." With each item her firm but delicate fingertip traced a firm, sensuous lap around Shell's softer sensuous mouth. "And then of course, seems that when you get into your slut mode, you *are* rather forward. Aren't you?"

Shell fitted her mouth to Astrid's: "Am I?"

Shell heard the words and felt Astrid's answer moving on her lips. "You are." They both explored the shared sensations together. And at some length.

"You mind?"

Astrid kept her mouth where it was but, eyes closed, drew a finger from Shelley's lip to her chin, then down her neck and across her collarbone. There the one digit grew into five and all five slid with gentle authority under her blouse. "So, you see? Angel and slut. You add up ... to ..." (she was whispering now into Shelley's nearest ear) "'Enchanting': tah-dah." (Those two syllables now released two pleasing puffs of air, blending Shell's aural and tactile senses in delighted cahoots.)

The palm now ran back and forth. "Say, now. *Me* too forward?" Astrid prevented an answer to her own question when she stole Shell's breath with a new kiss. Shelley found herself craving that aggressive affection, more with each ticking second.

* * * * *

After a long, leisurely, indulgent minute, Shell knew a heroic effort was again required. "Hey, sweet. 'Enchanting' or not; 'forward' or not: this isn't getting us fed."

As Shell stood up, Astrid sighed at the deprivation. But her personal star-chef insisted: "Listen up. Our menu: hot moussaka, cool cucumber rounds, cold vanilla ice cream with some fruit or other, and some getting-cool, fresh-squeezed lemonade—"

"Oink, oink, lady. Just a cucumber round. Maybe something to wash it down. Enough! Don't need a feast, Shell."

"All right, all right. Leave it to me. But first go apologize to the fish." As she traipsed off to the kitchen, Shell thought she detected a strong, even more chocolaty whiff, no doubt just more quantum foam passing through that enriching universe of hers (theirs, now). Disobeying her implied promise, however, she took the moussaka from the oven, her latest *piece de resistance*, unshipped the cuke plate from the fridge, and set it on the tray she'd set out. Two glasses of lemonade, and two napkins, neatly folded. Hand on hip, and foot tapping that beat she'd been working on all day, she let the casserole cool. "Come on, damn you!"

She squared her shoulders, licked her lips, hefted the tray onto her shoulder—lighter than she'd planned, but weightier than Astrid's request. She strode to the den where she found … an *empty* couch.

Before deprivation (or anger at her guest's disobedience) could take hold, her eye quickly located Astrid on the floor by the bookcase, leg extended. She was engulfed in a Niagara of photos.

"Shell! These are *terrific*." Astrid met her host's genial glare. "Okay, I confess. I got up. But look what I found! They yours?"

Shelley gave a proud nod.

"Marvelous. Oh, look. *This* one. You. Staring at us. Like you want to absorb the whole world. I love it."

"Wonder where that was. When I shoot, it's spur of the moment—take 'em, forget 'em. I wonder, now. Who'd I get to shoot that one?"

"Whatever! But look …" Astrid selected seven or eight and riffled them: "You can make 'em into a story. The tale of Shell. For your kids someday?" She returned with the handful to the couch, fanning the story at Shell's face, making her eyelashes vibrate. "Got to get 'em organized. An *album*. Or maybe a *projector*."

"Ooh, my own movie theatre!" She snuggled up to Astrid, pulled the tray toward them, but kept reviewing the shots. "Wow. That one. Sharing the beat. Some sophomore dance, I think. Who'd I go with?" (She found *she* was casting her mind back more and more, even without the photos. A fuzzy time-line grew sharper.) "The guy who took that one. Gorgeous. But..." She pulled the tray toward them. "Come on."

"Cool. I'm ready." Astrid bit into half of one then slid the rest of it all the way into her mouth and directed a smile at Shell. "Perfect fit, perfect taste." She directed a smile. "Shh. No backtalk: 'Star' speaks."

Shelley zipped her lips with mock obedience. Then she picked another treat from the platter, popped it into her own mouth, slid an arm around Astrid's waist and said, "Now. Let me."

"Let you what?"

"Watch and learn." She reached for another and held it to Astrid's lips. "Take."

Astrid parted her lips. Shelley slid it onto Astrid's moist pink tongue, then whispered, "Eat."

Astrid let her body sink farther into Shelley's comfortable arc, both mouths still in gentle motion.

"See," Astrid slid her mouth back toward the other's ear. "Perfect again." She kissed the hand that had just fed her, seized it, reached down for the other and brought both hands behind Shell's back.

"See. You *didn't* lie to Jay. You *are* tied up." Acquiescing in her arrest, Shell lowered her lips into Astrid's palm. Shell didn't know it (beginner's luck?) but that palm was one of Astrid's most sensual zones. So, within a half-second, she slid two digits into

55

Shelley's mouth, caressing that pale blue scar with her thumb. She posed a question: "Seems I'm stuck with you here, and since it's just the two of us... I'll be a pushy guest. There a more comfortable room?"

"Ah cah taw—"

"Sorry?" Astrid removed her fingers. "What? Another room?"

"Oh yes. Answer is yep."

"Then shall we ..."

"Yes?" Tides of desire were sloshing back and forth. "Yes?"

"Shall we head up?"

"Well, er—" Shell broke the rhythm. "No."

"No?"

"Nope." An impasse? "Can't."

"But I thought ..."

"Sorry, sweet. I'm being a tease." Desire resumed its flow. "It's just that we can't go *up*. Our ranch house; one level." (This was another conversation she'd be recalling the evening Astrid came for dinner.)

Astrid's eyes flared. "You lead," releasing her prisoner's hands.

"I obey, dear ma'am, hon', babe."

When she paused to pour a large glass of apple juice, Astrid began to tap her foot. Then Shell folded Astrid's arm into hers, to lend her support as they edged through the den door. "Later, then, fishies—" a plaintive farewell at the tank.

In her room, they found her one bed, which not only *felt* more spacious than the stool but proved to be. In spades. (Would 'in hearts" be more apt?) Under its cool sheets, their bodies quickly found a perfect rhythm. Their lips and hands were soon matching their legs' long-distance harmony.

Morning After and Forest Park Picnic

They slept in late next morning—no surprise, considering their strenuous five days of track, and their equally strenuous recent hours of discovery. It is true that, around dawn, Shell woke long enough to pull back their sheets to check on Astrid's scar, first with her eyes, soon with her tongue. The move woke first the limb, then the woman, into a sensuous stretch. A slitted eye grew into a loving gaze—like a sandy promontory bared to the sun at low tide—before sinking and dissolving into a sleepy smile.

Two hours later, Astrid awoke fully refreshed. On the spot she invented an unorthodox approach to that unconsumed apple juice. She reached across Shell and dipped two fingers into the crystal glass. She painted the dozing Shell's upper lip, then her lower, whispering "treat time." Shell first licked her two lips then proceeded to suck Astrid's two fingers dry.

A second immersion allowed Astrid to draw a fragrant "x" across Shelley's nearest nipple and, soon enough, across the other. She then helped herself to slow, alternating sips. Neither appeared to regret the deliberate pace of consumption.

Astrid cradled her chin in her hand and loomed over Shell. She announced, "Dear babe. You've given me *so much*. Medicine" (pointing to her knee), "food" (patting her mouth then rubbing her belly), "and lodging" waving at their shared bed. "So, in return, let me ..." She prevented Shell's motion to object, "Shh. No backtalk. Here's a little something, compliments of Mark. Let's see, now. Oh, yes. First, he'd put his ..."

In time, Astrid's memory and Shell and Astrid's practice got the move right. Mark's expert method, like the directives of any strong faith, got transmitted from expert disciple to eager novice. Those ten minutes re-confirmed Shell's discovery the night before that, while sex was a reliably terrific journey, prolonged intimacy with a loving partner—in this case, an amusing, fit, seductive, and experienced woman—was the gift to be treasured.

* * * * *

Saturday afternoon, they feasted beside Shell's new favorite spot, the waterfalls where Shelley had run her daily March wind sprints, where she began proving herself to herself. All the while hoping Astrid in time would notice. (Astrid's intimate presence offered ample confirmation of the success of those efforts.) The vestigial majesty of Forest Park, a massive green space at the city's heart, meant little to Shell. Of its noble civic history she knew nothing. No, what *she'd* loved, after her full month of healthful conditioning there, was the endless play of the water, cascading gently from level to level down the steep, wooded hillside. It seconded the intense satisfactions her conditioning was yielding.

In honor of that first movable feast, Shell surveyed her closet and selected a bright, emerald-green top. It was an item she'd bought a year before for her third date with Mike, a wrestler upon whom she had developed an extravagant Spring crush. Its three turquoise strings in back made what proved to be unsuccessful efforts to keep its two soft flaps closed. In the course of the evening Mike had displayed his genuine admiration first of the garment and—soon enough—of the svelte, firm body it both covered and disclosed. (That paradox afforded the two affectionate novices considerable delight.) Shell hoped Astrid would concur with Mike's judgment.

The relationship with Mike had burned for just a season but its failure proved a godsend. It whispered a vital message to her young heart: Brief but intense flings, even with stunning, muscular and admiring young men, might be delightful indulgences. Oh yes. But they were not, at length, the be-all of dating. The insight, slow to arrive, served to unloose that vast undersea mesa of desire. With Shell's first full view of Astrid in the gym on that cold afternoon, and the drama of the exciting tale she told, the massive ledge breached the surface of conscious desire like a whale, golden water cascading from its sides.

Astrid's good taste in due course confirmed Mike's. Time and again.

* * * * *

Their first wonderful day did have one sad moment. (Life, the precocious senior was discovering, can be that way.) It happened an hour or so later when Astrid finally made herself unhook herself from Shelley's hands and lips: "Listen. Coach Winter. He assures me I'm the older and wiser one."

"Yeah, I *used* to think so. But ..."

Astrid's kisses kept her from finishing the thought. But then she leaned above Shell's reclining body. "Seriously, Shell. Hon'. It's been what? Twelve hours? And here I am. Head over heels."

"Yes," she pulled Astrid close. "I've been noticing."

"God you are amazing, sweet. Makes it even harder to say this. Just now. But..." She took Shell's two hands and held her at arm's length. "Listen. What we're doing here is marvelous. But we should think. It may just be a stage, a phase, in each of our lives. It's *glorious*; you're *incredible*. Oh, my yes. But while we're indulging, we should try—fuck! *Damn* it all—to think. Slow down and think."

Shell, her eyes misting, reached up to squeeze Astrid's lips tight.

"No no no. No talk about phases, babe. Focus on now. Hosmer track, for one thing." (She pressed a thumb on Astrid's thumb.) "And our food cravings." (Index fingers.) "And sex, especially that move of Mark's. Wow." (Middle fingers, appropriately). "And oh yeah, that bicycle dude." (Fourths.) "And oh yes. I forgot sex." (By then two palms did a full embrace.)

"Uh, no, Shell. You didn't forget." (Astrid lifted their entwined hands and kissed the back of Shell's.) "But now, now, sweet. Sure, I know, I know. We must enjoy our special season. No pacing for *us*. But we have to keep in mind—" (time sounded its tyrannical chime) "come August, me in Ohio. You here, Wash U. Separate *futures*, babe."

"Yeah, but wait. Wait! Even after you scoot off and heartlessly abandon me... well, there's phones. And email. And cars."

"I know, I know. Still, trust me, fall's going to bring you a *new* world. Antire has for me. You'll start shedding an old skin. You *should*."

Shell harrumphed. "You seemed to enjoy that 'old skin' last night." When Astrid growled in agreement and renewed desire,

Shell took advantage. "And one thing I know. I'll be a better summer fling than your Mark."

"You win. Hands down." As Astrid renewed that enjoyment, Shell resumed what was becoming a new favorite occupation, moving aside Astrid's abundant hair. It had been displaying the most damnable habit—assisted now by the sprightly April breeze—of getting between their mouths. So she laid Astrid's glass aside and reached into the wicker cornucopia she'd brought. She premiered—"Look, hon'"— a bright green ribbon. Then a firm command, "Sit up a sec," allowed her to net Astrid's rich cascade into a dainty ponytail.

"Now for that mouth."

They then sank back slowly onto the blanket, and enjoyed again the taste of each other's lips, neat now. Lying side by side, they started their ten fingers dancing in place above them, now like a dainty spider doing push-ups on a mirror. The veins and muscles in those dancing, twining arms, came and went, came and went, a loving tangle.

One second, she was beholding Astrid's firm but delicately tapered digits and inhaling the perfume from her wrists. A second later came a moment of rich *sfumato*. Their encounter unloosed waves of memories through Shell, a blur of distinct images: winter wrestlers straining in tight grips; the relay squad doing spring leg-lifts; Mike's pushed-up sleeves when he saw, explored and disassembled her top. That guy on the bike.

Her pulsing fingers froze into a loving grip around Astrid's hand, which she guided yet once more into that vivid green top. Astrid's palm became a pulsating second heart, now gently seductive, now boldly authoritative.

Follow-Up Days after the Picnic

Shell had to re-adjust to an empty bed in her still empty house Saturday night. (She made herself set Astrid free, so she could pursue her get-out-the-vote dedication.) But she had a dream that almost compensated. She couldn't figure it out then, but a pass-fail college Physics course sophomore year would help. She saw Astrid—well, some regal figure anyway—standing on a chariot, mastering a team of horses. But, well, they weren't quite horses. With a flick of her firm bare wrists, Astrid created what that course would suggest to the imaginative Shell were wormholes that ran (circulated? whispered?) between the steeds: her mind leaping from one foaming one to another, snagged in a single instant into an instant within an earlier world. The effect may have been, yes, mysterious and cosmic, but in our down-to-earth world Shell awoke aroused. Nothing new, there. By now *everything* aroused her: Astrid's image, the memory of Astrid, dreams of Astrid. Even cucumber rounds on a plate *near* Astrid.

So, the next evening, when she heard her phone ring, Shell knew. She'd been sitting on her now-favorite kitchen stool, slicing apples for Ben's cocktail hour. She was entertaining the other four members of her family (just back) with tales—selected, sure; censored, a bit—of her twenty-two hours and eighteen minutes with Astrid.

"*You* remember. Our incredible coach?" They sighed, rolled their eyes. "Boy, you guys! She's even neater in person. Came over Friday after practice; I fixed her dinner. Right here! She'd hurt herself on the hurdles, so I made her my blueberry potion."

"Like you fixed for my ankle that time?" Angie asked. "Lucky Astrid."

"That's the one, my steppie." (Ang' giggled.) "Well, it got so late, she slept over."

"And then yesterday ..." she paused. Ben blew a kiss as he walked past her with his briefcase to the den. She pointed at the array of carved apples and back at him. "Right back, hon. Keep talking."

"So, yesterday…" she resumed, looking to the other three. Her eyes shimmered as she began her tale. "We visited my waterfall. I made us a picnic." Three nods at *that*.

That was when the phone interrupted her memory. It rang in real time. At that time, on that day, it was "now". Shell instantly grabbed it and cradled it under her chin as she finished slicing the rich cheddar.

"I never want to do this again, Shell-bell." The dulcet voice made the warm earpiece vibrate.

"Well, neither do I. I really don't. But—" her eye twinkled, "Who is this? Jay?"

"I hate you."

"Did I" (lowered voice, mouthpiece cupped) "fuck up again?" (Louder) "Were we on for today? Cosines?"

"Damn you."

"*Oh.*" She winked at the six eyes that swung her way. "It's *Astrid!* Hi. We were just discussing you. But what's…" she lowered her voice and swung away, "with the nickname?"

"'Shell-bell'? Oh, just something to mark our first phone call. Deal with it, babe. (I know *'babe's'* okay.)"

"Of course." She backed toward their stool and sank into its welcoming cushion.

"Good thing."

"Now, what is it you don't want to do?"

"*That?* Oh, go for a whole day without you." Shelley's heart prodded her rib-cage. "Yep. Ignoring my own advice about trying new stuff. God, I love repeating all your instant traditions.

Now, you *know* I hated to beg off after your—our—picnic," Astrid went on. "Those damned reports. Worked all afternoon, stayed up late, got up early, did 'em. Then I even got started on the precinct voting stats for the staff this summer. Impressed?"

"Impressed, not surprised." She lowered her voice. "I love to hear you say 'summer'. You'll *be* here."

"Yes, babe; yes, hon'. 'Til August. But after I got that all done... I was useless. I just gazed out from my balcony."

"Useless? You? Never"

"You are sweet. But then guess what?"

"What?"

"Saw your face. In the clouds." (Shell's heart resumed the lively beat.) "And sometimes all of you, head to toe. Naked, two feet away, like yesterday morning. And then—well, *you* know."

"I do?" Flattered by the artesian well of praise, Shelley arose from the stool and began a slow spin in place. She wanted to hear her Astrid say out loud what, *yes of course,* she knew. (She was still a woman after all. Even young, strong, and independent women can still indulge in some vanity.) Yes, even play coy in pursuit of a higher mission.

"'And then' what? Say it!"

68

"Well, then, sweet. Turned on."

Shelley emitted a rare blush and pivoted deliberately out into the hallway. The cord became a kitten, curling affectionately around her ankle. She had to sidle past her dad and raise the cord over his head as he returned from the den. She lowered her voice again.

"Now *that's* my horny sweet." (Then, in an even softer whisper,) "And guess what? *I'm* feeling it too. Twins!"

Just as she said it, Ashley and Angie peeked their heads around the doorway, stuck out their tongues; then popped out of sight, like bubbles of foam, gales of giggles the only rack left behind.

"I want to say more. Some folks around here, though—" she hinted.

"So you're in the nook? *Our* nook?"

The plural pronoun had two instant effects: aroused her still more and moistened her eyes. "Real close, hon'."

"They're back?"

"Exactly," (lower voice again) "... babe."

"In that case, I got another question."

69

"Which is?"

"Which is, 'Where *can* we get together?' Could—"

Shelley lifted her newly firm calves on tiptoes of anticipation. "Could—?" She'd exerted herself as a wooer all Friday and much of Saturday. Time to *be* courted.

"You could come *here.*"

"And *here* means—?"

"'Here' means my place. Oh, Lord: I smell a Shell quiz coming. Her next probe is 'when?' My answer: 'after practice'. 'And on what day?' '*Tomorrow*, babe.' Asked and answered,' as my dad says in court."

"Nice one-lady dialogue, hon'. But here's a question you didn't consider: will Mark be there?"

"No, hon'. No Mark. Merely Astrid and her belle." Now it was her voice that dropped lower. "I want you, sweet Shell."

Shelley looked affectionately on the doorjamb as Astrid issued her first official invitation, a pedestrian sight that became for her a subliminal image the rest of the summer. Whenever Astrid called, Shell would start "jambing."

"Well, then ..." She stopped in space, shoulders back, satisfied. "Yes."

* * * * *

"Tomorrow after practice," Shell was relieved to find Astrid's condo door at ground level. But she felt just a twinge of an old chill when she saw that its inside was a two-story affair. But she sussed that, just visible through the high balcony's railings, was Astrid's bedroom. So eagerness (and, let's be frank, desire) dispelled the chill. (Astrid's parents were treating her to a place of her own, a reward for her initiative in landing the spring job.)

They kissed. They talked about their first day back at school. They kissed. They sipped some wine. They kissed.

Astrid took charge. "Know something? I think you'd look good in a hat. I love your flowing hair (well, it's *starting* to, *trying* to), but I want to bunch it all up. Oh, look! That Cardinal hat, maybe?"

She pointed to one on her coat-stand. "I'll make you my track dude."

"Sure, sweet. So now I'm your *guy*?

One hand piled the hair into a mop. The other performed two erotic services. It caged the hair with the cap and then it grabbed Shell by the neck. By now Shelley was always craving the feel of that strong, delicate hand. Astrid's supple but determined lips were, next and immediately, providing a wonderful bonus.

71

Then, "Now, what? Do some climbing?" She pointed up to the first landing, then to the balcony.

"Oh, what the hell babe." Curiosity and appetite dispelled any doubts. "Up it is."

"The whole way?"

"Don't you always?"

"We do."

* * * * *

An hour or so later, Astrid had dozed off, hair streaming. The lights were off and the curtains drawn, but Shell still thought the room glowed. The moment offered her a perfect opportunity, gratis. From that Alumnae Hall plaque she knew (she'd memorized) the slew of awards Astrid had won. So here was a chance for Shell to try out her version of the scientific method: match certain Astrid body-parts and muscles to each award. Naturally, the experiment required that she revisit, in minute and sequential detail, that glorious body.

She pulled down the sheet and began her inventory. "The mile? That'd be those thighs and calves. Like La Shonda's. Hmm, Mike's too. Oh, yes." She reached out to stroke that sheen of golden skin and smiled when she noticed that the red scar had nearly dissolved. ("God, I'm good.") Astrid birthed the tiniest smile, mid-doze.

"And the pole vault? Upper arms. Chest and shoulders. Like Jean's." While Shell's experiment was quenching her curiosity, it was also, no surprise, kindling her desire. Within ten seconds—well, call it thirty—she'd started to reacquaint her lips with each muscled but sensuous area.

So much for Astrid's doze.

Reorders

Back home, in her own room after dinner (her conscience had been reminding her that she should spend *some* time at home), Shell knelt down to poke through her chifforobe. In its lower drawer were the (now stacked and rubber-banded) collection of photos she'd retrieved from the den. Next to them, a rolled calendar, a Christmas present she'd unwrapped but stowed there, out of mind. "Hey! I can use it. Keep a record. Of us: my Astrid and her Ashella." She entered an "X" in that April day's square.

She retreated to her bed, sat against the headboard and began a sensuous spool of the last ten days. Before long, she had nearly every square bulging. She drew a "smile for the days when I just *thought* about her. Then a '!' for... yeah. (Steps won't know what it means)" (giggle.) "Today gets two."

The budding scientist was discovering that, true, life offers only momentary pleasures, but the best of them could be saved and re-experienced if *recorded*. Who knew she could become her own historian?

* * * * *

Astrid met Mark for drinks mid-week. She explained they'd have to re-retrieve their old, safe friendship. "I've met someone. Suddenly, old babe, I'm involved."

"Do I know the guy?"

"No."

* * * * *

That week at the track, Astrid divided her time among the vaulter, hurdler and distance squads. When consulting, she would lean an occasional elbow or hand on a shoulder explaining— always patiently, usually firmly, occasionally playfully— various techniques of leg extension, foot striking, and timing. ("Ya' listening now, Josh? Okay, one more time…"). Rarely, between heats or drills, she would look up and across the northern quadrant of the in-field—where the milers and relay team usually gathered. Where Shelley was practicing wind sprints or doing push-ups or extra crunches in between her relays. If Astrid caught Shelley's face turned in her direction, she'd usually give her ponytail a toss or two and pull its green ribbon tighter. If Shell saw, she'd dab her neck with her towel.

When she jogged over to advise the LDs, Astrid stood in the center of the infield, to assess Jessie, Shelley, La Shonda and Amy as they ran their daily mile. She'd stand there, surrounded by the other attentive squad members. She'd slowly rotate during each circuit, a firm knot to which the four runners were tethered.

Shelley's mile that day was her "personal best." True, she crossed the line three seconds behind LaShonda, but she had run the trial heat in 5 minutes, 10 sec—her fastest by an impressive 6 seconds. As she began pacing around the infield, panting heavily and edging with the squad toward Astrid, she stopped to remove her shoe. She examined it and ended up poking a finger through it from inside. Astrid complimented her on her time but, seeing that wriggling finger, added, "And just think, Jaspar—the time you could make with two *good* shoes?"

Shelley nodded, but lacked the oxygen to laugh.

"Now, young ladies," Astrid turned to her acolytes. "Remember what I was telling those guys? Lap 2 and 3? Pacing! And try out that foot-strike method from last week. Then for that last circuit, all out! You heard?"

They had. But now Astrid had more to say. "Now when you head out for the next run—groups of four—I want you to let what I've been telling you travel from your ears ..." (she tapped Nina's left ear) "up into your brains," (she pantomimed rubbing Miriam's forehead, as if to call up a genie), "then down to your legs, yes even miler you" (pointing her finger at the top of Jean's upper calf, and gesturing to the group). "Got it?"

"Yes, ma'am."

"Yes, who?"

76

"Yes, coach Astrid." They met her half-way.

Shelley, still panting, tagged on her own comic echo, "Yes, ma'am—" but she let a smile frog-kick to the surface.

"Winded?" Astrid leaned a sharp and professional arm on her shoulder. Shelley's red face supplied the answer as she bent over, holding her side tightly. "Next time, you'll feel it less. Less the time after that."

She turned to the full group. "Know what else I think, all you ladies?"

"What's that, coach?"

"I think you're ready."

"For tomorrow, Astrid?"

"Of course. But more."

"Districts?"

"Districts for sure; *I'm* thinking state, ladies!"

"Really, coach?" a wide smile overspread Shell's face.

"Really, Astrid?" asked the other three with three wide smiles.

"Really," Astrid confirmed. "Today, Jaspar; your five-ten? It's competitive. And *all of you* beat five-thirty. A new plateau, my Hosmeys! When I'm back next Christmas, bet your names'll be on that plaque."

Universal delight.

* * * * *

Toward the end of practice, an hour later, something remarkable occurred. Several guys on the squad often pestered Coach Winter to ask Astrid to demonstrate one of her several track specialties. Now and again, he'd agree. (By mid-April, a typical Perot "demo" grew from a small master class into a communal and educational gala.) This time he whispered, "pole vault?" She readily agreed. Though the team's vaulters were all male, she hoped one of the underclass women observers would be inspired for next season. "Plant seeds" was her daily mission.

Shelley, from the infield's far end, saw the pulsing swarm of bodies around the runway and pit. Her eyes lit up with a mischievous notion: capture her woman on tape. A dose of her own medicine. Appraise *her!* She could already predict Astrid's silken outrage. "Horny voyeur!"

She nudged a couple of relay buddies and disclosed her plan.

"You go, girl!" Three conspiratorial fist-bumps.

She retrieved the camera from the coach's well-stuffed duffel bag and scurried to the infield's north end. There the assistant coach was making practice feints, each one tuning the observers' murmurs to an ever higher pitch. One more. Then, at last, she dashed down the runway—feet pounding, dust swirling.

At the last possible moment, with her hair unloosed from that green ribbon, she launched herself into space. Or so it seemed to the earth-bound witnesses. She was soaring, soaring, soaring … until for an infinitesimal instant she hung, her hair streaming, her body suspended in both space and time. (She seemed to hang motionless above the crossbar, like that mammoth Webb space telescope. They say it'll bask, farther up—or out, if demanding readers insist—than Scott's Gavin, a million miles out, in a magic equipoise between sun, earth and moon.)

Another micro-instant, she'd cleared the bar and was descending, a glittering blond arc, into the pit of cedar chips where she inflicted geological trauma. Her body set their aromatic billows free. The entire squad stirred their various pitches of voice and echoes of slapping hands into the airy melee.

Shelley caught it on tape, though she almost didn't. A guy kneeling beside her pointed to the lens cap she'd failed to remove. (When she smiled her thanks, he grinned but looked away.)

In her room that very evening, she discovered how much she treasured the stop-action feature of the recorder-player. As a budding scientist (as she called herself with a wink) she could watch, frame by frame, those muscles in action that, at rest, she delighted to "inspect". As the full-length video spooled, she could see, and almost *feel,* the hard biceps gripping the vertical pole, and the full breasts swiveling in the sleeveless track shirt during the ascent. On not a few subsequent nights, she replayed it. Each time she brought time to a halt, she let herself indulge in some ecstatic motion.

* * * * *

That evening—it was a Wednesday—Shelley called Astrid. She had news. So *much* news. "Hey, lady."

"My sweet belle."

In the background Shell heard some music and her foot began to pulse. "What is that? Neat!"

"That's ragtime, sweet."

"Cool. I like! Whatever *that* means. Say, you busy?"

"Now wait. Who *is* this? Jean? Aims?"

"Bitch."

"Oh, sorry: *Is* this Shell?"

"Who else? How many girlfriends you got? *You* pretended I was Jay. Well, *I* can play the game, hon.'"

"Just one, hon'. Just one. *You*. So then, if it is my dear Shell, how could I *ever* be busy?"

Shelley blushed. "God you are wonderful. I'm so crazy about you."

Astrid matched Shell's new sweet tone. "And *I'm* so lucky."

"God you were splendid today."

"Today?"

"Your demo, that vault. I wouldn't have missed it, my sweet star. And guess what?"

"What's that? Did, um, something come for you?"

"Come for me? What do you mean?"

"Never mind. Nothing. So what is it I should guess?"

"This. I stole your video cam. Now I have *you* on tape."

"Ah. My sex buddy turns thief. Nice. Guess it's my corrupting influence, eh?"

"No, sweet. It was my own initiative. And, my sweet, video's way better than a snapshot, right? You're so big on making all my shots tell a story."

Astrid harrumphed.

"You mad?"

"Nah. It's cool." Then she added, in the melodic *sotto voce* Shelley was inspiring in *her*, "Horny voyeur."

Shell laughed to herself but returned to business. "There's one other reason I'm calling, besides to hear your voice. Oops, wait. I heard a good one from dad last night at dinner. Ready?"

"Hard to keep up, hon'. But spill, babe. Spill!"

"It's a sign on a church he drove by. It reads, 'Tired of sin? Come hear Pastor Einhardt preach on 'Reforming the Broken spirit.'"

"Sounds heavy, that!"

"Don't it? Well, under it someone had scrawled: 'If not, call 878-4320.'" She gave a pregnant pause. "You like?"

Astrid's hearty laugh gave the answer. "I like him already." After a brief pause, Astrid asked: "Say, my sweet hot Shell: *you* tired of sin?"

Shell supplied a throaty growl of desire, sliding seamlessly into a laugh.

"Man, my young lady, you don't know how hard that was today. So proud of your best time, but all I could throw at you was words." She sighed. "Even our afternoons aren't enough for me right now. Sitting with Mark that time, sipping our cosmos—"

"What? You two were swilling the universe? Major appetites, hon."

"No, no, no you dim auburn! Cosmo*politans*. They're drinks. Someday, *you* may be old enough."

"Oh, yeah. Like *you're* so legal."

"Yeah, well, at least I *look* old enough."

"Fuck you."

"Would you?"

Their matched hearty laugh lasted two or three seconds.

"But listen. Let *me* finish. I just wanted it to be you next to me there, your lips drying mine, sip after sip."

"Christ! You let Mark do all that in public?"

"No, no. It's a fantasy I'm working on. For *us*. No, *we* behaved. *He* behaved."

Shelley breathed out. "Ah. Much better."

"I miss you."

"Yeah, well. I have a plan."

"Ta- da! Your nook free?"

"No. Not quite. But listen!" (She paused.) *"Here's* why I called."

"Finally, the point! My wonderful and disorganized darling babe."

"May be that's because you're inspiring me. So many ways. Now listen: I want you to come over. I want you to meet my folks—Dad, Averill, the 'Steps'. I want to introduce them to my girl, woman, coach, hon. To my babe. Do ya' *hear* me, sweet?"

Shell lay on her bed, phone against her ear, resting on her chest. Her foot was beating to Astrid's ragtime music, her eyes roaming across her open closet. She was already selecting, rejecting, combining a Friday outfit. (Not organized? Ha. All it takes is the right inspiration.)

"You think they're ready?"

"They will be. I got them pretty-well tamed with my guys. The minute I hang up, I'll go tell 'em. They'll just have to deal with it: their girl has moved on. On, hon, *and* up." Her mind drifted to her lover's lofty queen bed. "Up to my star. Show 'em why I'm so proud of you."

"Well, sweet, I'll try."

"Try? Simple. Just be Astrid."

"That easy, huh?"

"Oh, yes. Yes, yes."

New Shoes

Off the phone, she headed straight to the house's bustling center, her fingers snapping to that new ragtime tune pulsing in her brain.

(Astrid later informed her it was the "Maple-leaf Rag" by Scott Joplin. Some later historical research helped her discover that he was a fellow Missourian. More, he was from Sedalia, her grandfather's home-town. So, the budding history buff scored a trifecta: lively music, Missouri history, a family tradition.)

From the Jaspar-Grimm's sizable freezer she extracted a blue plastic tub. Within its icy glaze, its insides glowed orange. Then she swung into the for-once deserted kitchen and snagged a saucepan from the rack suspended above the center island. Its extraction left the others to sway and tap in random syncopation, a seven-second distraction. She reached for the flour canister, prized off its top, and checked its moisture with two fingers. (When she meets Scott, she'll've become a past-master of floury textures.)

Then her toes did a push up, lifting those calves to help her reach the nutmeg and cinnamon. She flipped their lids, shook a dash into each palm, and did a quick lick. From another gleaming rack, this one above the sideboard, she grabbed a whisk and proceeded up the hall, beating dotted eight notes on the bottom of the pan. (She didn't know that term either, but a music professor would identify and demonstrate it for her three years later). Bubbling into her dad's den, she found the steps hovering near his couch. She crooked a finger at them: "Ladies! A new recipe."

"But we're watching..." Angie began.

"Oh, yes. Yes," Ashley drowned her out. "What is it?"

Next instant, Shell was leading them down the hall, compliant field mice trailing a spicy pied-piper (well, -drummer). Then Ashley hurled a concern. "Hey, Shell. We always cook for dinner. Dinner's *over*."

"Not this time, my steppies. Something new. For later. If you *can* wait up till midnight, it'll be ready, like magic, at the stroke of twelve." Shelley started to count the "dongs" with a faux baritone voice.

"Oh, no, Shell. Papa Ben won't let us. Too late."

"Well, I'll see if I can work on him. Or for tomorrow: an afternoon snack. Plus, you can lick the bowl."

"Oh, all right," Angie yielded. "So what's in it, big sis?"

"It's going to be bread, flavored with pumpkins. Pumpkin bread. Sound neat?"

"Pumpkins? That's Halloween. You need a calendar, Shell." The reproof produced a smile.

"No, it's something new and different. Look. Here's the sugar pumpkin puree from last October. Angie? Water faucet. Let's bring it back to life!"

With a mischievous cackle, she began to juggle the jars of cinnamon and nutmeg, entrancing the two girls with the whir of her hands and the arcs of the air-tight plastic bottles. Then, without warning, she flipped one to Ashley and—just as she had opened her mouth to wail—the other to Angie. Each caught her own flawlessly. (Clearly it was not a new routine.)

"So, then. Tonight we blend and then we bake, okay?"

"Okay. But after, will you read to us? In bed?" asked Ashley.

"Yeah, the Aslan one again, can we?" chimed in Angie. "Will you, huh?"

"Of *course*. But now, you guys are in charge again. You're getting so good! Our two new kitchen queens."

Two sad looks. "Yeah. College girl."

"Right, my sweet-hearts. But I'll still be in town. So now. Ash? Mix! Angelina? Thaw! Then I'll come read. Deal?"

It was. And the timing freed Shell to walk to the den to fetch her Dad. As she passed the fish, she smacked her hands together, scattering a few spicy grains into their watery demesne. They rose to the surface, first to investigate, then to revel.

"Dad, it's time."

"Time? For what?"

"For a chat, okay?"

He looked up from his computer, sliding a mouse in erratic circles across its pad, holding it, eying it and blowing on it.

"Chat? Sure, sure. Just get me away from this."

"Turn it off and try later. Wait while I get mom. For a family consult. Got the steps busy so I can tell you and Ave' some stuff."

She scurried down the long hallway that led to the west end of the house. As her bare toes curled into the plush carpet, she found she was looking up at the flat, white ceiling. She noticed, for the first time, the creamy, pebbly swirl of its paint.

"I wonder, could it hold a balcony?" She nearly stopped in transit. "Or why not an attic? That'd be so handy for..."

Not pausing to analyze the disquieting image or explore the incomplete hypothesis, she proceeded to summon Averill. Then, back in the den, she pulled her dad to his feet and led him to his wife on the couch. Shell drew up a hassock to sit before them with silent anticipation. Her eyes bounced steadily back and forth, cautious but eager.

"Well, I told you coach Astrid came over, right? Two weeks ago?"

"Such a nice gesture," Averill offered her usual compliment.

"'Astrid'? Remind me please," said Ben.

"*Astrid*, dad! *Astrid*. That computer's addled your brain. My track coach? And mom: I wasn't just being nice."

"No?"

"Well, not *just*. There's more to tell. Have you noticed? Been getting in from school later than usual?"

"Well," Averill admitted. "I *have* been seeing more of the girlies in the kitchen without you. Your wonderful influence."

"Well, yeah, I leave them special orders; new recipes; new ingredients to try out. But here's why. I've been dropping by *her* place. Lots. First time she asked me over, she used a word. What was it? 'Sip-pro'? Something sipping?"

"Could it be reciprocate?" Ben suggested.

"That's it. Said she was re*ciproc*ating. For when I played host."

"Well, that's great Shell," offered Averill. "It's good to have an older friend. Some good advice on college. Your *next chapter*."

"She's been great. But listen. Listen—"

Ben put a finger on his wife's lips and tilted his head toward Shelley. "I think there's more."

"Yes there is. Oh daddy, yes!"

"Okay, Shell of my life." Ben took charge. "Enough suspense."

"You're right. Well, then. About Astrid." She placed both hands on her knees and drew herself up to her full sitting height. "She's mine."

"Yours?" Averill asked.

"Yes. She's my *woman*!"

"How's that?" Ben sat forward to study her eyes.

She stared back and squeezed his hand tighter. "*You'd* probably call it a crush. But no. It's more. I cannot get enough of her!"

"You're dating your coach?" Averill struggled with the novel idea.

"Yes and no. I'm *seeing, spending time with* ... okay: *dating* a cool woman named *Astrid*. Just so *happens* she's the coach."

The clarification brought things to a silent halt. Shelley resumed: "And there's even more ..."

Ben held up a cautionary finger. "Now wait. Before the 'more,' when did all this get started? Was it the time she came over—when we, *conveniently*, were gone?"

"Well, maybe that's when it started for *us*. Or for *her*. But for *me*, it started that day of the chalk talk. *You* know. All I could talk about."

Two sighs. "Who could forget?"

"Well, I had eyes for her from that day. But I couldn't get *her* to pay any attention until—yes, dad. It *was* convenient you were gone. Perfect chance. And I made my move."

"*That* sounds like you," Ben conceded. "Especially lately. Our about-to-graduate Shell."

"You've noticed? Yes. And we had so much fun 'hanging' the first evening, that I made her stay. Then, next day..."

"Your picnic."

"Right, mom. In the Park. And, while we sat and talked, would you believe she had the—what's that fancy phrase of yours, dad? Un- mitty-something gall..."

"Unmitigated gall?"

"Fine. The whatever you said *gall* to declare that, get this— she'd. never. much. *noticed.* me."

"You sound hurt, hon. Is that how love works nowadays?"

"Ben, I believe it's irony?"

"Right, Mom Ave. You got it. Something *else* I'm picking up from my sweet Astrid. *Teasing.* She's *so* cool."

"Stop again. By 'cool', you mean ..."

"What do I mean?" She closed her eyes and began to enumerate, squeezing one right hand finger after another with her left thumb and forefinger. "I'll *tell* you what I mean. She's cool because she likes to tease me; cool, cuz she knows her track stuff

93

and *teaches* us, the whole squad; cool, a super *athlete*. A great student too, by the way. And cool, so *gorgeous*! But," she borrowed Ben's thumb to continue the count, "coolest of all, daddy, she really cares for me, your daughter." She opened her eyes and gazed at them both. "'Cool' enough?"

"Yes, hon. Way cool." Ben smiled. "But how about the stuffy Hosmer world. *They* might not find it 'cool.'"

"Fuck. Let 'em." She released Ben's thumb.

"Ashella!"

"No, mom. It's *our* business. She's wonderful. Forceful. Athletic. I was *attracted*. I wanted her. I seized my opportunity and stole her heart. *Pretty* sure I did. So. Well. If they can't appreciate us, it's *their* loss."

"Sure, Shell. I guess…" Averill began.

But Shell was determined. "No, I mean it. And, anyway: Another month, we'll just be two college kids. Adult women! No, dad. The *truth* is, they'll be jealous," she chortled. "The *guys* will, for sure." The laugh settled happily into a satisfied smirk. "I repeat. *Their* loss. Hah."

"Well, my wee Shell. Oops, that's you from ten years ago. I better say, my young woman. You know I trust your judgment, and you clearly know your mind here."

Shell reached for his hand and squeezed it.

"But listen to your father. Be careful, hon. Life can play hardball, even with a special, first-time-ever crush. And true love's hard at *any* time."

"I know, dad. *She* knows. We've *talked*."

"Well…"

"Now next: the point. No more 'wells.' I want you to meet her. So *you* can see. Friday. I've already invited her."

Averill grasped Shelley's hands. Ben shrugged two helpless shoulders. "Fine. Fine. *We* have no social life. Right, dear?"

* * * * *

From down the hall, the doorbell's loud chime. (Not the "bong" of time, but the "ding" of opportunity.)

"I'll get it," shouted Ashley from the kitchen.

"Be careful dear. Look out the window."

She stuck her head inside the door *en route*, her nose and cheeks spangled with cinnamon. "I'm Ashley. I'm always careful."

Ten seconds later, she flopped back into the room with a "Look! A package. Who's it for, Shell? You?"

"Is there a name on it?" Averill asked.

"Dunno. But I signed for it! Aren't I great?"

"Yes dear. *So* grown up."

Ashley beamed.

Angie then appeared, a crease of flour across her chest. "Whatisit, whatisit? Sign what? Who from?"

"A package. No name, just our address."

As Shell surveyed the brown parcel, bound with vivid teal and gold ribbons, her eyes widened. A smile did a bench press among her bubbling features.

"Can *I* see? Let *me* open it." Angie was begging.

"Yes, yes! Open it, my Angelina!" A triumphant Shelley ran her hand through Angie's thick hair.

"Can I?"

Three adults nodded. Ash hovered over her to be sure she got it right. Angie slid the twining ribbons off, then tore off the brown wrapping. From it emerged ... what? A clear turquoise sleeve, shaped like a cornucopia. Into its depths Angie plunged her hands and a small geyser of golden paper began to spurt. Up from the bright innards her tiny hands re-emerged. In them, a pair of shoes—track shoes, royal blue with creamy white stripes.

Shell's eyes swam some more laps and her smile grew beatific. Then some restraint. She grew playful. "Well, nothing says they're for me. Hold up *your* foot, Ash."

She held the shoe up to the older stepsister's right sole. "Nope, no fit."

Ashley sighed but understood. "Nope. Way too big. And no, Angie, they can't be for you either. Mine'r bigger than yours."

"But can't I try? Please?" She flopped onto her back and waved her two stockinged feet like a grasshopper's antennae.

Ashley offered sigh number two and held one shoe up to her younger sister's right foot. "See, Angie. I *told* you. They're for *you*, big Shell."

"Well, wait." Shell did love prolonging the suspense, another variation on that trick she'd been acquiring under or on or in Astrid's sheets. "One last thought. Pa Ben? Sure this isn't some anniversary gift?"

Ben looked at Averill. "Now Shell. You know our anniversary's June 23 and *not* April 29. No, honey. Those are clearly track shoes. And, as of now, there's only one track star around here."

Shelley sighed in calm acquiescence, then let out a scream worthy of an eighth-grader spying her favorite rock star, live.

The new shoes from her athletic princess fit perfectly of course. As each foot eased like magic into each, she couldn't help adding, "*Told* you she's cool. She's wonderful." She didn't even worry about the steps hearing. She was too enthralled with her first girl-friend's professional and loving gesture. "She saw me stick my finger through one of my track shoes. Couldn't wait to fix the problem. See?"

The two adults nodded. The two young girls bubbled. So did the fish.

(Bubble, not nod.)

She carried the shoes in her arms up to her bed. As she lay there, she kept trying them on, one after the other. She called it "changing shoes." Then she stashed them under her other pillow, next to that calendar. But not before she'd drawn a throbbing heart on that day's square, pierced by an exquisitely painful arrow. She sketched in shoe-laces dancing on either side.

Awaiting Astrid for that Dinner

Shell was eager to see the effect the 20-year-old would have on dad, step-mom, and step-sisters. So tonight (back in real time now, as she sits by the hearth keeping a relaxed but eager look-out for Scott), she keeps returning to the instigating memory that's flooding through her. (What may have taken patient readers a good while to find and absorb, Shell's memory reclaimed and harvested in milliseconds.)

To the Hosmer manner born, Astrid knew to arrive politely late. But Shelley, born to that same manner, still couldn't help stealing an anxious glance starting at 5:30 to the circular drive out her bedroom window. Five minutes later she was parting those sun-yellow curtains in the kitchen's breakfast nook, leaning affectionately on that padded stool to peer again. She knew better but she peered. (And did so again at 5:40)

She really hadn't much to do in the kitchen. Her share of the meal was the *hors d'oeuvre*—she'd chosen hummus and had prepared it the night before. But a minute ago her eyes lit up with a last-minute addition: cucumber sandwiches.

Averill said, "Why, dear? It's just more work."

"Oh," she smiled. "Call it a whim. Oh, okay. I'll confess. It's what I fixed for her that first time. Only thing I could get her to take a bite of." She lowered her voice, "Fucking diet."

"Yeah, fucking diet," piped up Ashley. She'd been lurking near-by, basting the flock of Cornish hens she'd named as the night's entree.

"Don't say as we say," Shell and Averill answered in well-practiced unison.

After peeling the dark rind from the cucumber, Shell began slicing moist paper-thin slices. As she perches on the department chair's hearth three years later (now), the cuke's sweet whiff still thrills her memory. It evokes, in turn and just as vividly—yep, still another wormhole—an intense but luxurious afternoon tied up with Astrid and her sheets. (Two afternoons, actually. Remarkable, the way the brain can meld a host of distinct memories for an inspection that's both simultaneous *and* sequential.)

Shell fitted the round slices to the perfect rounds of bread she'd carved, then dressed and plated them. Then to her room for a second deliberation before her closet. No point, really. She'd already decided: that wrap-around green blouse (as she eyed it, no surprise that additional vivid memories jostled for notice). For her proper dad she wore it over a black turtleneck, the effect suitably

100

conservative, moderately inventive, and, like anything Shell chose, undeniably alluring.

Next she decamped to her dad's and Averill's room, to be sure he'd put on the clothes she'd laid out.

"Dad, don't you look great!"

"Now, now hon'. Fishing for compliments on *your* wardrobe orders."

"True, dad. So true." She patted herself on the back. "But seriously, are you sure you can handle this? Your daughter's new beau (or is it 'belle')"?

"My dear daughter, I'll manage. Your grandma did teach me some manners. I *won't* embarrass you. But, I repeat, I *am* going to set her down for that chat—man to...um, woman."

"Yes, sir. And when you do, you'll love her. You too."

"Well, dear Shell, you're hardly unbiased. But I do have to admit: you look fetching. Plan to sweep her off her feet?"

"No, dad. I already did."

* * * * *

Her perpetual motion swirled Shelley back to the living room, where both Steps were dawdling after their kitchen labors. She started in on one last lecture: deportment.

"Relax, Shell."

"Yeah. Relax, Shell."

"We'll be nice to your friend. We'll make you proud."

"Yeah, we'll be nice for—" Angie began. Then their joined voices went from E-flat to C, imitating the minor third motto of some TV thriller— "your *star*light."

"Now, *where* did you come up with *that*?" Shelley blushed briefly but resumed. "Huh, pudding? Eh, pigeon?"

"Heard you on the phone last night." Angie's soprano voice slid into an alto imitation of their big sis. "Can't wait until *tomorrow,* 'sunshine.' *Puh-leez* don't be late, 'starlight.'"

Ashley joined in: "Shell and starlight, sitting in a tree, K – I – ..."

"Okay, you two!" She threw each a stern glance. "And I'd appreciate it if you two'd stop eavesdropping. I mean it."

"Okay, Shell. We're sorry."

"Yeah, really."

"Well, then, baby lentil. Prove it. Tell. Me. Her. Name."

"Her name's *Astrid,*" Ashley recited, eyes downcast.

"Well, then," Shelley couldn't help smiling. "Try to remember. Both of you."

"Okay, big sis," Ash revived. "Be cool."

"Yeah, be cool," Angie echoed.

"We won't embarrass you in front of your *girl*friend."

"But I just wish—" the incorrigible Ashley took her two index fingers to twist a pair of indentations into Shelley's cheeks—"you had a dimple or two. Then you'd be cute. Maybe she'd like you then."

That Dinner

All in good if deliberate time arrives the Astrid meal, the feast whose sights, smells and tastes Shelley is spooling once more in these instants as she sits by the hearth, half a house from Scott. Shell did adopt Astrid's advice about photos—to capture those single caught moments and arrange them into a flowing narrative. But *this* festive night of true memories remains even now a string of recollected shots, a scintillant necklace of single, brief, bright recollections. They're still vibrant, and self-evidently fresh after three years, as the hearth-toasty college junior is revisiting her impatient high-school senior chrysalis.

A resplendently sunny May evening, Astrid at the front door. Svelte slacks of shimmering lemon; sleeveless black blouse. And that backpack: turquoise. Once in the door, she shucks it gently to the ground. From its bulging innards she proceeds to dispense gifts until its copious womb deflates.

For Averill, a packet of bouquet for the kitchen. As she passes the ribboned package to her, Ben looks at Shell, eyebrows raised.

"Not shoes, I hope."

"Dad! Behave yourself."

Ben winks at Astrid, reaching a finger to her which she promptly sizzles.

For him, a bottle of fine Missouri wine ("you legal?"; "Nah. My private stash"; Ben roared); for the two girls, bright green ribbons, handed over with a wink at Shelley.

Then, as she looks to Ben and Averill, "And now for you, Shell. Guess."

"*Can't* guess." Her eyes lose themselves in Astrid's.

Into the now-limp backpack she plunges her hand one last time and retrieves a dainty but thick album with an intricate paisley design of rich blues and greens. "Something to organize all those scattered pictures. See? Can you say 'album'? Hope you like the colors—my faves."

"See?" Shell crows to all. "Considerate, like I told you. And she knows exactly what I need. She *reads* me." As she reaches for the album, her fingers stroke the back of Astrid's hand. "I better borrow your fancy Nikon, Dad. Okay?"

* * * * *

Father in his armchair, Averill on its wide arm; Shelley across from them; Angie and Ashley simmering like popcorn kernels beside her, zipping periodically into the kitchen to check on "things." They'd given Astrid the comfy swivel chair.

Averill cleared her throat, "Shell? Think it might be time...?"

"—My special treat? Yeah; you're right."

"Can I help?" queried Astrid. "Let me help."

"If ya' helped, it wouldn't be a treat."

"I bet I know what it is. I bet it's the—" Angie's inevitable interruption provoked Averill and Shelley's tandem shush. "Angela! Remember s-e-c-r-e-t?"

Angie paused, her finger in the air, walking through each letter, eyes clenched. Enlightenment dawned. "Oh, okay. Her *secret* treat. For Star—I mean, for Astrid. I know."

"Yeah, and I know too." (Reliable Ash).

Shell returned with the plate of sandwiches, covered with a bright emerald cloth.

"Something special, Ms. Perot. You get to unveil." She went down on one knee and gazed into her babe's face. "*Bet* you like. *Hope* you like. *Know* you'll like."

"Me the honor? Well, *if* you insist." Four voices did.

"Tah-*dah,"* mimed Astrid and she made a great show of displaying the sandwiches. Her eyes lit up.

"Now," Shelley's blue eyes oscillated like slow billiard balls between Astrid's hazel ones, breathless (the woman, not her eyes) with anticipation. "Sample."

"Wondrous. But *this* time," she threw Shelley a mischievous look, "do I get to feed myself?"

Shelley hid a blush by standing up and placing her hands in comic ostentation on her hips. "Shall we peel you a grape too? Jeez."

"Okay, okay." Astrid took one perfect circle from the pile, bit off half of it, chewed with deliberation.

"Full bite, woman. No diets tonight."

"Pay no attention, Astrid," Averill interrupted. "Sometimes, she and good manners forget they're acquainted."

"Mom! Irony? Remember?"

"Effing diet." Ashley managed a whispered chortle to Angie.

* * * * *

107

Over dinner, twenty minutes later.

"Well, now, Ms.—is it Parrot?..."

"Astrid, sir. Please. Per-*oh* if you want to be formal, but Astrid, please."

"Sorry. Well, 'Astrid' then. And it's Ben. Please."

"Ben, Ben" the youngest two whooped. "Call him Ben."

"Okay, sir; Ben, I mean—" Astrid ignored the renewed giggles. "'Well, now' you said?"

"Yes. 'Well, now...' Please tell us more about the track squad. And your season."

"Ben, sweetie. Haven't you heard Shell over dinner for weeks now?"

"Of course, of course, hon. Just want to check *her* story." Loud stage whisper, hand beside his mouth. He waved a thumb at Shelley. "See if it matches."

"Right, Dad. Can't have me dating just *anyone*, can we?" Shell reached across the table and curled two fingers around Astrid's wrist.

"Oh, all right," Ben shrugged. "I yield. Your witness, dear," Ben looked with melodramatic helplessness at Astrid.

Averill grabbed the passed baton. "Our Shelley does tell us lots about track. Also her jogs up those falls—and of course you."

"Oh, Mother!"

"Oh. Admit it, Step-Shell," Ashley erupted. "Mom's right," she giggled. "Remember back in the winter? Mom made chili. You came home so excited we couldn't even get you to slice and peel." She turned to Astrid to recreate the moment. "She sat us at the table. To talk and talk about the coach and *her* 'talk'. Aren't I right? And you got out all our yearbooks. Right?"

"See what I put up with?" she whined to Astrid. "Every day. But it wasn't winter. It was March 22. First day of Spring! Barely a month ago."

"Suddenly Shell's made herself the team calendar, Ben." Astrid reached across the table to pet the back of Shelley's hand. "You tell 'em, Shell-bell."

"'Shell-bell!" Angie and Ashley nearly choked.

"What's the prob, dear young ladies?" Astrid came to her own rescue. "Can't big people have nicknames too? Eh, Piglet?" (She paused significantly and stared at Ashley.) "Eh, Pudding?" (Her eyes crossed to Angie.)

Both turned deep red. "Shell! You *told*. You *told*."

Shelley laughed. "See what happens to you when you start spilling secrets? Anyway, you guys are interrupting. Astrid? You were saying?"

"Not Astrid. It's 'star'," came their unison revenge. "'Star-shine'?"

Shelley made her spoon a catapult and prepared to fling a couple of peas their way.

Astrid defused the moment. "Yes, *ma belle,* I was saying—" (more suppressed laughter). "Nice to be noticed. And I heard about that table chat before, you know, from you. Right? And our picnic? They know about our picnic?"

* * * * *

A few minutes later, while Averill with her daughters are putting the finishing touches on dessert, Ben is in his den, trying to play both host and concerned father. Shelley looking eagerly from one to the other and shrewdly building suspense by pretending to zip her mouth slowly shut.

"So, a peaceful five minutes. Now, Miss Perot. Shell says it's okay for me to, well can I say 'interview?' To 'interview' her new—what's the best word? …" He looked expectantly from Astrid to Shell and back. "What *is* she, Shell?"

Shelley pursed her lips tight and gestured to Astrid.

"—friend?" he tried first.

"Sure. But that's just *starters,* sir—"

"'For starters, Ben'…"

"'For starters, Ben.' Right. So, 'new friend?' Sure." She consulted Shelley. Shelley nodded but stayed mum.

"Ah, then. 'Interview' Shell's 'new friend'. 'New friend, for starters.'"

Two nods.

"Well, then, new friend-plus. Any summer plans? Back to Ohio?"

"No, Ben. Things to do here. Different. I'm working in the West End and in the near North Side for the August primary. Do you know about Prop D?"

"Let's see. Prop D? The one on voting rights?"

"Phew! Glad *someone's* informed."

Shelley was tickled to see the new friend impressing her dad. (He her, of course, but no surprise there.)

"—Yes. It's a national effort. Identify low-income women, gather names, track them down, ward by ward. *I'm* assigned to expand the rolls in the city. But the real pay-off, after we get 'em registered: getting them to the polls."

Shell was intrigued too. She'd been trying to avoid thinking about summer; all she cared was that Astrid would be hers until August. Doing what, she hadn't thought to explore. She sat up and tuned in.

"So let me get this straight. You go from track coach at century-old stuffy Hosmer in the Spring to a summer of radical politics. That it? Think you'll make politics your major? Even your life?"

"Could be. Could be. I want to see if it appeals. It's great so far. It's one reason I chose Antire—their off-campus work program. How about *that*?" (A rare moment of self-deprecating irony.) "Pretty wild for a stuffy Hosmer preppie. Agree, Ben?"

"Yeah, dad." Shelley had to pipe up. "Think you should let your only daughter hang with a revolutionary like her?"

"And here I'd been so impressed. Should I reconsider?"

"No." Two firm objections.

"Well, I'm sure Shelley's glad you won't be scooting off to Ohio, come June. Right, Shell?"

"Dad, I made that the first of many conditions." She stood and ran a light hand through Astrid's thick tresses.

She then excused herself to "go help the Grimm reapers with dessert. Now listen you two; no fighting. And Astrid, be nice. Try anyway."

Ben began "To hear" followed in sync by Astrid, "Is to obey."

* * * * *

Ben moved to the padded desk chair in front of his computer console, and waved Astrid to an armchair. Nearby, the aquarium's friendly natives bubble busily. Astrid waved a friendly hand their way.

"Ah. So you've met?"

"Yep. Shell's filled me in: the fish, the float trip, blueberries. Unusual honeymoon, sir."

"Told you all *that*? You should be flattered—the girl keeps a lot bottled up, frankly." Then, with a calm and quiet look: "But now let's continue our talk, as I warned Shell, 'man to … um woman.'"

"Right, sir." Astrid leaned forward. "We should, Ben."

"First off, and above all. Astrid, I find you wonderful. An absolute delight. But Shell is my daughter. It's my job to ask things. I'd put frank questions to some serious or smitten guy she brought over—there've been a few by the way."

Astrid leaned into him. "No surprise there. What else would you expect? No jealousy here! But," she laid a warm palm on his wrist, "What you want to know is 'what's what?' With us. And me most of all."

"Exactly. And please speak frankly."

"'Frankly's' my thing, Ben. So, then: frankly I find your Shell irresistible. Smitten? Damn right! My *god,* Ben. Gorgeous *and* thoughtful. And those are just 'for starters'."

Her eyes grew distant as she continued. "When I drove in last December, there was some glorious meteor shower going. It lit up fifty miles of Illinois highway. It should have *told* me a miracle lay in wait. It took a while (darn it all), but two weeks ago, Shell the splendid athlete rescued me, the coach. And I knew. Gorgeous, sure. But she's determined. And—when she's reminded—she's disciplined. I was captivated. Still am, 'case you can't tell."

"Yes indeed. I can. But a girl—sorry, a woman—no matter how wonderful, how delightful at 20 can hardly be as cautious as a dad at 50. About *her.* Her *future.*"

"Absolutely. And to me, that's a 'new friend's' job too. Oh, hell. Ben. I have to be frank: it's also a *lover's* job. So: yes, I'm crazy about her, but I'm cautious. I recognize my responsibility. It's *her* journey. So, part of my job—dammit, dammit—is to *get out of* her way. Let her find her future for herself."

"Ah, Astrid. Twenty years old. Five decades of wisdom. I am *so* impressed!"

Astrid gave a grateful smile. "Thanks. But damn! *Why* would we have to meet now? I know I have to keep from suffocating her. But God it's hard. Hate it but have to. I mean it. What I want for her is what I want for myself. Me and my friends. We have so many passions. One of mine now, more each day, is education. Teaching kids. Perhaps a calling, like for politics. But still: you can't expect me to be a *saint,* can you? Around *her*? So forgive me if it's asking too much. Forgive me if I get too public with my affection."

"Ah well, I guess it's a new world. Nowadays, it seems, girls will be girls. (That's what my pop and grandpa used to say about boys.)"

"Yes indeed, Ben, sir, things are really changing. Kids my age, maybe we're different? Like freer. We don't hide our affections. And we are (you can see it Ben!) maybe even *charting* some new territory. Boy likes boy, girl girl. You guys find it weird, but, well, it's happening. We 'kids' are at ease with it."

"So I see. Boy, the world does change. Hell, at this rate, any day now, two girls may want to *marry*. Not ready for *that*, sorry. You two might just change my mind. But I doubt it."

"Oh sir Ben. That's so far away. But hey, one night at Antire we were talking about this. A guy, get this, was all *for* us, actually for all of us. Wrote a paper for a seminar—the plusses of guys marrying guys, girls, girls. Things like, lower the birth rate, slow down over-population. And increase adoptions. And, since women can—I really do think this, Ben— be more loving than guys, a baby raised by two women'll get four times the usual "daddy" loving. We laughed at him, but I thought about it. Still do."

Ben's smile yielded to concern.

"But, no sir. No plans that way. Not for *now*, Ben. I just want the best for her. So if I can love her but, same time, get her ready for future loves, for when I bow out, come August, or with luck *next* August, that's my job. *Until* then, though, I just want to hang with her. Guide her, sure, but take a long delightful look while I do. And get a few hugs. And, well, yeah—other stuff."

"Yes, yes. I get it. But for my wonderful steps, please, some self-restraint."

"Of course, sir. Of course. And if we *are* twins for life, I figure we'll know it even better in two, three, four years. Til then, I really do want her to explore the competition. And seek out *her* path."

Post-Prandial Consults

In the kitchen, while Astrid's magic was percolating at a distance, Averill put a hand around Shelley's shoulder, "Now, my dear—my, uh, *what* did she call you? 'Shell-bell?'—There is no need to tell you: your Astrid is simply superb."

"Hurray! She noticed!" Shell's hyperbole subsided into a warm smile. "I told you, mother."

"Yes, baby, you did. You were right. I'm even a bit jealous."

"Jealous? *You?* Why on earth? You and dad are so …"

"Yes?..."

"Well, just so happy. You talk. Laugh. Take float trips. You share things—those TV murder mysteries. Even opera—I just don't get that." She hugged her second mom. "I can tell. I see it every day. You're still in love."

"Yes. Still! Your dad's been magical. And of course the incredible daughter he brought with him. I couldn't be happier. But I think he'd agree: ours was, is, a second love. Not a first, like yours. Time brings different moments, different feels."

"Mom! Ave'! Sure you want to tell me all this?"

"Yes, my Ashella. You're eighteen, you're a senior. And this time it's *you* that are in love. Yes, it's time."

Shell nodded. "Maybe I should hear it. A month or two ago, I don't think so. But ..." she gestured toward the den, "*She* happened."

"You know the wonderful things your father is. But there's something else; even now, the man still grieves. Over his Annie, your mom. I realized from the start that he *knew* there'd never be another. But yes we were drawn to one another. Shared interests. And, Lord, what I didn't expect, just hoped: the way he's cared for those two—your favorite sacks of chick-peas."

"Name *I* gave 'em."

"Yes. And what you've *done* for them—like they're your sisters from another dad."

"They are. So how couldn't I do for them? But about Annie. If I ever start to ask about her, he shuts down. And it hurts.

She was my mom. I loved her. I was only four, but I remember her."

Averill sighed. "I know, I know you do. And he's still in pain. Every once in a while, I pass the den, and I see that look."

"Oh, yes. *I've* seen it. But I also see his love for *you*." Shelley hugged her step-mother. They stood quietly.

Still, Shell being Shell, still eighteen, and newly in love— fully smitten—rotated Averill and looked her in the eyes: "But hey, now. My Astrid. Tell me more. *Tell* me."

"I see you with her, dear. Such gentle affection. But also such intensity—yeah, even in your teasing, I see it. Same you give our 'steps'. *And* your hummus ..."

"Sure, and my *cukes*." She gestured at the mixer blades and the empty plate by the sink.

"Yes. Those cukes. Well, you've found someone. *I* thought it might be Mike."

"Yeah. He sure took off like a rocket, didn't he? And so built," she closed her eyes and sighed. "Oops, sorry mom. Can't help remembering. But compared to *Astrid*? She's gorgeous too— broad shoulders, keen muscles, wondrous lips. Oops, sorry: TMI. But here's the key: she *gets* me."

"Know what, hon'? Everyone you've met—Mike, too—it's like they reach you just when you're ready for new things. They move you along. Then *they* move on. Make way for the next one."

"Damn."

"What?"

"It's what *she* said. New futures. But, mom! I don't *want* her to move on."

"Of course, but Shell. Your world feels perfect right now. And for you it is. But *sometimes* even the perfect ones don't work. Like Bill and me. So we … hmm, well, we need some safe place, some retreat. So, sure: jump into your new love, no holds barred. But—hard I know—try to let part of you stand clear. Be wild, but be safe."

"Well I've got the wild half down perfect. Oh, man, lady: I'm jumpin' in! But that second step, mom, I'm not ready for it. Fact, I'm going to do back there and jump in some more—get my heart pounding. She's probably busy stealing *your* man."

* * * * *

Ben and Astrid knew the two women would come fetch them. So the efficient step-dad asked. "Now, before they shout at us: 'one more thing,' you said?"

120

"No, better not yet. I need time to think it through and say it right. Let me email you. Tomorrow, say? And, sir … And, sir" (she tapped his hand and pointed to his keyboard) "a chance, Ben, to polish your expertise?"

"Shell's got you just right: quite the teaser." Astrid chortled. "But yes, do write." He stood up, put two hands on her shoulders, "I respect, I value your judgment." Her smile grew even wider when he added, "But for now, 'Welcome to the clan'."

She smiled warmly, then giggled. "Dare I say 'Thanks, new and temporary pop-in-law'?"

He guffawed and returned to his chair. They sat silently. Astrid, with her usual calm smile, enjoying her quiet bond with her babe's dad, and relishing her newly acquired family. The rain-bowing clouds of fish darted in miniature schools, surfacing now and then to nose and nibble once more at Shell's treat. When that provider reappeared to announce dessert for the humans, their tank grew still more agitated.

* * * * *

The four who were still awake ate dessert family-style on laps. Ashley had fallen asleep on Averill's lap, Angie on Shelley's. Shell laid her gently aside as Averill said, "Well, I think we better get these two into their beds. Thank you, Astrid for being with us tonight," and she started to lay Ashley aside to stand up.

"Oh, please, ma'am. Averill. Don't get up. This has been *the. Most. Delightful"* (she gave a squeeze after each word). "evening since I left for college. Really. You are *just* the wonderful crew la belle Shell led me to expect."

Ben intervened. "Now come on, dear," as he turned to her. "Let's let these two say their good-nights."

He transferred his arm from Astrid's waist to Averill's, hovering in mid-flight to tap Shelley on the nose. "If you can spare a goodnight hug before you hit the hay, young Miss, swing by our room will you? 'Night again, Astrid."

Astrid's "Good night" blended seamlessly into Shelley's "Sure will, mom and dad." Then she added, with that hands-on-hips routine: "Yes—I *will* do the fish. You didn't need to ask."

Each thumbed a nose at her as each lugged a Grimm up the hallway.

* * * * *

Shelley and Astrid stood near the door. "I'll help with our finny friends. If you insist."

"No. Much as I love to coddle those fat, happy and spoiled fishies, got something I'd rather do."

Astrid gave a shrug of exaggerated perplexity. "*No* idea what you mean."

"Shall I tell you?" Shell came nearer.

"Do." Astrid took a step her way. "Please."

"Well, 'for starters', this." Shell put two arms around her. "Oh, sweet star. I am *so* proud of you. So in love with you. If I hadn't already had a crush … man! And step-mom thinks you're great. Thinks *we're* great. Cool, huh?"

"Oh, my sweet, sweet babe. I see where a lot of you comes from."

"I hope, I hope." She rubbed Astrid's neck and ruffled her hair. "But now guess what?"

"You just love to ask the easy ones. You want a kiss."

"Of course." (Astrid complied.) "But one *more* thing, sweet babe."

"Greedy tonight, eh, sweet slut? *What* thing?"

"*This* thing, I'm going to go up there and tell 'em—*damn* it, Shell, you did it again. *In* there. I'm going *in* there. Tell 'em I've invited myself over. Perfect end, perfect evening. They'll understand."

"Were you planning to ask *me?*"

"What? Nah. *You* never say no."

The final gem on the evening's necklace—and the memory she'd revisit the most in future years—began sparkling thirty minutes later. They had clambered onto Astrid's platform bed in her upstairs bedroom. Shell (no need to be coy now) straddled her, pinning her under a rolling avalanche of kisses—on her love's throat, mouth, cheek, lips and, yes, throat again. She could not get enough of that firm soft throat. Then came ...

Well, it wasn't a move she'd learned from Mike. Nor was it inspired by one of Astrid's. Nor from Astrid via Mark. No: it was her own, *s*pur-of-the-moment. She found herself doing it and she found herself loving it. Who was Astrid to disagree?

Shell gazed down at her, gazed all around the now-familiar room of robin's egg blue, gazed once or twice through the cream-colored banister posts down to the living room below. She may have shivered once or twice, that old but fading habit, but she exulted. She felt, she *knew*: she was on top of the world.

Email Exchange: Ben and Astrid

In keeping with her gentle threat, Astrid did in fact email Ben Monday afternoon.

"Good day, hey, Ben, sir. Guess if you're reading this you figured out how to open it. So now. About 'our' Shelley. It's a sense I have, though of course I'm basing it on—I still can*not* believe it—only sixteen days and by my count, a hundred minutes with her.

"Friday, you were frank with me. In fair exchange, *I'll* be frank. Woman to um … man, eh? Here it is: I think Shelley misses her mom. Not your wonderful Averill, of course. No, her *mom*. I've noticed she avoids the subject even when she is opening up about so much. (She tells me I'm helping her with *that*. I hope so.) But, it's like she's orbiting some unseen collapsed star. What we see and love is that glorious non-stop fountain of activity, oh my yes. But maybe it's helping her forget there's something lonely at her heart. (Amateur psychology here. Sorry.)

"Why do I say that? I say it *because of* all that bubbling. And the cooking and tidying and caring. Thank the goddess for it, of course. But it's like she just has *to be* in motion. I wonder if maybe it's why she's an LD—She goes long distances, not those quick dashes. (Wish she'd *pace* herself better, though. Whisper that word to her once in a while, will you?) … Sorry, email makes me chatty.

"And something else. Listen to this, Ben. She was over here one day. I came in and found her looking up at my ceiling. It's just this wide, flat, white surface. But she had this strange, frozen look. I asked her what was wrong. Said she'd started having these flashbacks. Most of 'em she loves, but not *this* one. It sounds crazy—a ceiling slamming shut? 'You're the first person I ever told. Not Averill. And never dad: my job's to keep him happy.'

"She also said, 'Don't breathe this to a soul.' Then of course her frown dissolved, she did her breathless laugh, punched me on the arm and started a tickle fight.

"Guess I'm being disloyal, but I think I should share this. I hate disloyal busybodies. But I want what's best for my—for *our* girl. Easy to make her feel loved. But here it's like I can't give her…. Is peace the word?

"You know from our heart-to-heart that I shouldn't—won't—be part of her life much longer. Not daily. And *you* will. She'll be in town. I can only be an 'LD'.

"And oh hey: something else. I notice she almost never wears jewelry. That's unusual. 'Course, anything she puts on just makes her more...uh well, 'scrumptious' is my word. (Sorry.) The woman in me wonders, is there something from her mother she'd like to have? Not to be pushy, sir. But sometimes we ladies can suss things guys miss. Yeah Ben, even dads!

"Well, sir. I've mailed you my thank-you note so I won't repeat what a great time I had. But boy, sir, Ben, Shell's dad, pop-in-law—did I have a great time.

):

(If you can't figure out how I did that, ask Shell to show you the icons bar. Even fuddy-duddies can learn...")

Ben smiled at the final challenge. But the comments about his first wife had touched a nerve.

He walked over to feed the fish, meditating. That night he slept on it. (He mentioned the email to Averill, but not everything in it.)

Early next morning, Tuesday, he approached the keyboard, tentative. "Hey, Miss Perot. Okay, Astrid. Thanks for writing. And how could I mind? Plus teaching an old geezer (my preferred term to 'fuddy-duddy') new things. [Hey, watch this: :)!]

"But now, seriously. I was taken aback when you asked about my first wife, Shell's mother. So personal. Sorry, I'm being frank too. But I thought about it. 'Come on, Ben. She cares. She's devoted to your Shell.' (You do, you are, and I—*we*—love you for it.)

"So I re-read it. That ceiling. Dope-slap! Yes, it was the week we moved out of that house. Where my Annie died. Diagnosed at Christmas. Died in March. I was in such pain. I had to close the book on it all. (It's hard even now, after 14 years.) Shell remembers it? She was barely four.

"Later that day—I think she was out front supervising the movers—I made myself climb back up. I retrieved a small duffel-bag of Annie's things. Couldn't abandon them, so I brought them here. But I stowed them away, in the back of the garage, behind a musty tarp. Out of sight, out of mind? Well, turns out, guess not. So maybe it is time. I have an idea.

"*Thank you,* Astrid. I'll keep doing some thinking on this. When do we see you for dinner again? You're *our* 'new friend' too! You've captured *our* hearts too, you know."

"Geezer-Pop Ben."

* * * * *

At her end, as she reread the message, Astrid heard the door unlock and swing open. Then Shelley's insistent, silvery voice. Then her steps, lighter yet firmer each day, up those steep stairs. And then she was dragging Astrid from her keyboard. Barely enough time to switch off her screen.

Astrid stood up but resisted. She placed two firm hands on her lady's firm shoulders. "Wait, now. Wait. I've been thinking, hon. You come in here thinking you can have your way. You and your grabby hands."

"Saying I shouldn't?"

"Never. But let's find a way to keep it interesting. Listen: how about this? See if we can *plan* being spontaneous. Whoever, on a given day, attacks, it's the *other one* who gets to call the shots.

"What? Shots? Some Ohio drinking game?"

"No, you sweet, dim, hot babe. 'Gets to employ a special move'."

"Oh, wow! A two-woman relay? Cool!"

"Sure. Why not? Now watch. Here's me—" Astrid put her arms around her and began kissing her throat. "I'm on the prowl. You follah?" (She knew Shell loved, and often quoted, the villain in her dad's favorite movie, *The Sting*.)

Shell had her eyes closed in delighted suspense.

"No, no, no, *no*! *Don't* stand there, woman. *Me! I'm* on the prowl..." (she gave a fake-savage growl) "so *you* get to call the moves. And *I* have to comply. Got it?"

"Got it. Hmm..." Shell paused for a beat or two, then hooked Astrid's elbow with hers, and edged her toward the bed.

"I get it." Her eyes lit up, her mouth leered. "Well, then. First ..."

Party Shots

By the time the track team organized a post-season party (another Perot innovation), the seniors had graduated. So, it was a tribute to Astrid that even these newest alumni and alumnae (their dates too) were happy to come back and bask in what was by then a remarkable season's after-glow. It was Hosmer Academy's first-ever, co-ed "track bash." Shelley wouldn't be the only one for whom, whenever someone used the phrase "great party," this one leaped to mind. The tradition would spread to several colleges—both coasts, Ohio, Colorado—transplanted by these first participants.

Astrid sped back from Jeff City, where she'd spent three days deciphering unwieldy spread sheets of voter registrations provided by her state senator. They'd help make her summer canvassing more efficient. She hadn't seen Shell in five days, so her foot was fused to the pedal. Once arrived (her eagerness got her to the gala before Shell) she threw herself into assisting the other coaches—her teachers until two years before, now her colleagues. They set up tables, hung banners from various tree branches, and started welcoming the eager first arrivals.

The squad arrived in stages, most of them sober (also a respectful tribute to Astrid), though the usual few had the usual flasks stashed in the usual glove compartments. As always, she was totally at ease and proved a charming and gracious host to the dates whom many of the squad brought. A few guys came stag (fond hopes of time alone with Astrid?) Not Jeff, though: he'd managed to cajole a recent graduate named Meg to "hang" with him at "this track thing." ("Join me, alumna babe?" "Oh, what the hell: Sure, almost-junior babe." The group soon flowed across the picnic area, an oak grove at the far western end of the campus.

Things were at a merely gentle bubble. Until Shell's arrival caused a sea-change. The guys, to a man, dropped their respective jaws. Several girls too. For Astrid, perched high on a ladder, time stopped. First off, that dress. The two women had agreed, yes, to be spontaneous and, also yes, avoid the regular or predictable. But they could not prevent vivid recollections. Some memories last. If vivid and vigorous enough, they can shape us.

In choosing her apparel, Shell considered the green top from their Park picnic. A tempting choice: she knew its effect on Astrid (like on Mike). After that debut outing, Astrid kept hinting: "next time you're over, wear that tie thing, will you?" Shell's usual reply: "Might." (Even for today's new woman, coyness can serve sly erotic ends.) But since she rarely teased (Ben was right), she complied often, and more than often to their mutual satisfaction.

En route, Astrid had been hoping Shell'd wear it. She'd float the pedal whenever the hope took charge. But that recently minted fellow alumna was growing more original, inventive. Feisty, even. She'd been exploring in the Delmar Loop, where the Washington University crowd often hung out. (She wanted to catch an early whiff of her first non-Hosmer universe.) She'd found something in one of the Loop's trendy but off-beat shops: a sleeveless blue top with delicate spaghetti straps. Perhaps not ideal for an outdoor June picnic. But once she'd seen it, donned it, and glimpsed herself in it, she simply reflected: "Oh, fuck it."

Her hair, luxuriant by now, cascaded across her shoulders—time bestowing one of its more reliable services. She reveled in its silky feel and would launch periodic auburn tsunamis to enjoy the sensation. On her chest, tanned from daily two-mile runs and firm from daily sets of ten-minute bench presses, hung a vibrant turquoise pendant. It helped emphasize her bare shoulders and elegant neck. The chain's delicate "v" also invited any interested observers' eyes downward, an invitation many accepted.

Astrid's too. The gem intrigued her (Ben's doing?). From her stationary height she could observe the rolling wave of wonder and recognition that heralded Shell's progress. Inside her, pride did a do-si-do with desire. (For more than a few of the male sprinters, no surprise, desire ran a solo. No orderly square-dance steps for them.) As she made her way toward the festive table at the far end, the air filled with (mostly but not solely male) amazement: "Who's that dish?" "That babe rocks!" "You ass, that's Shelley." "Jaspar? *That?*" "Yeah." "Oh, man!"

They all began streaming her way at the center table. Her hand displayed a bulging black backpack. From it she unshipped an accordion of photos, neatly segmented into plastic sleeves. (She would decide, partly from their reactions and partly from her own judgment, which shots would earn a place in the new paisley album by her bed.) "Hey, running gang. Photos of us. Come look!" The squad boiled around her, the way they used to huddle around Astrid's awesome demos. Ten feet up was Astrid, in breathless, sensuous suspense.

Shell looked up, saw her, put two fingers into her mouth, gave a loud whistle. "Hey, Ms. Coach. You're in here too. Come on down!"

Astrid pushed in one last thumb-tack, descended, and hovered behind Shelley. She balanced an affectionate pair of stacked palms on Shell's noggin. Shelley looked up, eyes alive, and flung her hair to the side again. When she did, the guys who'd gathered around her let their focus drift away from the photos for a second or two. A couple of rising sophomore girls let their eyes feast too, and not much more shyly.

"Okay, tracksters"—significant pause as she looked up at Astrid: "Here goes." Jeff could on occasion be the gentleman his parents had tried to nurture, so, before he gathered 'round, he

134

offered Meg his soda. ("You okay for a minute or two?" She swatted his rear end: "Go, go.") She sidled over to a couple of other abandoned dates and fell into some pointed chat about "guys."

Shell opened her files to the first shot, two of her relay partners. LaShonda was handing off a baton to Janey—their specialty, the half-mile relay. (Shell had labeled each photo only by event, not names—advice from some manual she'd bought at the Wash. U bookstore.) Her camera's zoom lens, which she'd bought the week after Astrid gave her the album, focused on the two women's hands. One was extending the emerald baton for the other's grasp. Their ten digits blended and filled the frame.

A voice Shelley did not recognize was that of a young man a few bodies down, his eyes glued to the picture. "That's terrific. Masterful." She glanced over, but all she could see was a slender forearm, and a shock of non-descript hair edging over a collar.

She relished the praise but proceeded to flip the plastic sleeve. Three rows of five hurdles, seen from an angle. Above the two farthest ones, two muscled calves, probably male, extend over the two crossbars. At the far right, a bent knee and a rival runner's maroon shorts creep in, one row behind the other.

Next flip: Astrid, shot from behind, ready to click her stopwatch, her hair a golden spray eclipsing the sun.

Then: a male, clad only in the briefest of shorts, caught in mid-sit-up in a quiet corner of a green infield—biceps flexed, abs bulging. That shot elicited some whistles.

"Ooh, hot one, Shell," said one guy. "Who's the foxy dude? Zat you, Jimmy?"'

"Not me. Well-built like me for sure. But not me."

"Well, Al then?"

"Mighty studly dude. Must be me."

"So tell us, Shell," Jeff wheedled. "*Is* it Al? Got your eye on him?"

"Nah, it's a creative shot. *Art,* guys, not porn. Just another slice of—" she raised her voice in a gravelly Winters imitation, igniting general laughter "—-the rainbow of talent that is our squad." Then she drew herself up and sat tall. "Fact is, guys—" she glanced up at Astrid: "I got other plans." She reached back and squeezed one of Astrid's warm palms, which by now lay like a tamed ocelot on her shoulder. The move elicited a few falsetto oohs from a few of the guys, and an envious smile or two among the women.

"So it's true, eh?" Jeff voiced the general curiosity.

"What is?"

"You two. An item?"

Shelley smiled calmly, as Astrid's other palm smoothed her hair. What the hell? Shell had graduated. The season was over. These were her "buds." Her heart could declare itself: "We are."

"Way to go, coach. Sly devil." Jeff rotated in place and fake-punched Astrid's shoulder. "No wonder I wasn't making any progress."

"Hate to tell you, Jeff. There wasn't going to be any."

Ten couples laughing made him blush, but then, as usual, Jeff joined in and laughed it off.

* * * * *

Shell leaned her head back to look up at Astrid and say in a quieter voice, "Proud?"

Astrid's glow was answer enough.

Shell resumed with authority. "Hey come on, more shots. Here's Jessie."

"Nice shots, Shell" were Jessie's words—the "track" Jessie with thick shoulders and neck, and tightly bunched upper arms, who had just strolled over. ("Poet" Jessie ran the school's literary magazine.) She pumped a fist when she examined two matched shots. In the first: the right arm cradled against her neck, ready to spin herself into motion. The next, a handsome 3 by 5: her arm now outstretched, an imaginary arc guiding the viewer's eye to the now shrunken silver sphere, hanging, majestic but minute, in the upper right corner. "Space Shot" Shelley's caption read.

Next a full page (eight by ten) of—yes, Astrid again. To capture it, Shell must have crouched or lain in the cedar-chip pit under the pole-vault crossbar. She caught the athlete hefting her pole waist-high, its end angling toward the camera, its twelve-foot length foreshortened. Back leg flexed, calf muscle taut. Steel determination emerges from a rapturous smile. (So Shelley thought when she snapped it. She was right. She'd captured it.) Jeff turned ironic: "My, my, *my*. Another one of Coach Astrid. What a surprise! Bet there're more!"

The next shot contradicted him. The five-by-seven showed four male sprinters at the ready. The angle turned the foursome into a single organism, eight palms flat on the track. "I call this one 'The Octopus'. In honor of dates I've had with Hosmer guys." Several girls laughed knowingly. A guy or two growled. La Shanda uh-huh'ed her agreement.

Shell was all set to flip to another, but the fellow who had praised the earlier shot edged over to inspect this one, soothing the plastic casing down.

Shell turned to him, ready to pry his palm loose. "Mind if we move on?"

"Oops sorry. You're Shelley, right?"

"Shell. And you?"

"I'm Greg, sorry. But *this*!" (He gazed intently.) "Remarkable composition, neat angle." His eyes slid away, but he made himself edge them back.

"At last. *Some*one appreciates the art. *Thank* you."

The rest began to murmur impatiently. Jeff whispered—to whoever cared to listen: "I don't think it's the angle that's turned him on. Bet it's the guys." A few guys laughed; a few women said "Shh, behave."

Coach Winter, who'd stayed out of the buzzing hive, strode over. "We got burgers about ready over here. Show us that good speed of yours, will you Jaspar?"

"Will do, coach. Sir." She ruffled another six or seven too fast even for stop-action inspection. "Now, look here. An empty sleeve. Guess what it's for?"

A rising junior girl suggested, "Another shot of Coach Astrid?"

"Never a bad idea, but I have enough of *those*. For now."

Then a few guessed it. "How about *us*? Group shot!"

"Bingo. Group portrait. Come on, gather around."

"Hey, Shell," Astrid added. "Doesn't your camera have a timer?"

The new guy, Greg, confirmed. "Yes, here it is right here."

"Good. We want you in it too Shell." The entire group concurred.

They all put themselves into disorderly but focused motion, Astrid providing firm and gentle crowd control.

When Shelley clicked the timer and slipped into a vacant spot in the center, Astrid pulled from her pocket a bright green paisley "scrunchy" to net Shell's hair ("So we and the world can see your face.") The buzzer buzzed, the light exploded, and everyone froze in a timeless cheer.

* * * * *

The party began. Soon the fumes of charcoal, pizza, diet coke (beer, too, conscientiously ignored by Coach Winter and staff) made for an even more festive mood. Groups bonded, mingled, shifted, reformed.

At one point, Astrid saw Greg off by himself, riffling through the plastic accordion. She beckoned to him. They conferred in low tones and then strolled as a pair toward Shell.

"Hey," she tapped Shell's shoulder. "Here's Greg again. With a question."

"Just have to say again how impressed I am."

Suddenly Shell realized something else. "Now wait. *You're* the guy who—get this, Astrid. He saved me that day I videoed you. 'Better take the lens cap off,' he suggested. I owe him."

Greg gave a shy grin. "That was me."

"Well," Shell began, not sure how to continue. "Thanks, Greg. I like those shots too. But it was my Astrid here who got me started, encouraged me."

Astrid nodded, but kept the chat flowing. "Now, Shell. I've found something out about this fellow, this new admirer—"

Greg blushed but spoke up. "Wait. Let me step up to the plate here. Coach Perot says …

"Astrid says" Astrid interrupted him …

"Astrid says you're going to Wash U in the fall. So you'll be in town. I was thinking, me being a senior...Would you—"

Shell suspected a plot, but she was flattered (yes, hurt a bit, but still touched) by Astrid's effort. And flattered by Greg's interest (man, um, to, um, woman?)

141

"Would I what? Go on."

"I'm taking Stanard's studio course in the fall. Could I call you sometime? Tips from a master?"

Astrid put an affectionate arm around her girlfriend's waist. "You have a fan, woman. Might save you from turning into a dorm widow." She rotated Shell and tapped her arm. "Write your seven digits down for him."

Greg's brow furrowed. "Hey, wait. Just advice."

"Sorry, Greg. We're being silly. But here," Shelley reached out for his hand and pulled a felt-tipped pen from her pocket. "Hope you can read it. I'd enjoy a chat."

The fellow surprised himself—and impressed the two women—by using that now sacred hand to lift Shell's to his gallant lips. "I'll guard it with my life." He bowed and disappeared into the swarm, pocketing the marked hand for safe-keeping.

The two women laughed, but then Astrid seized their first private moment and took Shell's elbow. "Remember what we said? Never being apart for one day again?"

"Of course, sweet. *You're* the one who traipsed off to Jeff City."

"Ah, yes. Guilty. But imagine *me. Five* days, babe. No you."

"And not for *me? I* can tell time. So can this lonely body."

"Shh. Here." She deposited a shiny new metal key onto her lover's palm. (Shell had found from experience that her palm was also one of *her* erotic locales.) "You go on. I better help Coach. Then I'm free. I'll be there in thirty, okay?"

Shell lowered her voice, but only marginally. "And in case you're interested—in fact even if you aren't. It's my turn to prowl tonight. Start planning."

"I already have one in mind. A surprise. But don't take off that pendant. Hear?"

"I hear, I obey."

Astrid's eyelids creased with anticipation. "Make it fifteen."

Their Last Summer Days

Astrid and Shelley were living their first and last summer together at warp speed, but all the while certain truths were gnawing into Shelley, gnawing like those undersea currents that strafe an elegant coral reef with their caustic debris.

While they tried to let spontaneity guide their days, their brave women's world soon developed a few reliably pleasurable habits. Certain moves that each tried out more than repaid revisits. (And became part of a wide repertoire. Later the rather opinionated amateur anthropologist Shell would whisper to Scott some lessons she'd inferred about a culture and its customs. "Hey, Look! A couple's private behavior is a tiny model for a village. Things they love to do—see, sweet?— they keep doing. A shared habit can become a wider custom. Others see it. Emulate." Scott might admire the insight, but most times he'd have another mission in mind. He'd tongue her whisper into silence and cut their dialogue short.)

More than once, Astrid called Shelley after a satisfying but tiring Monday at "Work the Vote". "I'm missing those lips. Come over, won't you?" Or on a Wednesday or Thursday, Shell might call to invite her for dinner. "We miss you. All five of us." More than one Friday, Shelley called and put more of that unmitigated gall to work and invite herself over. "Oh, and ... forgot to ask: Mind if I stay till Sunday? I'm planning for your next stalk."

Astrid spent most of her days working on that initiative, which meant she also had to go to in Jeff City every other week, to report to that senator. Often, feeling deprived, Shelley would ask her to "tell me more about what you're doing. I'm intrigued." And one day Astrid called, her voice bubbling.

"Come over, will you? I have a surprise."

"My, my. What *could* it be?"

"Not what you're thinking, shameless ho. No, as you told dear Ang', if I told you it wouldn't *be* a surprise, now, would it?"

An hour later, as they sat at Astrid's kitchen table, her host held Shelley's hands, unable to control her delight. "I have a grant for you."

"Grant? And that would be—?"

"For you to work for us—to help with the project. They'll give you $100 for five afternoons at Mo Hist."

"Boo hiss? What's that? Some kind of snake?"

"God, you're a silly. Not 'boo'. 'Mo'. That would be Missouri. And 'Hist' is 'History'." She proceeded to enunciate each syllable of "The Missouri Historical Society. You'll look up and copy old voting stats, pre- and post-20th amendment. Got it? So you see: no more being my 'widow'."

Shelley, pleased by Astrid's special effort, was all the more eager to please her. Of course just *getting* to the Archives library offered yet another challenge, which Astrid redefined as a "learning opportunity". When she'd first gotten her license, age 16, all too often she'd drive down streets like a pinball, veering from side to side, query feeding on query. Now, for Shelley age 18, Astrid as usual had a solution for her: make a map. And then: practice. On Saturday, she drew the route from Shell's house to the library. They drove it once, to give Shell the feel. By the end of the day, snuggling comfortably in Astrid's living room, Shell felt some progress in internalizing her city's layout. By the time she found her way to the place Monday, her geography was firmer and the work made her enthusiastic.

The place itself was invigorating. The handsome former synagogue had been handsomely redesigned. Tall volumes and squat volumes, some encased in dust, some newly scrubbed, ringed the reading area like an arena. Its central hall reverberated. Then there was the woman at the desk, with delicate and distinctive features, thirty-ish, with dark, pulled-back hair. She was more than helpful. She set Shelley up at her own study table, showed her how to look up the needed materials and bring the call slips up to the desk. She even, when her own assistant was serving other members, brought Shelly the various sheaves herself.

Shell reveled in the smells of the dust from the documents and relished even the stale air that clung to the hand-written census sheets newly freed from 19th century vaults. She admired the feel of the Victorian bindings and the colorful swirl of the end-papers. She was also deeply impressed to see the ten or so older men and women, hunched every morning over yellowing documents, taking notes, peering at ancient city maps. Her widening eyes saw these graying people digging into their city's origins and history, fitting their family histories into the city's vast earlier life. Their silent, diligent dedication set up permanent shop in the novice research assistant's mind and heart.

If nothing else, her days among the archives proved a cool way (cool literally, not Astrid-cool) to escape the oppressive and hot (literally hot, not Astrid-hot) summer outdoors.

On her last day of work, Shelley brought the librarian a small tub of *saag* with chickpeas (her and the steps' most recent experiment). Ingrid put her two hands over her heart and bowed. *That* week, at least, positively winged past. Shell's work did wonders (tiny ones, but wonders nonetheless) to push aside her sadness. Then, of course, it hit her with redoubled force on Friday when she realized that she'd let another week with her sweetheart evaporate. ("Your sweetheart" was phrase her dad used for Astrid when he'd tease Shell about her unusual romantic involvement. Shell, knowing how much he admired her, came to like it.)

Much as she loved marking her personal calendar with her private love code, she hated seeing each month's thirty-some squares fill up, knowing that soon, sooner every day, she'd have to fold over the next leaf. As May grew full, she sighed. To turn June over was painful. But July's completion gave her bones a shiver. In August's first square she saw the "sad face" she'd drawn weeks before (when August seemed forever away). One line below it, an even sadder one, tears trickling, for the next Sunday—("*this* Sunday, dammit.") Unlike those Cardinals' scorecards that she'd record every summer but feed to a February bonfire, this calendar she'd lock away.

* * * * *

The pool at Astrid's condo had become a favorite haunt. They loved resting on air mattresses, suspended in the deep end's slow circulation, or basting their two muscled, slender bodies while sharing a large beach towel of creamy fuchsia on the terraced sunning platforms. Most of the pool-goers were regulars so, after the first week or two, when the women each got hit on maybe five or ten times a day (high-school guys, college-guys, even an eligible bachelor or two—well, they *claimed* to be single) they were left to themselves. The Saturday after her history assignment ended, Shell lay on one platform, Astrid on the one beside it, as they tried to squeeze in as many final minutes as possible.

Their gazes plunged into each other.

"Guess what, lady?" Usually their chat flowed like a brook; today it was more like a guttering spigot.

"What's that, Shell?"

"Know what today is?"

"Damn. No. Did I forget something?"

"You sure did. It's six months to the day since our track sign-up. That memorable first day I saw you, dear coach. See, I *knew* you weren't the sentimental one."

"You know better, sweetheart." (Astrid liked the term too. A few years later, the first time she murmured it to her fiancé, it exuded a gingery aroma and administered a small twist to her heart.)

"Hmm. I'm not so sure now. But do you know how I know?"

"No, babe. How do you know?

"From my sharp memory first, but also from my calendar. I have the two days circled. February 2. flip, flip, flip, August 2."

"Brava, hon'. Getting *so* organized. Okay, now. *My* turn. Know how I'm always whispering to you, 'take American history'?"

"Yeah, yeah, sweet mentor. You won't let it go. You murmur it over breakfast. You mouth it, *sotto voce,* over lunch. Then, late afternoon, you pin me down, start doing that throat thing of mine on *me.* And then …? You stop. And then you whisper it again. *Such* a history slut."

"Well, yes, my dear. I do try to choose the ideal moments for planting that seed. But see? Your calendar just proves it's starting to work. You're" (her voice lowered to a sober alto) "'creating a document'. My history prof's phrase."

Shelley reached over and tapped the tip of her forefinger on Astrid's knee. Out of courtesy to the people around them (firm but loving advice from Shell's dad), and to maintain a smidgen of emotional distance, they restrained their appetites. Outdoors anyway.

As they dozed, their minds and appetites took a leisurely shuffle through a host of impulses, some of them sad, some exhilarating. A tiny slice of Shelley, in fact, *was* growing excited about her own start of college. The feeling slowly trickled its warm way onto that heavy, sad block of ice.

"Babe, babe, oh babe." Her sigh was genuine. "What will I *do*, sweet babe? No you to hang with. Or talk with. No you to *play* with?" (Her eyes blazed at the last infinitive.)

"And I won't be deprived? Want my best advice? Do what I did, freshman fall at Antire. Plunge into your new world."

Their talk ebbed. The afternoon shadows lengthened; the population of young kids around the pool slowly diminished; Shell tried to work on her fall schedule. But that effort faded in its turn.

Astrid began appraising one or two of the young bodies that remained. "Let's distract ourselves. Some mental exercise. See that one there?"

"The guy?"

"No. Girl past him. Tan suit."

"Far too young, old star. Even for you…"

"Hush, my sweet. It's another teaching moment. A chance to extrapolate, to untangle and unravel the future curled up tight inside her: I bet you even do that with sophomore Jay, your peer tutoring victim."

"Bet I don't." Her firm denial subsided for a second: "Or, well, okay. This one time, I was helping him with Trig. He looks up with an answer and his eyes burrow into mine. Checking his

151

answer was all *he* was doing. But those eyes! They're hazel. Like yours. I hadn't noticed."

"But you were strong, I bet."

"Yep. I was. Stayed cool. True, my eyes longed to scamper through his hair and stroll down his neck. Course with you I get a bonus. I can use my hands."

"Oh, boy, girl, do you! But wait, wait. Apply the lesson from the ripening Jay to this young lady here. She's a mere chrysalis. Look at that straight waist. See it?"

"I do."

"Right. Well, now. Picture her when her gene-clock starts ticking. Starts to swell the hips. To broaden her shoulders, sculpt her breasts. And the face: pouty mouth already. Bright green eyes. Ah, and the hair. It'll probably start to cascade in what? … two or three summers?"

"Yeah, cascading hair. It's always about *you*, ain't it?" She reached over to fluff her lover's blond hair that was pasted to her damp forehead. Can you spell 'narcissist'?"

"Now, listen. Stay with me. Her looks do nothing for you, right? And nothing, looks like, for that gaggle of boys over there. But just visualize the—what do our lads say—the dish?—she's going to be at fourteen. Three, four years: time will tick and work its magic."

"'Time, tick, time.' Can you drop it? You're like a warped c.d. Dad calls them broken records. Says *his* dad said 'broken needle'. Gee, now that I think about it—was gramps into drugs? Anyway, please. Can we turn it off? Just for one week?"

"But *hon*. It *does* tick. If you doubt me, *take* that freshman history. The wiser college junior-to-be now lectures the naïve high-school girl. *Take* philosophy. *Read* Heraclitus. Just inside that— God! that scrumptious sleek neck of yours (I'm already planning some moves for later), wrinkles are lining up for their turn at bat. The ovaries plunk down a monthly mini you, but only a limited supply. And all our lovely eyes— yours, mine too, even that young one over there—they'll grow crow's feet. They'll grow dim."

(Those creases in Astrid's eyelids that first afternoon at the track flickered across Shelley's mind. She squelched a small gloat before smiling sadly.)

"But that's only half the tale," Astrid continued. "More fun to imagine the feast waiting to rise to the surface. Skip the wrinkles. Think of all the gorgeous Shelley's waiting to rise to nature's surface and please hundreds of young men—"

"No women?"

153

"Oh, yes, my gorgeous one. Handfuls." She gave Shell's knee a reassuring pat. "Well, but for now, I'm melting. Join me in a dip?"

"Maybe in a few. Got to sort this schedule." She picked up her pencil and dabbed her head with the damp towel she lay on. "You go on, sweet, but walk slow and seductive. Let me enjoy the view."

"You know I'd do anything to please you. But—"she edged one foot off the wide towel they shared—"feel *that!* I refuse to just pace and burn my soles, even for you. No, I'll be moving fast."

"Well then, I'll just have to enjoy you, *fast* and seductive."

"Just proving that *anything* I do arouses you. Well, we still have late afternoon and evening. You'll stay over?"

In reply, Shelley blew a kiss toward the already receding figure, whose answering smile dissolved into a grimace as she executed a rapid tip-toe toward the cooling water. She followed it with a splash-less dive into the depths.

Shelley sighed but continued to pore over the various course offerings, striving with furrowed brow to sort through the vast raft of courses—including, of course, History. She had to admit several of them "sound neat."

But now and again she dabbed at her glistening chest with a towel, sighing. She put herself through a delicious hell by letting her eyes wander over to Astrid, whose churnings were leaving a turquoise wake. It kept slapping loud, time and again, against the pool's edge.

Then, as she held the handbook up to block the sun, she noticed the shadows. During her early visits in June, 4 p.m., they'd barely nibbled at the edge of the terraced incline. Now, August 2 at 4 p.m., they were creeping up to her knees. With a new eruption of misery, she made the extrapolation.

Her own eyes grew watery as she looked over just in time to see Astrid's muscled arms lever her sleek shape out of the water. To see the water that flowed, trickled, ran down her chest, her arms, her legs. As she gazed, even saltier water began to flow. As those svelte and muscled legs walked her way, steamy vapors began to shroud Astrid's body, and her footprints to evaporate the second they formed. She became a walking, luminous lesson.

Shell wiped her eyes and knew. Through that window of air, like a tiny gravitational lens, Shell saw, magnified, the group of girls they'd recently inspected. They sat now on the edge of the diving platform, holding hands and swinging legs.

During a mere second or two of real time, she saw them wave at a larger group of boys near the pool, the full group smiling up a storm, shimmering like a field of windy corn. One of the lads elbowed two of the others while the gaggle of girls swung their knees. Shelley saw one guy waving back avidly, another studiedly turning away his face, his eyes slinking back to check it out. The unwelcome sight let Shell see farther and wider. In a flicker, she nodded at the sad lesson. Girls would grow into women, boys into men. Friendships form—yeah, flourish for a bit—but then fade. All of it. All of them.

"Oh, sweetheart." She reached for Astrid's hand just as she sat down, and her tears began to bathe it. "Oh my baby," her shoulders shook. "Think I'll ever meet a you, an Astrid who won't turn to air? *Is* there such a thing?"

"Oh, yes." Astrid edged closer, massaging her neck. "Oh, sweet Shell, *yes*. For the you that you are, the you that I love, there *will* be. He's out there. She's out there. *Has* to be. Just Give. Them. Time."

Now, twenty yards away, the two groups were dissipating. The guys, on some shared whim, ran off, back to the locker rooms. The girls looked at one another, sighed once or twice, completed one more dive apiece, and then traipsed off—all of them—to those shadowy changing rooms at the pool's farthest end.

STAGE TWO: Scott and Gavin

Time halts when memory (that mixed blessing—unruly but persistent, fallible but insistent) wants to be consulted. Wants to have its say. Those seeming hours of recollections that Shell spun in an instant cascade as she was collecting herself on the professor's hearth serve as eloquent witnesses. And those recollections were (they still are) but small slivers of her first eighteen years. Now, the first-year college woman will be plunging into busy eddies of new roommates, swirls of new and newer friends, and, before long, academic do-si-dos. We may catch sight of her but any glimpse will be rare, fleeting, elusive—nearly out of sight, practically out of mind. Naturally, a highly perceptive reader (of either sex; he or she will probably know which she or he is) will nod in occasional recognition. *Or*, she or he may well shake a head in sad disbelief. "I can see her, plain as ...well, early dawn. Can't they? Can't *he*?"

As Shelley began to embrace that first year of new though relative independence, Scott was pacing through his last year of college in the East. Two-plus years of harkening to literature's soft, dynamic embrace whetted the English major's appetite. So, a year after Shell had arrived on campus, Scott did too, a first-year grad student in English. He was also a novice teacher—a Teaching Assistant, a "T.A."—handling one section of first-year Composition. It was a mutually beneficial arrangement: for the department, cut-rate instruction; for him, a chance to see if teaching called him.

During college, Scott lost his aging parents (he was a late-in-life, though fondly embraced, surprise), but early on he'd absorbed their cautious and deliberate ways. His father died of the cancer he'd fought since before Scott had gone East; his mother, the summer he graduated, after an undiagnosed, progressive decline. Perhaps he should have stayed East and begun a new life, but he felt drawn (family tradition still thrives here and there) to follow in his parents' footsteps—college elsewhere, then life back home. Scott was once again solo.

Meeting in Holmes

Men do fine with spatial relationships, but how they grasp abstract things can vary from the way women, masters of the brain's imaginative half, intuitively inspect and "get" the world. (That's why men make more reliable disciples; women, better gnostics.)

On a shivery March morning, there was no way that Scott could know that a seismic churn in his life lay in wait. Nor know how soon (May Day, the planetary year's second "crossing day") a second joyful shudder would deliver his hand to Shelley's. The links between then and now were curled up far too tight—mere buds, or (a more precise if recherche metaphor), clogged wormholes on time's abundant and greening twigs.

On that unseasonally raw morning the sun was stealing across the Equator. Within half a year, Gavin (the fellow striding toward Holmes Lounge from the University's noble Quadrangle) would be able to observe the star's motions from his special foothold—his *space*-hold as he will delight to term it. But that was (would be) then. This is (was) now.

And, as so often, "now" rules.

The campus was wrapped in gray, Scott in his usual white shirt, subdued tie, wool coat, white socks, tasseled loafers. The unspoken college uniform his fellow undergraduates had worn now guided the graduate student's habits.

This morning he was moving toward one of several round tables at the still, far back of the University's coffee lounge, Holmes Lounge. That's where Shell, the year before, did take Greg once for coffee. It was a place where, in time, she made many new friends and, often enough (no slouch, she), romantic partners. For Scott, barely a one-semester veteran, Holmes was one of a thin handful of places he'd retreat to after his teaching duties freed him from his classroom, chair, office, study. He usually chose a time when most students were in class or their dorms. That end, at that table, was his spot. On a daring morning, he might select a different chair, and seat himself at say eight o'clock on the table's circumference, not at his usual six. But he always faced the east entrance, keeping the cold, bare, but intricately carved hearth at his back.

He initiated his usual chews, took a standard-volume sip after each swallow, squared up his stack of papers. He reached into his shirt's pocket-protector for his red pen and got set to, as a fellow T. A. once remarked in loving jest, "make those essays bleed"—critique word choice and phrasing, mark grammar and

160

usage errors. Assign grades. Today, though, he felt an indefinable, a barely detectable, tremor. It made him glance up before he'd drawn any meaningful blood.

Choked on gray vapor, the feeble glow of the March sun bled through the windows at the hall's east end—where rows of mullioned windows faced out on that elegant quadrangle. His gaze stopped in its tracks as it caught sight of—no, not the sun. Why'd he think …? Someone was entering through the doors. Who was she? Slender, lithe, with a cascade of glowing hair. That brightening ember sliding in from the cold.

No. The creature was a guy. The man was handsome and well-built—features Scott rarely noticed in a man. (If he did, he'd clear his throat, avert his glance, and feign distraction. The culture of his single-sex high-school discouraged mutual attractions.) This time, though (a new stage) he kept his eyes fixed: fixed on the blond traveler's beard, spangled with golden flecks; fixed on the smile that glittered as the fellow wafted down the hall. The heads of long-haired men and buzz-cut women swayed and nodded toward him. On a raised palm, he balanced a tray loaded with steaming croissants. "Hey, perfesser" "far out, dude," "back for more, doc?"

Scott was so engaged by these sights and sounds that he failed to note that, at a low table on one far side which sported a coffee warmer and microwave, stood two women. One, her thick auburn hair interwoven with clicking cornrows (a new experiment) had also tipped her head toward the new man. He responded with a smiling bow as his steady transit continued. Her eyes danced back to the sounding digits of the microwave. She tapped a patient foot in time to the beeps and leaned an elbow on her companion's shoulder.

To them and the beeps, Scott remained oblivious, riveted by the "perfesser's" progress down the hall. The man's motion kept currents of air rippling through his loose chemise, providing brief glimpses of firm and elegantly sculpted ribs and a slender, delicately-muscled waist. The man's free hand swirled a sibilant cup of ice, from which, during his otherwise stately journey, occasional slivers cascaded, and vapor sprang from his mouth as he saluted a fellow professor here, a table of sophomore women there.

"Hey, mi-lord John." (The man's first words, Scott would recall. A musical baritone.) John salaamed from his perch of coffee and books and raised a thumb. "Break from the labors?" The thumb waffled, then tipped sideways and wilted onto the pile of books before him.

"Ah. Sorry, mate. But you'll revive. Any minute now."

"Ladies—" inclining his head toward the group of three at the next table. "I hope that's Canto Four you're into?" One stuck her tongue out. The second gazed at him, silent. "Sorry," said the more vocal third. "Sorry, Dr. K. T'ain't."

"What? Not yet?" Mock pain near his eyes. "Tick tock," he suggested. "One p.m. tomorrow."

Six helpless shoulders arose in unison. In his wake, the women burst into amorous hilarity: "*Nearly* stopped." .... "So *cool*." ... "The *eyes!*" "How long til one p.m. tomorrow?"

Now as for this Dr. K (Scott now had a partial name for this traveling man): his lean hips oscillated in that leisurely but purposeful stride. He arced closer to the hall's back, while Scott, that red pen arrested in mid-air, jaws arrested in mid-chew, was entranced by those worn jeans embracing those slim thighs. Scott felt divided in two —one half, pure attraction. The other half was envy. Of? Of the man's effortless rapport—with colleagues, with students.

The voyager's trek was at once regal and companionable. It brought him toward Scott nesting at his silent hearth. A particularly hearty hail of the cup to a corner party of juniors released another icy shower; it haloed his grinning face before cascading in a musical tinkle. Scott's eyes, their will suddenly their own, walked up the man—hips, shoulders, beard, shoulders—and locked onto two brilliant green eyes. He hoped he'd stop. He felt his ancient continent of self-effacement subsiding and, rising in its place, a long-sunken mantle of craving.

163

"Think you've snowed enough ice for one day?" Scott *thought* he recognized his own voice. "Care to reheat yourself here by the—" he gestured over his shoulder at the ornate fireplace.

"Ah. At last a warm welcome for a chilled wanderer. I see you are speaking from" (pause, wink) "—the hearth."

"You might *thay* that," was Scott's comic answering lisp, masking a heart jogging wildly. "*I* wouldn't, but *you* might. But *would* you, um, like—?" His word-hoard depleted, he managed a second gesture toward an empty seat across from him.

"Would I um what? Supply an infinitive?"

Scott, his tongue stilled, brain frozen but grammatically impressed, contrived another nod.

"I'd call that a yes. Well, then: how about 'to sit'? Too presumptuous?"

"Sit? Yes." Scott unfolded a palm. "Presumptuous? No," the smile still a poor index to his inner turmoil.

"Well, then. Third time charms. Ta." The man's accent was distinctive. Scott couldn't quite place it, but it had a lilt (was it Irish? Antipodean? From Hong Kong, maybe?). He flipped through his fairly full catalog of inflections but came up empty. But there was one thing he did know: he was drawn to the sound of that rich baritone.

164

The man somehow found a way to bow yet keep the laden tray level. The scant remaining ice in his cup still whispered. As he slid across from Scott, his lips' last vapor trails subsided and the smock-like shirt settled (leaving the chiseled belly but a vibrant memory). The visitor shelved that abundant tray (three croissants, some apples that wobbled invitingly, books, wallet, a storehouse of tiny jellies), then slid the cup between them.

The golden hairs that spangled his (surprisingly delicate) wrist drew Scott's eyes to the (similarly delicate) fingers. Drew them in turn to the smile spreading across the man's face, drawing his eyes tight, dimpling his cheeks. In a twinkling Scott had piled his neat array of papers into a disordered heap and flung the mess onto a chair beside him.

"I go by Gavin." He extended his right hand to Scott's, etching an elegant diameter across the table (the accent still a mystery).

Their fingers tangled, their palms met. Scott felt his hand hatching in the other's firm yet refined grip.

"Scott…. Pleasure."

"Most intriguing," the man replied. "Scott Pleasure. Is that a name, or a priority?" Scott blushed, and his eyes skittered to the still nodding array of ripe apples. "Or maybe an offer?" The blush blushed brighter.

He tried out some conventional dodges. "No, just a standard, concise Missouri intro" and his embarrassment began a delighted waltz at the teasing. "And oh yeah, the real name's Preston. Plain old Preston."

He wanted that ten-word intro (yes he was counting) to balloon. So: "Say, I'm a Holmes regular. The whole world here seems to know you. Why don't I?"

The question arrested time. (It was an early, moderate version of Shelley's later effect). For him anyway. Redoubling their earlier brief appraisal, his eyes caressed the man's shoulders, then vaulted to the rich shock of bright blond hair around the delicate face; darted again to the remarkably tanned cheeks, slid down the firm neck to the bare triangle of skin above the chemise. (Apparently cold Missouri mornings didn't register on his system.) The cascade of glances was the work of an instant, but the riffle coalesced into an enduring portrait. (Much later, and more than once, Scott would remind Shelley of his first sighting of Gavin. She'd nod in aroused agreement, then cup his neck with some preliminary fingers.)

Time's sometimes errant ratchets slipped back into gear. He felt Gavin's eyes boring into him while his mouth was bathing his ears with autobiography. "No. More of an errant visitor I guess; eccentric orbit. Only here since January. Visiting Scholar. Know the program?"

166

"No, one more area of vast ignorance. 'Visitor' from where?"

"Short answer: 'all over.'"

Scott waited for a longer one but earned merely an enigmatic smile. In time, though, Gavin added, "Here I teach some, write some. They lend me out to school districts roundabout. So," he winked a gesture of endless reassurance, "you're correct. Rarely here. *Bravo,* shrewd observer." (Impeccable Italian.) He bowed, and that hair fell into a curtain that tented his smile. In keeping with the paradox that less is more, the camouflage that made it all the more appealing.

At that very second, the microwave woman—cornrows clicking, mug full, pal in tow—swung near. Her open palm proffered a paper saucer wreathed in steam. She danced her eyes in their direction, and then tipped another genial nod toward Gavin. He reciprocated. And then—or so she would later insist, much much later—her eyes bubbled over to Scott.

Scott in all honesty could never confirm her story. Frankly, he never noticed her. (When in due course they revisited that first—well, call it an encounter—she understood and, after some self-indulgent grumbling, forgave.) She raised her eyebrows at her buddy, who shrugged and nodded toward a corner table. The pair arced past.

Scott, focused solely on the nearer enchantment, didn't know what he'd missed. He realized he could both mask and feed his crush (he'd memorized the term "sfumato" in a college art course, but this was the first time he felt its wondrous force in real life) by asking this obvious master for advice. "What's your secret? How do you win them over like that? And so quickly. Surely," his directness surprised himself "—surely it isn't just good looks?"

Gavin shook his head yes. "Well of *course*. That's all it takes." He smiled then grew serious. "No, lad. I think it just comes with time and experience—trade tricks you acquire. Plus, best of all, I love what I do."

Scott burst into a confession. "I wish I could. Well, I *think* so."

Gavin's widening eyes, nodding head and gesturing hands urged him to "spill," a popular verb in the university's idiolect which Gavin had quickly adopted.

"I'll try to. Trouble is, I'm new at this—teaching. First year. I feel so constrained. If I could just break free. One time, gosh it was maybe my fifth week—October—one day I suddenly felt I was getting them, catching their imaginations. Made a pun on some kid's name and they all hooted. Like a rocket going off. Sexy moment!" His eyes rose to Gavin's, then sank.

Gavin's laugh echoed loud and long. Then embarrassment arose again and Scott eddied into small talk.

"So. Well. Anyway. You arrived when? In January, you said?"

"January is in fact what I *said*." (Gavin's exquisite *savoir faire* adjusted to the conversational shift without comment. That grace brought relief and won another sliver of Scott's heart.) "But truth is I managed to sink down some shallow roots in December. In fact, I got the first invite to an interview in early November. The exact date's in my journal."

"Your Journal? That's a …?"

"Oh, a combo: a daily log but also a place for deep reflections. You don't *assign* them? I assume you *keep* one for yourself?"

Scott shook his head twice. A dark room in the attic of his brain took note: "journal."

"What I do recall, vividly, was your autumn sliding into winter, your sky showering golden arcs like an escort, night I flew in."

"Leonids?" Scott wondered to himself, an old memory stirring.

169

"Meteors, mate. The sky fairly glowed with 'em."

"Ah. Yes. Was it the Leonids?"

Gavin nodded but tapped his cheek thoughtfully. "Close, man. One month off. The Geminids, actually. The twins. So, *you* saw 'em? *Sans blague?*"

"Well, not that time but yeah, way back, I used to be *really* into that stuff. Ah well. Trivial childhood memories, huh?"

Gavin mixed concern with interest. "Now my friend, don't dismiss them. They're still *your past*. Always there, if you are willing to listen and heed."

* * * * *

Scott wanted to probe more. But small-talk was never his strength. At least it never *had* been. "But, well, so. Did you have any trouble finding a place here? You know. An apartment?"

"Oh, digs?" The man's eyes rolled back his way and came alive, sly laugh lines re-creasing. "'Digs,' yes. *Ein zimmer*. Took a day or two. Found a great place."

"Really? Whereabouts? Is it near here or would it be 'a fur piece'?" (His mind spooled a tape of his Dad's out-state drawl.)

"Now, wait. Wait!" Gavin leaned across the table and locked Scott's eyes in an emerald tractor beam. "Don't tell me.

170

'Fur piece'? More Missouri lingo, I bet. Not about nice clothes. Means 'a long way.' Yes?"

"Sorry, friend. Only half true. Sure, you've nailed it. But, sorry, for us locals it's '*Missouruh* lingo'." Some brave new impulse prompted him to hold up a thumb. Gavin reached right across to touch one of his own on it. Scott felt a new surge of— out of the blue, he remembered some lines his mother used to read at bedtime. The thoughts of his favorite childhood character flooded through him, the Mole from *The Wind in the Willows* when he first meets the creature who'll be his life-long friend, Ratty. His mind took time to spool it word-for-word. "The Mole waggled his toes from sheer happiness, spread his chest with a sigh of full contentment, and leaned back blissfully."

To himself (though with motionless toes), he wondered: "Now, where *did* that come from? Things are getting cooler. This hot man? Is he some lost twin?" To Gavin (more restraint), "Remarkable the interests we share, you agree?"

"Could be. Feels like. Time always tells."

Scott hoped so. "I see another one. Your tray there. You look like a walking cafeteria. Are you, like we say these days, into food?"

"By heaven, yes. Food? Absolutely. Item two."

Then Gavin's loose cuff whispered through the table's cinnamon dust and two fingers clasped Scott's wrist. Then the full hand closed over his again, and again he felt it stir.

"Well, say now, young Scott Pleasure." Scott glowed and blushed at the public airing of that new moniker. "Spur of the moment. But, so's life. Come see my place. Let's get 'into food' together. I have this terrific recipe I've been wanting to try. I need a 'Missourah' guinea pig."

At Gavin's riveting but gentle gaze Scott felt a new continental churn—South America yearning for Africa. At first he was speechless, so Gavin elaborated: "So rare to meet a kindred spirit. Some he, some she, some *one* to warm to."

"How can I resist?" was his first thought. "Why would I want to?" his soul replied. So, aloud, "When?"

"I'm off for my weekly visits this afternoon, but back as usual by week's end. Your pick. Friday? Or Saturday? Even Sunday if you prefer to delay gratification."

"Let's compromise," the careful Scott carefully began. But "Friday. Friday's good" came out.

"Ah ha: another 'Missourah compromise'?" Gavin's laugh subsided into a broad grin. "Friday it is, then. Now, one more favor: can we start before sundown? I have some views from my

172

balcony I want you to be my private Wikipedia for. We'll celebrate our own private Eid el-Fitr."

He saw a new furrow in his new friend's forehead. "The feast that marks the end of Ramadan. So, yeah, we're way late, but feh! It's the spirit that counts. And here, please, are your marching orders. A humble request: for three days, try to fast. And *then* slip on your feasting shoes, Scott P."

He took a final crunch of the cup's melting ice and breathed out more vapor. His breath bathed his invited guest with a warm, cooling, fragrant blast.

(Stage One Reappears): Final Exchanges

While Scott has disclosed himself briefly, through his life-changing visit to Holmes, we cannot wholly neglect Shell. (Depending on their speed and attentiveness, some sharp eyes may have detected her a minute or two ago.) In her own way, and on her own time, she'd become a regular at Holmes Lounge starting fifteen months before. Like memory, time does not always spool straight...

* * * * *

One afternoon about two weeks after Astrid's departure, her sisters came hallooing along the hall, eager to alert Shelley that they'd prepared the day's afternoon snack. They *were* taking over. They found her in front of the computer, weeping.

"Don't cry, Shell. Don't cry for your starshine." (They got her tears instinctively.)

They grabbed her from both sides and stroked her (at long last) long, silky hair: "Look what we made. Some hummus. Mom says it comes from chickpeas. We're your chickpeas, right? Or do you want something else? Since spring, you've been wild about apple juice."

A quick blush, then huge hugs. "Perfect, my steps. I don't need anything else."

In those first few days alone, Shelley sent wave upon wave of emails to Astrid. But she soon thought to save copies, a novice historian's new instinct. She printed them out then clasped them all into her shiny new accordion folder of bright lemon (along with Astrid's frequently soothing, always loving replies).

Here's an early one…

Well damn your sweet eyes anyway. I'm feeling a bit like my old self; only cried twice today. In between, I had to drive down to campus. Once I move in down there, I think I'll get me a bike. No more track—or you—to keep me in shape. I'll pump those pedals and try to forget you. Think it'll work? Hmm...Now, these emails to you. I've started saving them. Then when it's a complete package (never I hope), I'll stick that calendar in it too. Primary documents for my files: my forever best "summer of love".

A week later:

Guess who called me? Our sweetie, Greg. <u>You</u> know, my sweet bitch. You tried to set me up with him at the solstice party? Took me a sec to remember him. "You probably don't recall. I

175

liked your pictures, remember? You wrote your number on my hand?" He teased me about that lens cap.

Said he didn't want to intrude in my life, but you'd said you were leaving about now. Thought I might "become what Astrid calls a widow." Plus. Get this. "I hope you'll understand this. Recall those shots?" I said yeah and there was this pause. "Hard to get this out, but easier over the phone and with you. Jeff was right. The sit-up guy? I did like the view. You follow?"

I followed. So he won't be another handsy Mike. (Probably not I bet.) What a relief. ('Course, I thought you were so innocent. Such the professional.) Well, I was too blue to hold up my end of the chat for long. But I thanked him. He may just be that rare thing, sweetheart—a sweet and thoughtful male. I gave him my campus email. Maybe I'll invite him to Holmes. They told us that's where the younger undergrads (like me in a week) hang out. Some professors too. Maybe he'd enjoy being on a big campus and away from Hosmer? Who knows, maybe he'll get hit on by some sensitive frat guy (is there such a thing?).

Two days later:

Wednesday, I got to campus and it helped. They let us newbies tour our dorm rooms; mingle; get keys. I put on a brave face. You'd be proud. All these activities had their tables and posters in the gym. (Guess they do it same way there?) One table was "Women in Action". That sounded cool. Another was campus

176

ministry. But it wasn't for religion—more about community service, food pantries, adult literacy, stuff like that. I put my name down.

Oh, and there was the gay / lesbian table. Well, wouldn't you know it, the guy manning it was this incredible hunk. Just my luck I guess. (God, sweet, it's been too long.) I guess I'd've had a pretty <u>limp</u> reception. ('Least my sense of humor's back.) But, now, get this: the girl beside him? Polite, and encouraging. Neat eyes. The girl, Jodie, wrote her number on the flier she handed me. Guess I still have what it takes. Or she's just desperate. (No, I know better; you taught me <u>that</u>.)

Say, but now one more thing to make you jealous. Damn, though, it'll probably please you. Both. Today I went back to those Archives on Skinker where I did your research. (A good, painful way to deal with you: visit all our special spots.) Well, I ran into the woman who was so helpful to me. Boo hiss lady? She remembered me from July.

"All your hard work. Did your research stick with you?" I told her matter of fact it did. "I think I'll pursue it at Wash. U." (It's true babe. You at work on me again.) "So the summer amateur's becoming an activist? That's wonderful, Miss Jaspar!" She remembered my name. Quaint lady. I felt so grown up.

She invited me for tea. I just got back. Actually, we ended up sharing a sherry at Duff's. Say, babe, <u>*there's*</u> *a West End place* we missed. Outdoor tables, too; like in the Loop. They didn't even card me. (I'll take you at Christmas, count on it.) I wondered if she would take it any further. She didn't, but after you, I never know what "older" women have on their minds. "Well, you're so close, come drop by. Let's do this again." She gave me her card. So, now I have a contact—I'm an official Astrid research disciple.

Tomorrow I go back to our Falls. More pain, but it's pain I want to feel.

A week later:

Hey, there, dear Ms. Perot! Yeah, getting formal on your ass. Your heartless advice is starting to percolate. I came across that video last night. I was sorting through all those summer photos—to put into the album. By the pool. You and me on our patio. Saved the most flattering on a special page, but sorry, babe, I pitched some. Focus. Composition. Yeah, and once I got up to number six of you and your smile, I stopped. Could I be developing good taste? Should have waited and asked Greg. Nope. Made my own calls.

And that pole vault video? The first few days you were gone, I'd just watch you, then sigh, then cry. I remember how I loved to slow-mo it, your head coming up, up, up, and then freeze-frame it: my own sun rising in my own east. I'd stop it at that split-second when you have that determined look on your face, like the *one when you'd pin me down, eyes on fire, hair streaming. And that was when, well—you can guess.*

But now, no. So I slid the cassette back into its sleeve. Found a bright green marker, and wrote "Astrid" on its spine. Shelved it. Ashley's gonna have my room during the semester. If she plays it, it's just a woman doing a pole vault. Her sis's starshine! Hope it'll inspire her—pole vaulting. Yet once more, my Astrid's eternal influence.

Next I picked up that duffle-bag that dad gave me—the one he'd stashed my mother's treasures in. He kept a few to put on his dresser. (Averill insisted.) I put in a couple of things for the dorm. My track trophies. My third place from state. Went to the Loop and bought an ornate box. For my mom's pendant. (The one you couldn't keep your hands off.) Also put in it two rings of hers that dad gave me just last night.

I purchased a nearly empty date book, goes a full eighteen months to the end of my sophomore year. Page in the back for new names, new friends. I put Greg's number in there. And Ingrid's. I'll see if the Jodie thing goes anywhere.

Something else funny at the dorm. As I walked down the hall, hefting the duffle, saw a guy, a shy freshman, but the hottest green eyes. Looked at me once, then away. Maybe I can bring him out? Have you inspired me to be a helpful busybody or just a slut? Next, rounded a corner and about slammed into this girl lugging three huge boxes. I offered to help with her stuff, and I started admiring the neat tank top and tight biking shorts. "They're way cool." "Thanks, and thanks for your help. Drop in some time."

My new life's sure bubblin', babe, lady, sweetheart...

Post Holmes Days

He scarcely recalled the rest of that day. He walked in a delighted stupor through his 10 am composition class, his students' faces a flickering tapestry, their voices a whir of bees in a downspout. Early afternoon he freed his car from the fading yellow lines that caged it on the university lot.

From nowhere a long-neglected memory floated front and center. See, guys have memories too and, from time to time, they arise and float.

His fingers made a safe, pale lattice for his eyes. Through them he could see, through his wide window, that huge sycamore in front, casting its cylindrical shade on the granite street. The sun-bathed window ledge was his favorite spot. He could peer through the clean square panes to the orderly row of cars lined along their street, a bright yellow line at its center.

His nest yielded comfort. On certain days, behind him in the kitchen, his father would turn on that old, old radio (his dad's in fact) and, as its hum signaled its coming to life, the voices of baseball filled the sunny room. Reassured by the steady play-by-

play, he loved to watch the rectangles of sun inch their way across the room; they'd twist and distend on the east wall, then crawl in time to the ceiling in a rosy fade.

An early outdoor visit stunned him, however. They were trying to walk him across the street, to cross that line, to meet some neighbors. "You'll be in school together. You should meet him." He strained backward like a cat on a leash; dug his heels in. Over his shoulder, a worse shock: he saw the stately tree, for the first time, up close. Its trunk was blotchy, its bark peeling. Moss oozed out of its slimy crevices.

He gazed into the leaden sky and saw what seemed another world, an alien world, pivoting around that utterly strange tree. The withered leaves still shook and whispered, yes, but its shape was wrong. The wide and stately tree now looked lean, bent, and tapered. From this new position, its branches poked the air at savage angles.

As he drove, he gave a quick shiver at those old images, but let his soles begin a new dance on the accelerator. Propelled by the beat of a tuneless melody that start to flow through him, he got home, entered, his feet tapping a syncopated bee-line toward a rear alcove. It was usually concealed by a pale curtain, but he flung it aside and started rifling through some old trunks—some of them his, some his father's. More and more lately he'd tended to gather and store, like a determined but incurious pack-rat.

He'd always lived a precociously senescent life—his dad's phrase. He felt most at ease lolling in an easy chair, reading novels (usually historical). Much younger (that earlier vision brought it back), he'd sit quietly in the back yard and listen with his dad to a baseball game, his dad in turn recollecting from his youth memories of the Cardinals and even the long-departed Browns. (These were memories of a still earlier era, preserved in his dad's words, his actual voice.) His mother was always indoors, splicing yellowing family movies together. (It was she who'd introduced him to Mole, Toad, Ratty—and his favorite, the shy but self-sufficient Badger). When time came to start dating, it was a struggle; he did it mainly because his classmates were starting to. Sure, he liked to look at the girls, liked the habit almost enough to off-set the disconcerting novelty of the sensations.

Gavin's mention of a journal stirred a memory. He did a deep knee-bend to examine a moldy cardboard box, in it a dusty clasped volume with faded gilt lettering, "Five year diary." He stood to stretch his aching hams, then bent to lift out the small booklet. He shoved the rest of the contents out of sight and drew the curtains. He hefted the small box onto his shoulder, and, catching a glimpse of himself in a tarnished mirror, grinned. He recalled Gavin's groaning tray. "Pale imitation," he sighed.

He plopped the box onto the ottoman in front of his chair, blew dust off the lid, sat back and began to leaf.

"Aug 12. Cloudy day today. Sun for an hour or two this morning. Wind NW all day, and yet the temp got to 90. Perseid shower tonight. Barometer 30.12. Not much happening."

He flipped some pages.

"August 30. Cardinals had a good game; won third of four. Windy day. Temp reached 85, then turned cooler. Tomorrow starts sophomore year. Something coming? Time for bed."

Flipping the pages that followed yielded only a whir of white. Four and a quarter blank years beckoned. He drew a firm, black line across the page under that old entry from ten years before. He sprang up and took a stand at the make-shift table in his kitchen.

He laid the small book flat on the flat surface between his study and (on very rare occasions lately) his dining nook. He bent his knees for purchase (far more than he needed, but he wanted it to feel significant) and lifted the pen. Lifted the pen and

… Wrote. Effortless. Words quickly grew into phrases, phrases into sentences, like wine gurgling in delighted release from a jeroboam. The new words spilled out in total disregard of the diary's divisions of days, weeks, years.

"Before sunset." A direct quote from him! It hadn't taken much prompting. None. Him and his travels! I wonder, does he ever *get* where he's going? Keep writing, Scott. Open up! Well, then. I *like* the guy. I am drawn. Wonder, does he use his journal to record conquests? It must bulge.

Yes, Gavin. Was I just rechanneling my cravings? Should I respect the response? Back home, starting a new life. So I vote yes. Gorgeous. The smile; that wit. Some shared interests too. Yeah. Stuff to discuss with him.

A child of older parents, he'd been deprived of the easy raillery or mocking guidance about sexual matters a younger couple might have offered their sole offspring. All he had to rely on were overheard jests in the halls or in the senior lounge, or patient hints from his occasional girlfriends. His romantic life had always been a ricocheting cue ball; each new attraction intense but brief. He could always move on, and away—back into his own quiet world.

Until Gavin. In one day (hell, in ten seconds) Gavin blew his cover. That first splendid vision in Holmes started it; their chat just confirmed it. "I'm sold." *Fuck* what others might think.

He'd write more later. Entering his bedroom, he strode to his east-facing windows and flung open the sash, first time since November.

* * * * *

Later he slept. He pushed off from Monday and his imagination began to flow. A vivid dream. Trapped in murky

185

water; clammy weeds from a cold oozy bottom twined his legs. He kicked and kicked and, finally freeing himself, rose toward the brane of a watery universe; burst through it.

Now he was fully awake in real time. Eyes wide, on the windowsill he saw a bird, tapping conscientiously at a snail's carapace. Mild air lapped at his face. He leaped from bed.

His Diary. Even before he searched for something to nibble on, he reopened it, walked it to the kitchen table and resumed his scribbling. As he paused between jottings, he gazed in awakened wonder at his hand, splaying its fingers, first with knuckles up, then palm. He remembered that tingle. Then he contracted all five digits into a single smooth fist, marveling at the many shapes and textures it could assume. He actually turned over a blank sheet to trace his hand's full outline. Below it he wrote, "My hand" followed by the date and time. Then he flipped back to where he'd left off.

I can't wait. But got to play it cool. Don't show up too early. But I better go walk the route. I don't want him to wait.

The written word fathered the deed. He let go and let his rechristened journal guide his new day. He walked the four blocks to Gavin's, timing the trip with the hands on his watch.

His World Springs into Motion

(Post-Holmes)

Wednesday morning, the second dawn of Scott's Kuiper era, sixty hours until Friday evening, delivered a new discovery: how thrilling the early hour smelled. Thrilling, too, to experience what only a day before was the ungodly hour of seven a.m. He awoke and found himself wooed by some early rays spilling high on the wall of his front room. They were about to slide down the wall and lap at a large framed picture. One of his parents' most prized possessions. It was an early print by a Missouri artist, George Caleb Bingham: harmonious boatmen gliding down the wide Mississippi. Awakening some rusty astronomical skills, Scott did a quick and nerdy calculation of the earth's motion, its tilted axis, and extrapolated the results to his own early rising. "In a month that glass'll shimmer rose gold. I'll open the curtains and make it my alarm."

"Enough wallowing. I'm up. I need to get in shape." He slipped into some old shorts and a pair of battered tennis shoes, laces clicking, left on his t-shirt and headed out. As he began his jog he watched the fresh curtain of emergent green rolling across the varying hues of houses, pavement, cars in endless ripe rotation.

He looked to the west and saw a last few spangled stars, dimming. Old instincts, unpracticed for years, helped him locate the ecliptic, the sky's starry belt through which our (even Gavin says "our") sun journeys. He missed his childhood comrade, Orion, but he remembered that, come October, that hunter would peek out from behind the sun, and arise in the east, a reliable herald of winter.

Around him, squirrel upon squirrel boiled up from the fresh ground and exploded in rotating helixes up and down the mulberry trees. From a particularly opulent bush's womb vital twitters sang. As he jogged rather jaggedly down the street (this was all new to him), a canopy of blossoms showered aromas over him. Birds frolicked in birdbaths, ready in good time (he could predict) to spew droplets of red diamonds when the sun heaved itself up—yeah! Just over there. Across a grassy lot, he saw, as if his eyes had grown zoom lenses, the microscopic ecstasy of mating mantises. Nearby, hovering in two or three of the blossoms, caterpillars sported, testing their teeth on infant leaves, thin as tissues.

As he rounded a street that, he was fairly sure, would carry him back home, his legs began to ache. His splats of rubber on asphalt grew slower but more regular, and the rhythm summoned up a musical memory. A Bach chorale excerpt: first its regular and insistent pulse; then its rich melody. The spirited tune got him a good block farther. Then, as he picked up the pace again, the tune melted seamlessly into the steady but livelier, more syncopated beat of de Falla's "Miller's Dance." (He'd heard it on the local classical station the week before, one of his parents' old routines he was learning to adopt.)

And then... a remarkable thing. His splatting feet acquired a soft accompaniment. Yes. Beats with a metallic whine gaining on him. He pivoted his head and saw, like Venus dashing in its trek past the more leisurely earth, a young woman on a bike, her hair's cornrows curled up tight into a bright gold bandana. She biked intently, the pulsing clicks of her pedals matching his pedestrian jog. Her hands gripped the handlebars with firm authority, but her nicely muscled bare arms and firm legs moved to the very beat pulsing in his mind and on his soles. Coincidental? Or cosmic?

He summoned just enough breath to say "morning." She tipped her head a few inches to the side, mouthed "yes," the sibilant syllable dissolving as she and her passing smile sped past. The assured pumping made her calves, head, and shoulders a sensuous metronome. His eyes registered the long, well-muscled legs; relished the bright green shorts riding well up them; the angle of her body against the bright trees that the early sun was (bingo!) bathing with nascent gold.

Not for the first time lately, he could kick himself. Look at what the world had to offer, at what danced even at that hour. No, for an early Wednesday, the view on his street wasn't so bad. Did she bike every day?

189

* * * * *

The rest of Wednesday and Thursday were a blur. When he tried to read, the words swam laps across the page; when he taught, voices sluiced through his ears like water through a sieve. Both afternoons, trees blent with sky, squirrels with limbs, granite with grass. On Wednesday, a precocious (or merely negligent) lawnmower was threshing a few remains of last autumn's leaves. Suspended like a hologram in the rich brown tornado it spewed were Gavin's smile, eyes, hair: a sweet apparition upon a gauzy curtain, a living Turin shroud.

Thursday he awoke to a brighter dawn, as he glanced through his curtains. His first thought was the bicycle lady's pumping legs, but the image was immediately displaced by Gavin's face. It generated his usual responses. By Friday, Scott decided he would turn over his old self-conscious leaf and, dammit, respond to the guy.

His heart raced while he fretted. If the guy made a move? Where would the hands go? The lips? Wait, pause. "Hold on. You don't just want to go blasting into a new life, no holds barred, do you?" He was like a fall of snow after a spring cold snap, alternately caking and liquefying. "That's not you," he'd keep whispering to himself. "Careful." No. He'd be the restrained guest, merely polite, studiously curious.

Eight hours later, he consulted his watch and found the small hand at the six and the long one hovering over the 1. "Time to find out." Thanks to his test walk, he was not too early. So he gripped the door's golden handle. First stun. Locked! He should have checked *that*. Now what?

He hemmed and bridled at the doors, searching for the wanderer's name in the jamb's array of buttons. Damn. It suddenly dawned on him. All he knew was "Gavin." Gavin what? Oh, yeah. Dr. K. (Why not C? Cooper, right?)

The third button down looked promising: "Gavin Kuiper." So far, so good. Close enough, anyway. "Should I press it?"

Fortunately, and especially fortunate for our tale, he did. And a second later, that voice, musical even through the intercom's tinny rasp, rang out in a fused alto and soprano from the cold bricks.

"Yo. Scott there?"

He cleared his throat. "Yes," (strange flutter in his larynx) "it is. Scott."

"Great, mate. I'll buzz. Know the drill?

Shell Elbows Her Way in with Another Farewell to Astrid

Wait. Stop. Scott is indulging in his first, intense, adult relationship. Luck of the draw (or part of some larger design?) it's with a guy. But Shell, that newly confident (even headstrong?) eighteen-year-old, can't help elbowing her way in.

True, she won't meet Scott for nine months, and their first date—which *we* can foresee, though to them it's still-well-concealed—is a year and a half off. Still, her charm and vitality deserve and claim our attention. She's growing, and in real time, into the woman who'll trip Scott's heart into a head-over-heels tumble.

Time's engaging in its usual unruly somersaults, this time refusing even to ask our patience. While it seems we live our lives sequentially, our minds and hearts grow in a disordered fashion— spontaneous, with wild erratic connections and lapses. Here is Shell's for-now last message to Astrid, a healthful if sad sign. It shifts our gaze to Shell's first college semester. (Scott won't even reach campus for another year.)

Thursday, September 21.

Oh my dear Astrid,

Now here's something I bet you thought would never come from me. A real letter. And on the first day of fall: maybe in honor of the seasons changing? Or maybe just me. See that fancy, frilly monogram stuff at top? My mom's. Got home from the Loop last night, Dad disappeared—I heard him rummaging around in the garage—and brought in this dusty, fancy box with blue filigree initial inscribed on it. ACJ like on each sheet. Our initials match! ('Course I knew that, just never saw them in print.)

It makes me feel special to write you on it. I know she would have loved you, too. (Of course. Who doesn't?)

I've never really handwritten one of these. I'll probably come off sounding even worse than those "ready, shoot, aim" emails of mine. Already tore up two of these. Sorry. This is the one you'll get; Mom's notepaper is too precious. You've told me often enough to stop apologizing, so here it is.

I'll give you the whole story. Dad and I had a final Lebanese dinner outdoors in the Loop—Averill insisted: "Go, you two Jaspars!" (I even thought about asking Alicia, my new dorm friend along—my new style guru, too. But no: this was just me and your admirer, your "Ben, sir.") I treated: I'd saved some of that grant money, so dinner was on you. I can't escape you.

But I asked him for advice on untangling this heart of mine from you, like you whispered—gently, yes; lovingly yes—all summer. I figured he knew us two <u>sweethearts</u> better than anybody. Told him I should try to get the distance you say we need. He nodded (he remembered your talk), smiled and ran his hand through my hair. "Very wise, hon," he says. "But it hurts. I know." Then he smiled: "Seems my dear daughter's trying to write what her grandpa would've called a 'Dear John' letter." He looked down the bustling street. "'Cept, she's writing it to a woman. He'd have some questions!" (Darn, I wish I'd met him. Most girls have grandparents to run to, don't they? Guess you're kind of that for me. Hi, sweet granny Astrid!)

But I told him no. Never a 'Dear Astrid.' I'll always be yours, babe! Love! Sweet! But I think this frilly letter gives me a chance to, like, I don't know, shimmy up a tree; try for some distance. For a little distance. But wait, wait. Come December I'll climb down. So we can tell each other. Everything. Yes, even any new lovers—boy, girl, whatever. I'll swallow hard, but I'll want to hear.

Well, then that makes this sort of a formal declaration of ...well, not independence; never that (or always that—to be independent like you) ... no, maybe just a thoughtful, patient, brief, and (yes!) painful suspension.

There. I did it. But I'm not over you, love. Never. Sure, the taste and feel of your lips can fade. (Haven't yet but I know they might.) But there's the you that lasts—the laugh, the serious look, the teasing, the determination. You're still my direction. And my momentum.

Can't stop yet. I had a dream last night. Me sailing above the trees. Gazing down into a silver lake, streaked with showers of diamonds. And down there your sweet face, hair streaming, mouth smiling. But then I flew higher, and your face shrank and shrank. Became a diamond too, still glowing, but way down.

What can it mean? I woke up smiling but with wet eyes. Maybe I can at least get you to one side. I'm going to hold my heart and my breath until Christmas. Got it?

Always ... your...

Ashella

The Start of a Beautiful

With Shell's intrusion welcomed and her loving, painful declaration accomplished, the usually self-effacing Scott can earn fresh attention. We await Gavin's welcoming buzz.

Scott's gut somersaulted into excited anticipation. That state of mind used to be brought on by a higher (if not always more musical) voice, pert breasts, a slender build, firm abs, shapely thighs.

He spoke louder yet tried to sound cool. "Buzz away."

At the vibration, Scott rotated the handle firmly downward and pushed in. He found himself edging across the ornate Victorian tile pattern, as he heard his host clattering down the upper stairs at break-neck clip. That voice with a thousand overtones wafted its way down the shaft:

"Wait, wait, pal." The voice settled into a rich baritone: "I'll lead."

Scott had just reached the first landing when Gavin swung on one foot around the jamb of the second—a car cornering on two wheels, that Road Runner comet as its blur of motion ceases and its body reintegrates.

What the voice began, the sight completed. Any thought of staying cool melted. Shimmering above him half a flight up, Gavin glowed—his eyes hazel, the triangle of neck and upper chest bronze. A luminous bandana now seconded the aureole of thick blond hair. And his momentum set loose that shirt of his (emerald now) from—it reappeared and with interest—that slim but granitic belly.

By then Gavin was molding Scott's palm with his two. "'Tis you indeed. Welcome. But, wiki, wiki. I have sauce that's on the verge of sublimation. Follow the echo, young sir." As he sprang from stilled motion up three steps, that regal bandana danced. Gavin turned the corner and evaporated, but his scurrying feet made the stairwell vibrate.

* * * * *

Scott toiled in his wake, puffing his way up two more flights. There he found an ornate, curiously carved door swinging welcome on its hinges. Gavin's voice sang out ("Enter. Enter") from what cinnamony aromas announced was the kitchen and wove into the piano strains of a Debussy prelude ("my favorite and dad's, that sunken cathedral; how'd he guess?") caressing the air

197

from paired speakers. Though he didn't articulate the thought, Scott made the first of many novel discoveries: artistic or musical or literary tastes are not unique, not to an individual or a family. The species goes about acquiring a common heritage, here and there, now and again: multiple random exposure. Frequent, open, full and frank exchange. And, dotted here and there, separate islands of consensus.

On the stove bubbled three pots, their lids pulsing with fragrant gasps. His genial host gave each of them three quick whisks, lowered their three flames, and bestowed a trio of paternal gestures ("calme toi...et toi...et toi"). He then took Scott by the elbow and walked him to his fridge. From its freezer he drew forth two full, frosted goblets, their round bells snuggling in his palms. When he proffered one, the gelid wine sloshed slowly and invitingly.

Next his free hand scooped up a silver knife that gleamed on the sideboard and curled two fingers out to retrieve its whetstone buddy. His right hand balanced the other goblet on which a frosty glaze was forming.

"Follow, please." He lowered both hand and glass to the small of Scott's back and guided him through his living room, steered him past a hall down which the tail of his eye caught a trembling labyrinth of sheets. Upon them a host of intricate designs shifted shapes.

"First the view I promised." His deep red tongue swam slow laps across his lips as he rotated Scott's head from the hall to the western window. "Recall?"

By now the rumbling bass notes of the rising "Cathedral Englouti," announced its key melody. Gavin led Scott through the French windows, whose scrims those equinoctial breezes were puffing. The professor walked the grad student out onto the carved stone balcony; from its corners those warm breezes had just about finished scouring winter's last vestiges.

On a white trellis hung a pair of silver baskets, from which rich, purple blossoms cascaded. (Gavin had moved them outside for Scott's visit.) Beneath them, Gavin berthed his wine on a mahogany side table then swung his body behind Scott. Two soft steely hands steered Scott to the edge.

"Look." He shifted his palms to Scott's neck and swiveled his head to face east. "See." As Scott gazed, he felt his host undock, sensed his retreat, then heard an eerie yet melodious undertone, a sweet keen.

"I picked these digs for their history. So, now; while I hone, get oriented." Scott turned to see Gavin marrying the knife's blade to the whetstone and continuing to do so as request followed request. "And then the test. So. Report please." (Back and forth.) "Describe." (Back and forth.) "Explain." (And again.)

"I am at your service."

"Good. First tell me what you see there, to the east: educate me. Your city's your specialty, yes?"

"Ah. Well, then."

`Gavin's rented balcony was high enough to offer a dreamy distant perspective on the riverfront arch, some fifty blocks away. On its perfect parabola the western sun still glowed, rose gold on silver. "Heavens. Such a view you have here. Wonderful locale, Gav.'"

"Ta, sir. Here to please. And learn."

"Well, then. Our Arch. Expresses the city's mission: the gateway to, the promise of, America's western wonders. You chose well ..." Scott delighted to salute Gavin with one of Gavin's greetings, ". . . mate'"

Scott heard the air cease to throb. Instantly he felt a cool line drawn across the back of his neck. His first thought (some dim, ancient ritual?) was the knife. But then he knew: nah, just Gavin's chilled and winy finger. The pedestrian explanation, however, didn't erase the delightful sensation.

"Yes. One down, mate." Gavin's warm breath filled Scott's right ear. "Now pivot," he continued. "To the south—your Park."

Now Scott could put his parochial expertise to work. "Well, now, if you could gaze through that line of roofs there you'd see Lindell. It was our World's Fair's Main Street, the Pike. So again . . . it's a rich vein of history." In future weeks he'd provide his host a far more extensive sketch of that past, but just then his mind and heart were attuned to the now of the moment.

He dared to sidle onto a daring limb: "Bet you chose it just to impress me."

"Oh, of *course*. I was destined to meet, by sheer lucky timing, on one chance Holmes morning, the one man who can best explain my new world to me? (When I first heard the name I thought it was 'Homes.' It's what drew me there.)" A knowing and enigmatic smile rose to Gavin's lips and hung there, to delightful and mysterious effect. "Hmmm." The hum dissolved as his lips formed a perfect "o" and he began to whistle some elegant aria.

Scott's calm smile maintained a southerly stare to conceal his heart's thump. (He was becoming quite the expert at duplicity.) Meanwhile, that delightful cool finger kept itself moving and him guessing.

Enough. He turned to face his friendly tormentor. "Hold it. What's the test here—my knowledge or my self-discipline? You're making it hard. To concentrate, I mean."

"I know."

All words ceased for a second. For two. Three.

"Now again," Gavin resumed. "Vision number three. The west." He re-pivoted Scott another forty-five degrees. "Where your sun's last rosy fingers cast what one or two of your poets call a vernal glow—" It was not the sun's fingers but Gavin's that got to work. Its slow sensuous arcs were turning Scott's concentration to air.

"Very nice."

"What?"

"This."

"This what? Noun, please. View? Lesson? Or this finger, perhaps?" He slid it yet again, now even cooler and more delicious (how could that be?). Recalling some old moves of his own, Scott deciphered the moment.

Scott pictured Gavin's massaging hand as a mother cat preparing to heft a prodigal kitten back to its nest. Flocks of fingers were caressing first the left, then the right sides of his neck, and grazing as far as his chin.

"But first, old Scott, young archivist and historian *extraordinaire* ..."

(Scott's brain and veins shivered at the lengthy title and the newer moniker). "Pardon. Before we turn to us, I repeat: turn west. What's there?"

"What are we seeing?" Scott tried to calm the trembling that had seized his legs. "Let me think." He cleared his throat. Then, amazing himself again, he reached his two arms behind him to lasso Gavin. "Now, then. What you're seeing. Brookings Hall's noble entryway. Beyond it, but out of sight, is Holmes—our magical spot. And just beyond that is Duncker—our truer home."

"Home?" Gavin's tone had suddenly changed. "No."

"Sure it is. We work there."

"It's only temporary." Scott hands detected a sigh behind him. He felt the man ease backwards, though he remained comfortably caged. "Your world, not mine."

"Ah," Scott reminded him. "Not every homeless soul can boast digs like these."

"Perhaps. Perhaps so. But still. Listen up." Now he could feel Gavin's lungs breathe deep. "Vital early warning. What you've captured here—both by belt and by heart—is someone who's always and entirely *en route*. Heed the tip, *tovariche.*"

Scott concealed a pang but tried to complete his assignment. "Well, call it our office then. We do our English thing." He dropped his hands and turned to face the man, adding, "For a nomad, I repeat, you can create marvelous, sensuous homes out of nothing. Inside I saw one—" his thumb pointed in. "And—" he swiveled and laid his cheek against it—"That shoulder of yours there—or, rather, here."

"So, you like it?"

"Do I like this 'here'? Oh, yes." Scott moved his cheek around, like a Martian rover, pawing with its first curious foot. "*And* this one. Yes… And, oh yes yet again. *Another* 'here'."

"So, then. Well then. It seems you are here."

Scott Gives Birth to a Novel

He walked home next morning, the sun barely up. The privilege of seeing the world a third time at that fresh, cool hour felt like a new and delightful privilege. No girl on a bike that morning, but more than enough shimmering images of Gavin to breathe life into his blank pages. Within seconds he was feverishly scribbling, his tongue exploring the corners of his lips. As his cat wound herself with subtle persistence between his bare ankles, a frenzy of affectionate recollection was driving him. On several occasions, much later, Shelley loved to query him, "So, sweet man. How'd you get to be you, anyway?" Each time, he'd simply point to that blue Diary. Its dog-eared pages still sat well to the side and on a high shelf. "Showed me *getting* here anyway. Er, getting *there* anyway."

"So it's not for publication?"

"Not *that* version, no. That *stage*. But for you, sweetheart: bedtime reading, any time… After we 'talk' some."

So what now follows comes from a later reconsideration. As a preamble that night, he scribbled, "The evening, the night so perfect. I want to get it just right." "Just right" meant fifty detailed pages. So what follows is—contrary to appearances—a concise summary.

He recorded how they unwound their hands from each other's waists and adjourned down that windy hallway. To a kind of sheeted covey. Those sheets he'd noticed on entering divided the man's digs into numerous crannies; the eccentric arrangement offered a universe of tiny suggestive possibilities, a new surprise around every corner. To the sheets Gavin had fastened postcards or magazine images of Missouri in this, his latest home in transition.

Whenever Scott set down his goblet Gavin would snatch it up, go into momentary eclipse around a luffing white corner, and return with one (for Scott), often two (Scott and Gav'), charged beakers. Though still aroused from that balcony quiz, Scott found the time to be mesmerized by those fluttering holographs—the leisure to be jealous that, in three months, Gavin had accumulated a bigger slice of Missouriana than had he in a lifetime. There were even some Bingham images, enlarged into 8 x 10s, in color. Scott was especially drawn to the pair of meditative trappers (he adored the one in a vibrant teal shirt) who'd given the boat's bow privileges to what looked like a cat.

Shelley, the reliable regional historian would inform him that the ambiguous creature was a bear cub. She informed him further that, though yes the teal was alluring, she preferred the

"Jolly Boatmen in Port," with its dancing man at its center. "It's okay, sweet love. We share the color; but for me it's about dancin'. Remember our de Falla moment?" Scott had another tie to the painting, a personal one. His parents had met at their church a frail, elderly spinster whom, at age six, Bingham had in fact painted in a family portrait. Living genealogy and art history.

Gavin sat down beside him and—no coyness, just affection—hung a cool hand around Scott's shoulder. "Now, new man, Missouri fellow: I think, at short last, it's our time?"

Yet, when Scott turned toward that smiling gaze and nodded, the probing man, who seconds before had in his distinctive way been hitting on him, morphed into a solicitous, thoughtful companion.

"Comfortable?"

"The body is." His eyes craved that soft curve of Gavin's neck, yeah right there, just where it blended into, yeah, that firm jaw. (Gavin had erased his traveler's beard. Was it from gentlemanly courtesy? Or was it just another of his perpetual renewals?) "But," he added, "my spirit's glad you paused to ask. It's still a bit wary."

"Ah. Well, then. We'll take our time."

The rest of the evening would amaze Scott. Gavin's elegant but firm build kept him shivering with delight. His air of authority, loving but firm, captured his heart. So was he eager to dissolve in his embrace? Frankly, yes.

Yes, and yet. His old tentativeness and shyness arose. So as he drew close he was relieved when Gavin kindly melted. A true mentor, a loving guide, he was gently walking him through each moment. And, the lit professor was always quoting. And he had "this *penchant*" (perfectly elocuted French naturally) for 18th century English literature. And music and opera. He'd often quote; occasionally he'd sing. Pope's words and Handel's melodies were twin obsessions. Augustan formality put to the service of modern lust. Gavin, the sensuous pedant, saw the educational opportunity intimacy offered. Erotic pedagogy.

His loving and considerate tutor made Scott feel that the two of them were undertaking a joint adventure—fording new rivers, trekking frontier forests. Together they encountered some novel sensations and not a few astonishing new positions. (They astonished the novice Scott anyway.)

Gavin proved the perfect partner in their busy two-man "corps of discovery." He made it fun, imaginative. "Recall a favorite woman. Use your loving hands like you did on her. Say to me the things you said to her." Gavin professed as much surprise and pleasure as Scott did at the moves and endearments Scott hatched.

Or, "Now, me. I'm the guy. You the woman. Remember how *she* reacted to your charming self. Then extrapolate and reap the rewards." Scott played the assigned role to their mutual satisfaction.

Gavin's affectionate mastery was a work long-since-in-progress. That immense consideration of his he'd acquired bit by bit from his globe-girdling travels. That Norwegian woman he'd met in a Bangkok stop-over was proving indispensable again. He'd been *en route* to a three-month sojourn at Macquarie Island in Antarctica—an oceanographic laboratory where in time he'd meet a stunning Russian geologist. Inge taught him (and Mikhail in turn confirmed *how well* she'd taught him) how each stage of love-making can gain intensity through sensual negotiations. Lots of "may I?'s", "yeses", "wait a bits", "what ifs, and "oh, man!" As Gavin put that acquired expertise to use, each hour yielded agonizingly delicious moments. First, erotic suspense; fast on its heels (or simply in due course), carnal extravagance.

One time, the hesitant disciple made a feint to pull back from a burst of his guide's passion: "Sure about that? *Should* I stop?" Gavin asked, and Scott upon instant reflection was back instantly—like Heisenberg's cat, here and there at once.

He lost, for a space, all track of time. His mind's eye somehow rose above each sensuous moment. He glimpsed this new lover, this first man, in the past with his many others, then hopscotched again to the future where (and when) he knew that as many more bobbed expectantly. That new, multiple eye of his collapsed all these moments into a frantic held instant, a beehive of considerate, intense lovers swarming, swarming across the globe. And above it. *(Above* it? Come again?)

Throughout the evening, Gavin's CD player was clogging the air with successive melodies, alternating in random order— some vocal, some instrumental. Dixieland. "The Wabash Cannon Ball." "Brandy." The Beatles. "Zefiro Torna" (Monteverdi). "September Song." Janis Joplin. Several Strauss waltzes (*one*-two-three)—and a modern reggae cousin (one, two, *one*-to-three), "I can see clearly now." Scott took to them all and, all in good time, sang their praises to all-and-sundry—students, colleagues and disciples of his own. (And yes, yes: his wondrous Shell. They became each other's mutual disciples.)

Scott did take control of the player once, to introduce Gavin to one of his few provincial favorites. Not Janis but *Scott* Joplin: the black composer who, like Scott's dad, had hailed from out-state Missouri. (Family tradition had given Scott at least a sliver of musical exposure. The tale inspired Shell to explore still more on her own.) But Gavin was the evening's conductor, so over and over it was Debussy. That magical cathedral just kept rising and rising, a recurring coda.

Once, though, Scott heard some soprano trills. It was a Handel aria, as Gavin later confirmed in a cooler moment: Galatea warbling like a dove to her man, Acis. A tiny part of Scott's brain gasped at those warbled notes. How could two distinct tones dwell together as one? How can sequences collapse and fuse like that? (Amazing what the brain can pick up while the body's otherwise, even passionately, engaged.)

* * * * *

"Now," groaned Gavin as he let his kimono fall open over his now distended belly. "Baklava. Up for it?"

"No, no. Please. A digestive break. Unlike sex, there *is* such a thing as too much food."

"You too? Good, then. Care for a stroll? An orbit around my high-rise patio?"

Scott acquiesced. They'd barely covered half a circuit when Gavin paused, took Scott's arm with one elbow, and employed the other hand to swivel Scott's face upward. Among the tendrilling vines and blossoms glowed a brilliant, suspended point of red.

"Look there! See? That's Mars. May I introduce you?" The always-gallant Gavin bowed the planet toward Scott. The name and the orb sent Scott into a new recollection: his Dad and mom shivering around a telescope, patiently stamping their feet as Scott, age ten, sought to capture and bring into sharp focus that identical red blur.

"Yes?" Gavin instinctively detected Scott's pensive moment.

"Yes. Early days. A telescope. From my folks."

Gavin smiled knowingly. "Ah, they did their best. But, well, that was then?"

"That was then. And sure enough, not so many months later…"

"You…" Gavin prompted.

"… put away childish things.."

"So, farewell the heavens, hello books? Sky sewed up tight?"

"Guess so," Scott sighed. "But it was pleasantly replaced by documents, maps, books. Loved the tales; savored the dust."

Then a comic notion from nowhere glowed bright. "Say, world traveler." He imitated Gavin by tilting the man's head back up. "Think you'd like to go there some day?

For once in their time together, silence.

Then: "Go there? *Go* there? Go *there*?"

"Sure. Make like our Huck. Light out! Some new territory?"

"Ah." A split second of skiey contemplation. "I *do* wonder now and again. Where next? I often ask myself, '*Have* I filled all the available needy ears? Seeded and watered all available minds on *your* globe?' Hmm. But Mars? What would I do for food up there? Cucumbers from sunlight?" (Scott smiled at the reference to one of Gulliver's voyages. What *hadn't* Gavin gotten to know?)

"But by Allah and the Bodhisattva, what a trip *that* would be."

Scott hadn't meant his joke to bring such billowing clouds to life. "Is he serious?"

His laugh hid the pang and he took refuge in ill-usage. "Well, now, *great*. Four days ago you start a heart-theft. An hour or so ago you complete the robbery. Yep, and several completions since. And now, you contemplate escape? And not just down the road." His leg commenced that old involuntary jiggle. "Planetary?"

"No, no, no." Gavin's two arms circled Scott's waist as they continued their joint gaze. Then his hand slid down to massage Scott's upper thigh. "Just an intriguing thought. *You're* the one who brought it up, love."

His honeyed breath crept into Scott's ear, calmed the leg, and turned the knees back to water. "You know I never stay

213

anywhere very long. I'm always *en route*. But still. For *now*. No talk yet of leaving. *Not yet*."

Scott took his turn and breathed into his host's ear. "But listen. You *can* change old ways, break habits, reform. Hamlet bemoans 'the stamp of nature' that brands us. Well, dammit, he's wrong. Make a commitment. Start with Holmes, with Duncker: those guys and gals already love you."

Scott amazed himself. He reached for and turned Gavin's head away from that tiny crimson light and folded those rarely silent lips into his own.

His New Life

Scott saw how far caution got him that night, so he chucked it. Self-indulgence became his soft but insistent mantra. Soon the teaching novice and roving professor settled into a pattern that would stretch out until—well, Scott knew better than to try to rely on units of time to lasso these new wonders.

Gavin was delighted with Scott and found him a genuine partner whether in bed or the kitchen. But it was as a colleague that he was most eager to shepherd him. In bed, he always shunned the conventional. "Gav" would go all poetic on Scott—challenge him to grasp him like a cool cascade of water, or grow on him like a stand of corn, bursting nightly into tasseled splendor.

Gavin had a short-wave radio that at odd times of odd days picked up what Scott at first found unintelligible chirps and nasal snorts, beamed from places (Gavin translated all of them) like Kazakhstan, Uruguay, Micronesia, Kenya. They'd create their movable feasts in Gavin's kitchen. (Or in Scott's—a whim determined which.) They'd consume a cucumber *hors d'oeuvre* and plan the evening meal—or, whims ruling again—select items at random while Gavin opened Scott's ears and mind to news around the globe. Forever after (well so far anyway), when Scott would read or hear about, say, Bangladesh, he'd smell the aroma and feel the textures of, say, *saag alou*.

Endless conversations, catholic topics: Breughel's eccentric realism, or the way Dvorak's harmonies (whether Bohemian or Iowan) lit a path for Stravinsky or for Berg or for "his" Scott Joplin. Once or twice Gavin got going on Gnosticism. He'd insist that those early thinkers understood Christ better than he understood himself, or anyway better than any of his selves that the several gospels sought to report. Or—less theological—they'd agree to admire the engineering acumen of a Brunelleschi dome or be blown away by Dante's command of a host of Italian vernaculars.

Even movies. Scott admired the way certain directors would throw some "mythical shit" into popular fare—and he got Gavin to see it. "Like in 'Field of Dreams,' the obsession with threes. Mann slams his door in Ray's face three times. But Ray returns and returns. "A true hero's persistence and determination?" Gavin nodded. "Art at work, even in things commercial."

Gavin came to love a fluffy piece called "Notting Hill," especially the wordless scene—they're called *movies*, not wordies—that collapsed nine months of the hero's loveless life into thirty seconds of changing seasons—rainy fall, snowy winter, and the floral return of spring—all in a single walking "take." Scott wondered whether the real reason Gavin adored it—he was even proprietary about it—was because it reproduced a similar sequence from his favorite literary quest, *Sir Gawain and the Green Knight*.

Sometimes these sessions would go on and on to a new day. (On more than one Sunday midnight, Scott snuck a peek at the pendulum on the tall corner clock and cast a glance at his sheaf of ungraded papers). Scott would also recur with a martyr's regularity to Gav's adamant commitment to moving on.

"You always fit in, wherever you alight. Think you could ever screech to a halt?"

"Sorry, Scotty. I know I frustrate you, hon'. But no: that's not me."

"Yeah, yeah. But is there maybe a second you who *could*? Or couldn't you somehow duplicate yourself before you depart?"

"Produce a duplicate? No, luv, that's for *you* to discover. Not for me to provide."

* * * * *

Another Gavin query from out of the blue. "What if some thirtieth century reader flips some pages written today to try to recover and provide a glimpse of one of your 'chat rooms'? For them, a millennium from now, such a 'place' will feel as alien an

217

anachronism as tenth century monks illuminating a sermon from the third century Desert Fathers are to us today. No, love. All change is loss. And change is permanent."

But they did end up agreeing on some recurring fictional patterns. A motif or theme that resists nature's dedication to change. Quests recur, and they recur with only minor modifications. Gilgamesh's post-diluvian travels to recover Utnapatim; Elizabeth Bennet's witty but passive search for a mate; Huck's watery float. Chaucer's pilgrims. Sarty in the story Gavin most prized, "Barn Burning." Those quests hue to a pattern, however varied the worlds in which they vibrate or through which their participants travel—as excited, purposeful atoms.

Such debates were always at lust's option. But, sooner or later, sleep took charge. Scott inevitably awoke (sometimes at dawn, often earlier) to Gavin's raging blond cascades. They'd bring sunny life to their room long before our local star appeared.

A Class Act

It was Scott's classroom where Gavin left his most lasting imprint as he continued to shepherd his partner's and protégé's progress. For one thing, after those always astonishing and exhausting weekends, when Scott came to class, he … well, all too often, he didn't feel ready. What Scott came to call Gavin's tough love forced him to wing it, to abandon those leisurely lesson plans. Some Mondays he had barely enough time to review notes or jot bullets. So he performed it all from memory discovering an instinct to find and voice connections on the fly.

And? So?

So it went just fine. Went great, but with a rare glitch or stumble, sure. Best of all, or maybe as a result, his normally shy eyes began bursting their fetters. He'd no longer fix his gaze on his printed lecture sheet nor on the farthest windows. Now he began to let it roam. He saw the frown of that girl off to the side; the girl in the far back, eyes alert but hooded under her dark blue hat; a few inquisitive looks on some; the occasional elbow delivered by one guy to the fellow next to him; the sneer from the slender girl in slinky black to the girl two desks over.

Scott kept pumping Gavin for tips—on how to open them up, say, or for exercises to produce what expert manuals called "telling writing." Often the advice would flow pillow to pillow, Gavin whispering pearls of wisdom like a silent angel to Scott's half-conscious but delirious brain. Or—sweet conniving bastard— he'd make a move, arouse him, get him up to the verge, then … Pause.

"Yes? Yes? … Damn you! What?"

Then, after a pregnant pause, a whisper. "Try peer editing." Then they went back to their "work."

What surprised Scott the most, coming from such a devoted teacher, was his mentor's suggestion not to become too involved with the welfare of those students. Be more like a doctor, assessing the patient's health. Sure, get creative. Sure, be imaginative, but observe the results with a cool and calculating eye. See how they respond to the adventure you'd devised. Next semester, next term, you'll absorb, refine—you'll do it better.

Real progress one day with Huck Finn. He'd lectured them on Twain's writing style in his usual methodical way, but then he gave them a clever journal assignment (a journal was becoming good enough for him; why not them?) to write a first-person childhood memory. Now, as he was sounding them out, the back of his mind (another spacious locale Gavin kept urging him to explore) started percolating. The final image of Huck heading off to the new territory made Scott stop in mid-sentence. Out of the blue, a vision: blue and red and steaming white globes hanging in space, each spinning in separate rotations.

He could make nothing of the sight, only its intensity. Then out of the—well, the cosmic black—he suddenly blurted, "But, hey guys, why couldn't he go into space?"

They laughed. "Don't think so, sir. Horse and buggies to Mars?"

Their new and friendly mockery helped him relax and return to Twain's text. But he could not erase the play-action video his mind had spooled. He moved it, carefully tagged, to that mental Outback in amber suspension. His glance landed, for a bare second, on one fellow about halfway back who didn't join the derisive uproar. His face, darkly handsome within a rich, azure paisley bandana, assumed a sober and reflective cast. He hunched over his book and began to turn its pages, jotting notes.

A Starry Jaunt

It wasn't just in the twenty by twenty-five foot classroom that Gavin helped to free him. "We've got to get you out more." And Scott knew he was right: life can't just be golden tête-à-têtes, scattered among their intermittent honeymoons. What Gavin inspired had to seep out from bed and dinner table (vast as they felt) to the great wide world. One Sunday, Scott breathed deep and chose his poison. "What say I introduce you to the Science Center?"

Gavin was all nods.

As they stepped onto the moving stairs to carry them up to the Center's main level, Scott gave Gavin's arm a shy pat. (That was a public first.) Then, as they started upwards into the buzzing hive of fellow visitors, he amazed himself. He hooked his index finger into one of Gavin's belt-loops while his thumb quietly but fondly rubbed that firm lower back. He thought he heard a small snigger below him, but when he rotated his head his gaze met just an array of eyes—some distracted, some indifferent, one or two mildly attentive. He unhooked his arm quickly. Hovering further below, out of sight, a maroon cap quivered. Equally out of sight was the shy smile bubbling under it.

He kept his distance after that "Not quite ready for our debut, eh?" Scott felt a smile well up. Couldn't help it. Gavin was so unpredictable. "And so fucking irresistible," he admitted to himself. "Damn him."

Thirty seconds later he walked Gavin to the ticket booth, held up two fingers and paid the amount flashed on the electronic screen. Gavin took his elbow. "C'mon, mate. Let's head to your star show."

* * * * *

Still, in spite of their blessedly carnal home encounters, there was a wobble in their orbit. The tremor would vibrate whenever Scott recalled the message from that first balcony chat at that first sunset that first night. Yes, in spite of their most ebullient love-making, or as each spoon fed the other his latest creation, Scott sensed the merest pin-prick to the mind's conscious eye. Tomorrow or next month or next winter, Scott knew, Gavin *would* fold up his tents. Time or space *would* twinkle him out of their world, heading wherever. Even as he strove to harvest new sides of himself, he *knew* it would not keep his travellin' man around.

He knew Gavin was a godsend, levering him up, up and out of that old, dead security. But (none so blind) what he would not see, even if a brilliant laser had sculpted a hologram of it on his

223

cornea, was that by becoming the man Gavin was helping to sculpt, he'd outgrow his creator. He was already being forced to learn to mentor himself, shape himself. *That* much he could see.

Still, for now, these insights spurred only the faintest background hum, a low hiss that couldn't distract him from their blissful life. Scott was amazed more than once, when he awoke late in middle of the night, about to reach over to bring Gavin back to life, that what sprang to his mind was not a replay of any of the memorable moments from two or four or five hours before.

No. Instead he found his mind hanging, suspended in music, whether a Brahms intermezzo, Sinatra singing Gershwin (he loved the line, "There's a somebody I'm longing to see"), Louis Armstrong's trumpet, "Good Vibrations." He was amazed at how all the other memories of the night simply sloughed off and he lay there at perfect ease, melodies spooling, separating, coalescing. He felt lifted into a place of no time—no space, where now a voice, now a melody, vibrated the universe like a single but infinitely various string.

Scott Brings Fiction to Life

Much later, Shelley loved to urge Scott to tell her the tale of "that first meeting." The first time she asked, he launched into that miraculous "Gavin" morning in Holmes. She cut him off. "Now don't be coy. I mean *our* meeting. *Us*—you and me." But she did not mean the one when she, stranger at dawn, pedaled past. Sure, it was nice to recall that near-miss. Still, what she loved to revisit was the first time they actually grasped hands over that sizzling grill, that smoking and fiery fiesta pit. Nor did she long for the version recorded in his journal. "No, sweetheart. Do it from memory! The real moment." (Shell, thanks in part to Astrid's firm standards, could have her demanding moments.)

The brief public hour at the Science Center, though that daring moment had induced an immediate shiver, actually helped him grow more and more relaxed in the classroom. He even began to glow (minimal but a glow) like a stellar nursery within that old dusty pall of habit and restraint. Like the spoiled, unimaginative, but reforming Eustace Scrubb, in his favorite book from a childhood fantasy series, he became determined to peel those layers and layers of dead dragon skin. He wanted to dive down to some as yet indiscernible heart and discover what lay there. Remarkable and eye-opening the way a mere children's tale, and a fantasy no less, still whispered to, and worked to shape, the adult Scott years later.

He'd come to one day and found himself inside the front lip of desks, a daring hermit crab skittering along the front of a beachhead: testing the lapping waves before burrowing into a snug haven. On the Wednesday after the "star-show," something remarkable. It was destined to involve both men. (*And Shelley.*) Scott, though, was the only one present at its birth. He was dying to tell Gavin about it, but had to wait until Friday, so he planted it in that other new friend of his—that growing, bulging journal. That's where he recorded his life with some accuracy; it was an ear that recorded his life but withheld judgment.

He'd exhausted that old Diary long since and had bought a new, thick, deep blue one at the college store. As he nurtured the tale, he'd draft sentences, then draft more. He'd draw arrows from here to there; he'd edit and cross out, all the while trying to refashion his rather quotidian life into high art. Well, art anyway. So in the process it grew less factual, more imaginative.

Friday he was so wrapped up in this other new first that he lost track of the time. So by the time he slid Gavin's key into the man's third floor door and entered, sunset was hovering close. Even the rarely sarcastic Gavin commented: "At last." He stood and stretched out both hands. Scott yielded one but employed the other to start fanning Gavin's blond fall of hair. He stopped himself. He knew where that led. Report first, pleasure later.

"Get this. Something remarkable."

Gavin put a melodramatic back of his hand to his forehead and wailed, "Oh, no. You've met someone?"

Scott paused and folded his arms across his chest and let Gavin's feint subside. "Not to worry. It's a classroom event. Patience, sir, as I narrate."

"And I'll be surprised because …?"

"Because, this week, during your usual abandonment, I hit my fictional stride. Here!" (He flaunted the blue volume and now started fanning it.) "Best of all, it actually happened. And, just as best, we have an offer. A real one. But, since I've written the story before the event, what's in here is but an educated prediction. So you'll have to be patient here. Love me, love my prose. *And* love my exposition."

He was confident that the words he held would make it into print. (Subsequent events and relationships and his growing command of his craft would disabuse him of that confidence.)

"*Vraiment?*"

"Well," he added to the suspense, "it's an event both academic and social."

"Two in one? My breath abates."

Gavin's eyes ran rapid scampers from Scott's eyes to mouth to neck, but, though it had been five days, he let the instincts of friend and mentor win out. He passed him one of the two brimming red beakers.

"They're well-breathed. Now, roll on."

Scott grinned, sipped, complied.

As we walked home from the Park, wrapped again and again (and again) in joint embraces, our shirts drenched with the early St. Louis heat and humidity, I directed a healthy blast of breath at his tousled mane. "Well, I didn't think that would end so well."

"Well, yes," he replied—

"That's you, Gav. You, but modified; I'm me, ditto. See?"

Gavin nodded, smiling. "Doubles all 'round. You're here on my couch. And yet..." pointing at the azure journal... "There you are in there. In blue, no less. Heisenberg *redevivus*."

"Profoundly so. Now: '—*he replied with a cheerful but labored countenance*, "—yes, things got a tad bit unnerving

228

towards the end, true. But then, my young friend, consider how much worse it could have been."'"

"Ah, admirable. Commencing at the end. But don't spill *too* much, give away the pay-off?"

"Trust me, gentle reader."

"Good, fine. But this gentle one's getting eager. And curious. We've yet to walk in your Park. So what could '*that*' be?"

"Well, *calme toi.* I can dare to imagine, for it's lying in wait. If and when any of this *does* happen, I can revise. Or not. Maybe, even if it differs."

He ruffled Gavin's hair again. Oops, no. Stop. The tale takes precedence. He decamped to another chair, index finger in his volume.

This reflection did serve to put the evening's encounters in a somewhat rosier light, but in no way did it calm the shattered nerves, much less prepare the frame for a night's quiet repose. As usual, I looked to him.

Gavin smiled.

The whole business had begun not long before. The start, a rather festive one, seemed to follow on the recent sweet explosion of Gavin into his world—the chats; the saucepans; the pillows.

229

Gavin pantomimed laying a tally on an imagined blackboard, laid his head on his cheek with a sigh. Then sat up and gave the keep-moving signal, a rotating finger.

Yes, not long after I began those regular overnights with him, my students were starting to open up more, prying and prodding.

"Ah. More autobiographical? Really?" Gavin from his couch mimed a caress. "That *happened*?"

"Did." (A finger to his lips.) "I've told you, love. Just without detail, without drama. Nursed it in here, embroidered it."

I simply imagined it was spring getting into them too. What else? Surely not my connection with ... Gavin (I'm using your name for now. Need to find a "pretend" you for in here.) How could they know? Well, they say that folks can tell when love's hovering nearby. Could they? Or was I was growing approachable? Artesian springs of confidence and humor bubbling up? Could that be?

Gavin nodded, smiled knowingly. Stayed silent.

Well, on this day, I'd begin to find out how to, as Gavin puts it, "catch that new spirit."

Class over and discussion ended, they'd swarm their way up to my desk, where I sat in careful authority. They were asking

me questions, posing what-if's. "Hey, Mr. Preston" (that 'Mister'
threw me. First time one of them said it, I wondered if my dad had
materialized at the back of the room.) "Please check out this
transition?" "Can I show you this intro?" "That story about
Sarty? Why does he talk that way?" (I had learned to vary the
writing work with an occasional short story. Gavin sold me on it.)
A wave of bubbling inquiries foamed on my beach. I answered
what I could, but then amazed myself: "Come to my office. Better
yet, find me in Holmes some morning. We can talk."

Yes, the change in their manner was remarkable. Then I
saw, from the corner of the eye, this charming miss. She'd hung
around while the others approached, flowed and ebbed about my
desk; she sashayed to and fro, stalling until the others had
transacted their literary and compositional affairs—consulting her
book, fingering a bright blue Cubs hat.

"That hat, now. Is it real, or is it your art at work?"

"Patience, sweet. Seems I have you hooked?"

Gavin's salaam pumped Scott still more.

... letting the others go before her, hoping—or so I
assumed—that they'd dissipate. At long last, the air did in fact
become unclogged. Just us two, I stuffing papers into that old
leather case of my dad's—Gavin pointed to it across the room, and

231

Scott confirmed—*she flickering like St. Elmo's fire at the front of the desk.*

"Yes. Good day? Is it Lucy?"

"*Is* it?"

"What?"

"Is her name Lucy?"

"*Yes.*" (Lucy, alive within Scott's azure binding, answers Gavin's real question.) *Appreciative smile, nervous laugh.*

Gavin, chortling, employed a real hand to salute the fictional greeting.

"*Ah, Lucy! The Saint of returning light? Did you also invent Daylight Savings? Well done, missy.*"

She cocked an eyebrow my way and shrugged a shoulder or two. "Oh, sir. You're in your baffle mode."

Confusion mantled her features, driving my newly playful nature to cower in the damp sand. She cleared her throat. She meant to try again.

"*Can I ask a favor?*"

"*Favor? Sure.*" *Suddenly business like. "Oh, I know. You need that usage sheet? For the final?*"

"See what I'm doing here? Exaggerating the slow, dense, impersonal old me?"

"Exaggerating?" (Scott looked stricken.) "Kidding, kidding! A gentle evocation of the pompous novice." (The stricken look receded a tad.)

"Oh, gosh no. Sorry. You see, there's this ..." Slight blush. Small pause.

"Kind of in a hurry here, Luce. This?" My wit began to resurface. "This what? This porcupine? This steamboat? Okay, fine, I get it: this guy, right?" I plunged on, heedless. "But how can I help? Can't you—"

"No, but...But it's not a guy, see?"

"Well, if she's in our class, why wait for a formal introduction?"

Her eyes sank. "No, this woman. And she's not in our class."

"Oh, woman. Sorry. Another professor? You want me to intercede?"

"No." Her eyelashes grew damp. "I want to meet her."

"Come, come Lucille! Doesn't she have office hours? Like me to walk you up?"

By now she was shying like a startled colt. Even dense me could detect that our connections were fraying.

Gavin's real eyes by now were scampering across Scott, driven again by five days' deprivation. And his editor's eyes were seconding the emotion, scrunching tighter and tighter at the story's leisurely pace: "Enough suspense. Spill the beans, man."

Scott smiled. "My instinct exactly. Listen!"

After a few more false starts and jumbled intentions, I finally pieced the young lady's concerns together.

Gavin nodded, pressing hand to heart to beg forgiveness, but his eyes riveted tighter and tighter on Scott's mouth, eyes, neck as his concocted tale peaked.

She had, in the ancient, well-rehearsed Missouri parlance, this hankering for this other—not, it gradually dawned on me, the conventional "another" from a Harlequin romance, but a "one" like her. Another student. A girl. Girl named Hyacinth (it's actually your Shelley, okay?) And, wonderful coincidence, she was in Gavin's class.

Scott looked to Gavin as he finally let his shadowy tale break the real-world's surface, shearing its boiling blue.

Gavin's eyes grew wide at the girl's (for now merely parenthetical) name, but he spun his hand in a whir.

Scott longed to continue with his artistic debut, but his senses picked up on Gavin's enthusiasm, which made his artistic appreciation of the tale more intense. So he subsided.

"Done?"

"I don't have to be." He held up the journal and fanned the unread pages.

"Well. Honest, now... How much of that really happened?"

"But dear one, how can you ask? I just read it. Doesn't that make it real? Eh, professor of literature?"

Gavin grinned, sighed, and then retracted his hurry-up finger into his fist.

"Oh, all right. Fine. It captures the spirit of the day, not the facts. I confess, the real Lucy wasn't quite that shy. It didn't take that long to reach the nub. And in fact it was she who suggested the solution...."

"And at long last, sir what is that solution?" (Finger reappeared and spun.)

"Instant answer for you: a joint party. She heard you were planning an end-of-semester picnic—that's news to the real me, incidentally. And, well, couldn't we have one too? 'There's this cool sophomore I see a lot in Holmes. She's in Dr. Kuiper's class. I could meet her."

"That's it? The whole exchange?"

"It."

"And from that five-second molecule of chat you've inflated this vast and chatty universe?"

Scott basked in the implied compliment, but then he recalled something.

"Oh, yeah. Wait. Get this: she let fly an intriguing twist when I teased her about her woman. Let me see—" He flipped a few pages and swept his finger down the text. "yeah, here:

"Oh, but I thought, you see, that you could really relate." When she said it, blushes upholstered her face. But she was determined. "Have to confess: I was at the Science Center Sunday."

"She was?"

"She was."

"'Why didn't I see you?' I asked."

"Why didn't you tell me?"

"I *am* telling you. In living blue."

"So, where was she? Really?"

"'Really' is in the mind of the listener. Her words *in here,* are, *I was lurking way down on the escalator. You never saw.* Though what she *really* said to me was, 'The time you turned, I ducked. I was giggling but held it in. Your hand in his belt? So cute'."

"So what did you finally tell her?"

"Well—I'll be the narrator once again"—Scott held up his journal, like Perseus' mirror, to shield himself from Gavin's irresistible gaze.

—"I quote *assured her of my diligent commitment to her happiness and urged her to reconsult with me. She nodded, a hopeful smile starting to tug at her lips.*

"So now—" he lowered the book and gazed deep into Gavin's sparkling eyes, "the question now leaps, in *our* world, from me *and* Lucy: Are you willing to be my partner, pard'?"

"You mean, let your scruffy 'Comp One' minions crash our fancy sophomore dress ball of master students?"

Scott fired a thumbs-up stun-ray. "Precisely. And all in the service of love—of real longing in our real world."

"Well, okay. Fine. It does appeal to the Cupid in me. But here's a thought that I think is true for both worlds—yours there in your scruffy mitt and our real one here."[1]

The *facts* in both are that we're an *item*, man. Why hide it? Lucy knows. Here in black and white—and bound in blue. So, then. The Science Center was our official *premiere*. Means this fiesta can be our *deuxieme*."

"You *know* when you speak French I turn to mush. You *know* it. But still, this gala is for my students—well, *ours* now, you (and Lucy) being so pushy—not for us (you and me)."

Scott eyed the finger that beckoned, and the hand that patted the couch. He answered the summons.

"No, but wait." Gavin delayed the intimate moment. "First, about this Shelley (or Hyacinth if you must). Have to admit: Lucy has superb taste. Shell *would* be a catch. For *any* woman. Any man too, I'd wager."

---

[1] It seems honest to insert a pedestrian footnote at just this moment in *this* novel—the one in your hands, not Scott's initial fictional indulgence which has served here simply as another speaking character. It announces, in an appropriately formal manner, the author's withdrawal. Otherwise, what we are confronting here is the possibility of an endless succession of receding "truths." That thought experiment, pursued too diligently, might up-end any confidence in anything these pages in your hand—or words on your screen (who knows what methods of transmission future technologies will bring us?)—purport to report. We'll see him recording or inventing experiences, but mainly he'll become just another actor (important of course but only "another") in the story's final version. (Well, as final as I've ever let it get.)

238

Though his sight of her was still un-recollected, Scott was strangely stirred. This after all (this is still Shelley's favorite part of the still-born chapter he let her read one time) would yield their first encounter. Scott and Gavin's *deuxieme* will be their hands' *premiere*.

"And something else. I bet your Lucy doesn't know. This party, gala, fiesta? *Her* idea. Shelley's. (aka Hyacinth's now, of course.) One day she waved her hand, took the floor. Soon was shoving it down our throats. Some high school tradition she insisted we try out."

"And you swallowed?"

"She proposed, she described, she burbled. We cried uncle. (You need to explain *that* phrase someday.) So we're on."

He kissed Scott on the lips, less briefly than he'd planned but, before long, not long enough. Then ...

"She's remarkable. Our kind of dynamic mover."

Scott, in short, with other impulses stirring, resisted this further introduction to Shelley. (Shell would pretend to be jealous when she reached that part, but the teasing would yield soon enough to other pleasures, some of them familiar, some novel.) But had his metaphoric mind bothered to kick into higher gear—what a wide pulsating network might have radiated from that instant.

239

Nor could Gavin refrain. But he *did* take the time for a split-second vision that proved accurate: his man and his student—that auburn-haired Shelley—walking arm in arm through some unseasonal February warmth, suspended in rich and bracing aromas. As time paced backward, sweet strings began to sound.

End of Year Picnic

Scott would bring up the "picnic" idea in class the next Monday—"picnic," "party," "fiesta": each noun approximate, none exact. After a half hour of some timed, thirty-second free-writing exercises, then a pair of a three-minute joint editing drills (more of Gavin's ideas—"rat a tat, fast fast fast, get their brains steaming") Scott announced, "Enough. Take a break."

Cries of "Whew!" "Sore hands." "What's gotten into you, sir?"

"I been thinking. Do you realize? We're about done in here. Soon it's sayonara, Comp One."

Mock-groans bubbled up among the derisive cheers.

"Yeah, yeah. Well, before you celebrate, what would you all say to an end-of-term spring gala?" (Another proposed noun.) I'm told there's another class planning one, first Friday in May. Want to join them?"

Lucy had no idea that her notion had taken root; she'd entered, eyes downcast, and edged to her accustomed seat in the rear. Now she looked up, a sudden smile suddenly flashing.

For ten minutes, sad to report, the class showed more life than in the preceding fourteen weeks' dedication to noun clauses, intros that "grab," verbs that "show." They asked for details. They offered suggestions: about timing: about menu; about activities. He began pacing the front of the room and, as their eager artillery of inquiries began to patter, strode into the rows between their seats.

"So who's their teacher?" one asked.

He retreated a step and mumbled a quick "Oh, that's Doctor Kuiper."

A sly glance at Lucy's face revived him and generated a metaphor: She bubbled on a spit of sand just beyond the shore of the sea of voices and gestures that boiled between her and Scott. The devil in Scott—a miniature imp Gavin kept trying to set free—wanted to ask, "Why the big smile, Ms. Carson?" But he settled for delight at her delight.

"So, now, Mr. Pres—I mean Scott. So, man—" The guy's switch to informality startled, then thrilled him. (Gavin's advice was getting confirmed in spades: "You're only three years older. Don't get all stuffy. Show your expertise, and you'll *earn* their respect.") "Let's talk turkey. Any hot babes in that class?" The words came from a guy named Smits (Roger? Fred?), usually four rows back, always by the window, permanently disengaged.

Scott's devil surfaced. "Ah ha. Seems we've found Smits' real priorities. Topic sentences and transitional phrases, you doze; but babes and brews get you hard? That it?" He blushed when he heard himself say it, but the class hooted with delight. Scott let a smile migrate into view; so did Smits as he painted a sizzling finger on the air.

"Good one, teach! That's it. Define 'Social'? 'Cold brews and hot babes'."

Scott was doubly tickled—by the spirited ruckus and by the emerging Smits. His first good look at the young man revealed a pleasantly tan face (Spring break in Cancun or Florida, no doubt), firm jaw, smooth neck. And that disarming smile. He (Smits) should flash it more. Or maybe, he (Scott) should look up more. In fact, the room (*his* room) now seemed peopled with attractive and interesting folks—engaged, and simmering with bright chatter.

"Well," his mind finally got its arms around the guy's point, "Beer I'm afraid is out. College rules, you know." Frowns, nods. "Of course, nothing in my contract about checking every backpack that shows up." Sounds bubbling louder.

"Now, as for those babes. Is Mr. Smits—"

"It's Jonathan, sir. No. For *you,* Scott, it's 'Jon'."

243

"Ta, mate." (Gavin's influence.) "—Jon here on the money?"

Half the room (most of the guys) gave loud yeses. From the other half, though, silence. One woman, however—the always moody Esther—spoke up. "Well, now—me? I can take hot babes or I can leave hot babes. Sorry, Anita." She stuck out her tongue at the svelte but curvaceous girl in leather pants two seats over. Anita copied the gesture, coupled with a languid extension of her middle finger.

"No. What *I* want to know about," Esther went on "is, any cool *dudes* coming?" Several girls saluted one another, leaning across a guy or two to do so.

"Well, of course: fair enough." Scott leaned both palms on a front row desk, hovering coolly above its female occupant, and scanning the simmering crowd. "I haven't met his group. But I forgot to mention—it's sophomore lit, so there'll probably be a bunch of them planning to major in English. That of course means, by definition, that they're *all* brilliant—the cool babes *and* the hot dudes. Think you—we, I mean—can match that?"

They thought so.

As she left that day, Lucy didn't halt but, as she sidled past his desk, she looked him straight in the eye, to mouth a distinct "thank you." Scott bowed in reply, hand on heart.

Before she disappeared, eclipsed by the door's wooden jamb, he called out: "Say, Lucille! Any more sightings?"

"Of?" A blush rose then subsided.

"Of *her*. If the two of you could hook up beforehand, we could cancel this whole fiesta."

"No, Scott." She smiled as she found herself calling him by name. "Don't you dare." His answering smile encouraged her still more. "It is going to be one fine 'do.' Cancel it?" She filled her lungs with air for an aggressive order, quite a new impulse: "Get real, man!"

"I'm trying, I'm trying."

* * * * *

That evening, Gavin organized the two lists, and summoned Scott. "Look at this. Shelley again. My real one, not your pretend 'Hyacinth'. Your woman's woman, right? Still taking charge. I wrote—See? Here at the top? Quite specific: 'Main course or dessert.' So what does she write next to her name? 'Hummus! A feast needs an appetizer, Gav.' And next to it she scribbles 'Widen your food horizons, man.'" (Scott realized much later that these were Shell's first words, still unheard but at least visible, on paper. He liked them—their culinary wisdom, and what they promised about the writer's personality.)

Gavin continued, "I wouldn't have pegged her for passive-aggressive. Maybe you better warn what's her name."

"Lucy?"

"Lucy."

Their Fiesta (Part One)

In his sleepy life before college, Scott had spent hours at the Jefferson Memorial in Forest Park, "MoHist's" home headquarters, leafing through sheaves of early St. Louis maps, illustrations and photos. Many were of Forest Park. One time he grew daring; some instinct caused him to stack a passel of them, then riffle them at thumb speed (a primitive tiny version of the Lumiere brothers' invention.) What the experiment revealed, besides the spurting dust, was the way the Park held its magisterial place year upon year at the city's throbbing heart.

It drew matter to it. Fields, diggings, meadows, asphalt: all ebbed and flowed around it, first north, then west. The building that is now the Art Museum was built in 1903 (the centenary of President Jefferson's Louisiana Purchase), and served as a major reception hall for the 1904 World's Fair, attended by President Roosevelt and future leaders Taft and Wilson. (Half a century later came the Planetarium, joined in time to the Science Center. In due course the lush, verdant Park thus played host to dinosaurs, presidents and starbursts.)

Scott's distant, archival life continued to sway, like a massive, ornate but barely submerged cathedral, beneath the sparkling waves of his new life with Gavin. Choosing the Park as the setting for their fiesta (Gavin gave him free rein to select the locale) filled Scott with some proprietary confidence. The chosen spot was convenient—half a mile east of the campus, and barely a mile from his "digs."

They drove to the site (his journal was already wrong. There was no walking that evening—too many party items to transport). *En route,* historical time became an accordion, their journey a wormhole through civic history. Scott identified the various eras as they swung through and past. First the wide, northern entrance at Union Avenue, a grand Victorian boulevard of the Fair's vintage. Next, heading south-west, they came upon a pastoral-urban delicacy: a gazebo-cum-bandstand surrounded by a moat sumptuous with ducks. The moat lay before the Municipal Opera, a pre-Great War, Georgian amphitheater carved into a spacious and welcoming hillside. (The "Muny" offered reliable "commercial" entertainment—popular in its truest sense. After nearly a century, the place remained central to the culture of the sprawling metropolitan region.)

They sped farther west, then eased south behind the Art Museum, one of the Fair's handsome vestiges, and finally down a narrow, winding lane, a hill or two south and west of Shelley's waterfall. (Neither of the men knew that, of course, but Shell

248

would educate at least one of them, in due course.) The path nosed down through several strata and brought the co-hosts to the Park's most untouched sector—a tiny remainder of the dark, dense eponymous Forest that far antedated the city's 1764 founding. (He was pleased that night to see two sets of late 20th century students populating a green but ornate world that had been imagined and sculpted a century before.)

Scott, amateur historian, appreciated and reported this old old news. But the new him (the proud but skittish lover) could not help processing far more recent and far more pressing questions: "How should I act tonight? Just be his colleague? Has Lucy told anyone she saw us?" And finally (of more consequence) "what can I do, how can I behave, to keep him?" He knew better but that night his confidence ruled all.

As he fretted, Gavin was narrating an anecdote.

"Yesterday. That Shelley woman?"

Scott awoke from his historical excavations and current fears. "What?"

"Shelley?"

"Who?"

"Get with it. Lucy's Shelley. (Your Hyacinth, remember?) Truth is, *she's* really the founder of our feast." He tapped Scott's kneecap with each reminder. "Why. we're. doing. this."

"Oh, right. Lucy's 'Intended'."

"At *last*." Professor Gavin appreciated the noun from a story by Conrad and gave Scott's kneecap a warm massage. "Yesterday, as I was saying, she dropped off a container at the office. Told Betty to tell me she was meeting someone for tea, so she might run late—to tell *us* actually. She said 'them' not just 'him:' you're included." (When Scott and Shell tried to trace their history, Scott claimed that the plural pronoun here constituted her first words to him. Lovers get sentimental, even possessive, about every hint of their perceived inevitability.)

"Really?"

Yes, of course. As Shell had told Astrid. Ingrid, "MoHist."

"It's the truth. The sophomore woman leaves detailed messages. Even emailed me earlier."

"She does MoHist, huh?" A whiff of fragrant dust. "Clearly a woman of splendid taste. I wonder if she's... Never mind: Lucky Luce."

"She assured Betty she'd make it. 'Tell Gav—sorry, I meant tell Professor Kuiper, I'll *be* there. This is to tide him over.' What she said."

"Mighty considerate." But his heart suddenly sank on Lucy's behalf. "She's out cheating on my girl before they even meet?"

"Doubtful. Betty thinks she's on *my* trail. Believe *that?* 'She asked particularly about *you* and she smirked.'"

"No fear there, right?" said Scott, with a brave smile. (His view of Shelley was modifying, anecdote by anecdote—and not, at that moment, to her credit.)

Fiesta (Part Two)

As the two hosts arrived, the sun was drenching all those freshly-leaved trees in gold, greener and more golden than on their first night six weeks before. Gavin took advantage of the empty clearing—"this untended prairie of yours"—to request a hug. Scott, after a quick glance down the deserted slope, yielded.

As usual, the firm embrace and soft lips did their work: "And you wonder why I attacked you amongst the vegetables?" (The previous Friday he'd "leaped" Gavin, unannounced. Carrots and kohlrabi had erupted into a green and orange fountain, a cascading mixed salad.)

"Did I object? No. And now: may I register an early request? For, say, midnight?"

Scott took one of Gavin's arms and rotated into it, wrapping it around himself, bringing the man's palm to just below his right nipple. Had he been a woman, her breast would have craved some fondling. Gavin's palm was wonderful as always, but he knew that the move would have prompted a far more intense response from a she. Yes, anatomy, while not determinative, can give destiny a leg up. Or it can moderate a budding impulse.

Gavin then unwound his limb and, with a final squeeze, turned to the bar-b-q pit. Shrewd timing. Within three minutes, bikes, feet, backpacks, chatter began to fill the clearing, vibrating the air like a swarm of industrious bees. Scott felt he had multiple obligations on this critical night—as teacher, colleague, lover, and host. A chance to show what he'd learned, to "be de man," to make the evening a success. He took a determined breath and telegraphed Gavin's mind: "Time."

He leveled a well-directed elbow into the man's ribs and climbed onto a handy table as the arrivals edged their way toward them. Once up, he rested a calm hand atop Gavin's tousled mane, a move that stirred a scattering of "Aw's." He shivered but he warmed to the task. In spite of the handful of smirks among the guys, he made himself stand tall and cupped his hands.

Twenty or so freshmen and sophomores pressed around the two men, like stalks of corn curtseying to an August breeze. Gavin reached up and behind to hook a finger into the man's belt loop, an affectionate tether and thoughtful prop. Lucy, standing half-way back, hugged herself. Scott raised his eyes well above the assembled partiers to note the thickly forested hills that rose up from the clearing. They seemed to whisper to some deep part of

253

him even as he began to speak aloud to the assembled students. He resisted the summons, but took quick pains to file it.

"First, welcome. And, for half of you, an introduction. I'm Scott. Gavin ('Coops,' some of you call him?) and I have talked—"

"Talked? That *all* you did ?" someone barked out with jovial sarcasm. Laughter, nervous but affectionate, fanned out.

Scott, standing two or three feet above them, glanced down and breathed deep. He ruffled Gavin's hair once more and then threw back his shoulders. "True. But *then* we talked." A heartier laugh.

Gavin joined the laugh, a compliant verger just below an officiating priest. His eyes relished the growing congregation.

"And" (proud smile) "we came up with this—well, call it a game."

"Okay, fine," Smits bellowed, "It's a game." Incorrigible.

"Thanks, Jon. And it goes like this. Each man or woman of *mine* gets a gold post-it, pasted to her or his back. On it, a challenging literary quote. And for Coop's crowd, a green one with the name of a poet, playwright, author."

Esther had a hand on her hip and scorn on her lips. "Problem, Esther?"

"Yeah, sure. I get it. You're trying to set somebody up with Anita. Probably her only hope." When she parroted Anita's usual sneer, Anita laconically held up her three middle fingers and pivoted the hand at Esther: "Read between the lines."

"Seems Esther's distracted. Some personal axe to grind. But, yep, she's got the scent. Now. Before my colleague here pulls me over on him, I'd better, like you guys say, *spill*." (He'd always disliked the word. Or the males that used it: high school athletes, guys he both resented and envied for their effortless romantic successes.) You can't read your own back, right?—right—so you will all have to *ask. someone. else* for help. That means mix. Talk. Now, 'Why,' I hear you ask?"

One of Gavin's crew, a lad with a half-open black shirt, inviting smile and rich mustache, one arm around a woman's waist, rose to the occasion. "I'll bite, Professor. Tell us. Why?"

"Why *what?*" Scott now had two impatient hands on two hips as he'd reached the confident apogee of his explanation. His teacherly mode was engaged. He felt "pumped."

That by sheer chance (or was fate lending a hand?) was when Shelley eased into the clearing. She joined the crowd, resting two affectionate elbows on the nearest pair of partiers. She was tickled at the size of the turnout and impressed as well by the speaker's bumptious energy. Did he look familiar? Well maybe. But in any event this first sighting was in his favor.

"All right, then, old man," said the smiling fellow. "You tell *us. How* do they match?"

"'Old man.' I like that." He saluted the guy. "Your name?"

"Name's Alec."

"His name's Alec" the stunning woman beside him confirmed, curling a long, bare arm around his waist. "He's taken."

"Alec," Gavin nodded. "Taken."

"More than we needed to know. But, okay. *Here's* why. You have to keep mixing *and* meeting *and* asking until you find your match, green quote with gold author."

Gavin spoke up. "Scottie's right." (A garden of smirks.) "What we want for you is to *mingle*. In fact, with your permission, sir—" he nodded an inquiry up to Scott, "shall we?" Scott confirmed it.

Gavin waved to the crowd—"Let's do it. Come mosey on up here, pards."

Scott chortled at the traveler trying out more new slang, but he catapulted himself to the ground, disdaining Gavin's shoulder. "Time to break some ice."

"Well, *finally*," Smits declared.

The group slid forward, like a wave nudging foam onto a beach at high tide. Scott and Gavin, side by side, selected and pasted the various green and gold slips, each on the next respective back. Three or four women, and one guy from Gavin's class, dawdled around Gavin, but he moved them along toward Scott with adroit taps to the neck or palm prods to the lower back.

* * * * *

Scott found Lucy and crooked a beckoning finger to lure her from the gentle melee. Once she'd reached him he did one of Gavin's "hurry up" hand spins to get access to her back. Reaching into his pocket, he whispered to her (he couldn't resist) "Guard this with your life, you hear?" He signaled her to rotate and applied the gold rectangle to her left shoulder.

She turned around and beamed. "You *are* up to something."

Scott said nothing, folded his arms, and smiled. She stood on tiptoe, reached over that barricade of arms, and squeezed his two shoulders. "Thanks, Scottie." She nodded toward Gavin and, with a wink, patted Scott's nearest belt loop. "And thank him too, eh, 'pard'?"

"Well, sure, young 'pard.' But now, remember: Play the game first. Make some friends. You've got all night for your Shelley (Shelley, right?)"

"Yes, yes. Shelley." Then her mouth drooped. "But I can't wait."

"Oh, Lucille, Lucille. Just *try*." He slid his arm around her waist, a liberty he would not have dreamed of taking the first day (or first week, even first month) of class. "Builds character, Luce." He looked into her eyes directly. "College *means* making new friends. So, now. *How* do you think we can do that?"

"By mingling?"

"By mingling."

Lucy frowned but she did detach herself and began walking her muted enthusiasm toward the lapping pool of bodies. As she stirred herself into the mix, she turned and waved at him through some winking atoms of green and gold.

He reached over his shoulder to bestow a pat. "It's all working! Lucy. Our fiesta. These kids." He came up to Gavin whose cheeks puffed full as he blew the pit's brightening coals. "God, we're good. *I'm* good."

"Finally dawns on him. Bravo." He patted Scott's post-it-less back as well. "Now, let's *us* mingle."

"You go on." Scott resisted. (That inviting hillside was renewing its mute, vocal appeal.) "My work's done here. For now." He slapped his hands together with loud and comic satisfaction, as if to scatter all his old young and dusty years into smithereens.

Gavin rubbed Scott's forehead, like his personal genie, and then, like Lucy, melted into the swirl.

* * * * *

"Go up higher, man. Get you a look-see." And so he began to edge up the gentle slope, weaving like a May-pole dancer among young saplings and venerable oaks. He nosed along the path like a needle tracing the grooves on those old records on his dad's antique turntable. At last, he turned. Looking down from his dark vantage, he found that he could in fact start seeing. Too far up to decipher faces, he actually gained a better perspective of that hive-like swarm. He could see it coalescing into an orderly, deliberate portrait.

In one quadrant, he saw—he was tickled to see—Lucy trying some deliberate encounters, approaching, first, a single guy, then a retreat, then single girl, and then a couple, for inspection. Then, suddenly, not far from her, he saw—man, look at *that*?—a

259

gorgeous woman. "Shelley?" he guessed from Gavin and Lucy's descriptions—the flowing, radiant hair; her authoritative stride.

Those two glowing particles were tracing clear, elegant and gradual paths. They seemed at rest, and yet they danced, a Mozartean adagio (more of Gavin's tutelage). When Lucy reached the other, Scott was first delighted, then concerned, to see her arm wind around his protégée. "My, she works fast. Too fast? Hope she doesn't scare her off."

But then his eyes focused more tightly on that distant fall of bright hair, so remarkably blonde. *Was* that Shelley? ... No. Dammit! It's Gavin. *Damn* him. "Back off, will you?" (He whispered the words aloud.)

He took a deep breath and let his mind and memory reason that all was well. Gavin's assignment that evening was, like his, to reach out welcoming hands. And especially to Lucy, who was, after all, *their* project. "So why so jealous?"

As he stood there on high, his spirit tried to slough off those particulars. Here he was, in a joyous teeter on the cusp of a doubly new life: he was going public with his first guy, and celebrating, with a great class, some first successes as a teacher. And, be honest now, who was key to both? His Gavin. And what *he* adored in him others would as well—warmth, humor, generosity. So of course they'd also find him incredibly alluring. Why not Lucy, no matter her declared sexual wiring?

He felt warring emotions. An intense admiration and, side-by-side with it, admiration's shadow, that jealousy. Both so intense that his brain clenched. It was as if he could gaze deep into his soul just as he looked down from the wooded height on that swarming mass: Gavin's students and his students; the greens and the golds; bodies mingling. And oh yes: bodies drawing apart.

"Drawing apart." Oh, yes: that grain of mental sand began to scrape and claw inside him.

Fragments of Gavin's defining phrases bubbled in his head: "This cold, green world." "Not *here* I won't." "*Always* en route." He sighed and made (not for the first time) the insistent deduction: that damned glorious Gavin could only be who he was. And what Gavin was, he sighed with calm despair, "(that bitch, bastard, marvel) can't be mine."

The insight made him feel … how? He asked himself: abandoned? Sure. But yet somehow more secure. If he could not keep the man, he could try to take charge of, even *shape,* his man's departure. *That* might at least gain his first love's lasting admiration. No rapture, no. But some conditional, some moderate success.

A cloudy thought was born. It began to give off a thin glow, like an ember in an ashy fireplace, its presence more sensed than examined. From nowhere, the alternating two and three-beats of their most recent shared anthem, "I can see clearly now," pulsed through him.

In the meanwhile, for now, for this sharpening Scott, it was time—time to head back down there. And to mingle. That would be the ultimate if tentative flattery: to unfurl the wings Gavin had begun helping him fledge. Head back down to the world.

His mind turned to other childish lives. Of Mole, again. From *The Wind in the Willows* (his mother's favorite reading choice); and of Eustace on Aslan's mountain, the book his dad (the theologian of the family) used to read him. Would these new heavenly signs that he was absorbing up here lose their clarity down there? Could he be true to his sad commitment?

The only way he could find out was by finding out. He initiated a deliberate rush down.

Boys and Girls Together

With dusk fully welled up, Scott felt his steady way down the newly precarious slope. Once back on solid ground, he moved with all deliberate speed toward that cloud of mingling bodies.

One fellow on the clearing's edge—a stranger; no doubt one of Gavin's angels (um, students)—offered a jovial challenge. "Mind if I check you out?"

Scott froze, waited a beat, then with unsuspected confidence, raised his smiling eyes in mock horror. "Oh, sir. This is all so sudden."

A good sport, the fellow winked. "Sorry, man. Just your quote." He smiled, laid one hand on Scott's shoulder, then pointed a finger on his other hand downward, spiraling a request. "Turn, please."

Scott wanted to comply. He fixed his eyes on the younger guy's green ones, remarkably vivid even in the dusk, then took in the broad smile and the right ear's gold ring. Still, duty called: "I hate to disappoint you, but—meet your other host. I got no quote."

"Sorry, professor. I just got here." That broad smile stayed broad and he pivoted himself instead. "Check mine, anyway, please. Tell me who or what to look for."

"I will. But call me 'Scott'. 'Scott' gets results."

"Okay then, Scott. I'm Steve." Scott filed the name and face as the sophomore rotated.

While he made a leisurely examination of the gold post-it—"Lord Alfred"— Scott let his eyes start to enjoy the abundance of jet-black hair hugging Steve's neck. But he pried them loose and, another lucky result, they glommed onto Esther, alone in the clearing. She was poised behind Gavin, observing him as he tended to the smoking and ever-more-aromatic meats. Scott noticed for the first time the young woman's delicate and thoughtful face— thoughtful at least when she was not performing for classmates. Or in her default mode: frowning.

"Hey, Steve. Someone who *can* help." He pivoted him toward the girl. "Tell her I sent you. If she doesn't snarl at you, there's hope."

Steve's hearty laugh and a whiff of his body lotion made Scott wish he and Gavin had also decided to get tagged. But he gestured toward the woman, and offered "Or would you rather I…"

"Oh, I'm sure I can deal. But still, sure. *You* know her, sir–"

"Or as we say in Missouri, 'know her, Scott'?"

"Yes." He grinned. "Please, Scott. She *is* one of yours."

Scott fitted a palm to the small of Steve's back and guided him toward Esther, now wrapped in smoky fumes. She had a long, pronged fork at the ready.

"Ms. Somersby. An offering." Esther stared for a second, before a grin surfaced. "This is Steve. Pleasant lad, one of Gavin's. He's dying to get read. I'm told you can read, right?"

Esther frowned at Scott, surveyed the guy, and— remarkably—extended a hand. "I'll do what I can. Steve, is it?" She and her fork rotated toward him. "Esther here."

"So I've heard. A, um …" He pulled his face back a millimeter or two, "pleasure." (Scott laughed to himself at the familiar noun.)

Steve let loose an infectious smile but looked cross-eyed at the two hovering prongs. She hooted and shelved the weapon.

Scott faked a frown her way, directing a loud stage-whisper to Steve, "Careful now. She can *seem* harmless." When Esther slid out her tongue a full inch at him, Scott turned away, delighted.

Then his mind jumped, totally unbidden, to that silent kid in the back of the class-room—Rob, was it? Ron? He hadn't seen him yet, and it dawned on him that he was disappointed. "Should have emailed him a reminder. Damn. Sharp brain. Have to *get better* at drawing them out. Well, man: next year."

* * * * *

The object of Lucy's interest, all this while, was weaving with calm authority between the crowd's outer edges and its heart. She'd engaged with, then detached herself from, a succession of men and women—singles, pairs, threes. They'd all been eager to seek her out. Now she was momentarily solo and Lucy focused her eyes on her. Like a rocket that wobbles when set free from ground control until it acquires internal guidance, she arced unsteadily toward the woman.

Toward Shelley. "Hi."

Not too imaginative, no. But Lucy celebrated the lone syllable.

"I can match that." Shelley replied with a bemused furrow on her brow. She slid her voice down a register: "Hi."

"Hi, hi" was the girl's nervous reply. But she stood her ground. "And have you—" Lucy ran a nervous hand through her short-cropped hair "—been decoded yet?"

"Not yet, no. A bunch of you guys—eight? no, ten—made separate stabs but—*nada*." She rose up on her toes to look down at the girl. "Strange. Gavin *assured* us you guys were bright. Said your teacher'd assured him."

"Oh, really? Scott *said* that?" (Lucy's clear delight lit up a smile so genuine that it nudged Shell's heart. It was a second stroke in Scott's favor.)

During this first exchange, as she basked in the sophomore's radiance, even that scar beside Shelley's lip glowed, a quaint beauty mark. It made her eyes want to sink. She kept picturing her own horrid freckles; those flat, gray boring eyes; that awful slant in her nose.

But words that Scott had been throwing her way lately (thanks, Scottie) helped choke her diffidence. "You can do it, Carson. *Say* it." What *he* usually meant were her keen insights on Faulkner's lonely hero Sarty in "Barn Burning," or the way she could always supply a vivid illustration for a challenging topic sentence. But those tiny encouragements had begun to migrate to her spine for wider, more general use. (It also steadied her that Scott had just about assured her of her post-it's magical powers.) She re-collected herself and raised her eyes to Shelley's.

"Well we are. Really. Our Scott tells us."

"So kind of him to cheer up the hopeless. Ah well, maybe I've just been unlucky." Then (a habit that had become a natural part of her repertoire) she put her mouth in an exaggerated pout, "Sigh." The sweet sad shape sent a new raft of shivers through Lucy.

She breathed deep, "Hey, then. I'm Lucy. And..." (amazed at herself, she stood taller and let her smile bloom) "maybe your luck's about to change?"

Shelley's eyes twinkled and a shake of her head vibrated those auburn tresses, punctuated here and there by a few last beaded cornrows. "Maybe so, Luce. Let's try."

"Let's. Oh and also, by the way," Lucy actually heard herself say it, "boy do I love it when you do that."

"Do *what*? And when have you seen it? Or *me*?" Shelley's vanity tussled with impatience.

"It's that sulk, that sigh. It's—um, most becoming. And," she disclaimed her frequent sightings and gushed, "Shelley. It only took once." Her newly confident hand gave Shell's right elbow a tentative squeeze.

"Ah. So you *enjoy* suffering? Nice." A smile tugged the edge of her scowl. She was enjoying the other girl's interest and, thanks to Astrid's agenda to encourage *all* women, was impressed by the girl's sudden gush of confidence.

"Not at all. I just loved watching your mouth move. That's all. But," Lucy was acquiring sea legs, "I better watch it. Maybe praise goes to your head. We can't have *that*. So, let me i.d. you, please."

"Okay fine," Shell gestured toward the two men now tending the grill, "I'll let you. To please my Gavin." Lucy held the gaze and let her new courage infuse her tingling finger-tips. They reached out and turned Shelley around. "Let's see then. 'Mr. W. S.' it says. Now, that could either be my uncle, Walden Surrey—he writes these awful limericks for our family Thanksgivings. Or, oh look." She arrested Shelley as she started to turn back toward her. "There's more, under it: 'Sweet swan of Avon.' That could only be William Shakespeare, think?"

"My, my. I guess the *eleventh* try is the charm." She turned to pat Lucy's head. "Lucky I found you. *You*'re the brains."

"No, no. We *all* are." Recharged, she continued: "Well, assume it's right, shall we? Now read mine! For me, please. And for our, my, Scott."

"Scott? Oh yeah, Scott, right. Fine, let's make *him* happy too. Why not?" Shelley *was* enjoying the encounter. She wasn't aroused (when she was, her inner eye concocted a chimera that

269

fused Gavin and Astrid) but she was touched by the younger woman's evident attraction. And she continued to applaud the younger girl's growing assertiveness.

Lucy rotated a determined 180 degrees and took a firm backward step toward Shelley. In an instant, two warm hands were spreading her shoulder blades, like pulling (or so Lucy hoped) a ripe orange into fragrant slivers.

"Let's see then. It's—wait. Turn more toward that grill. Yes. 'Come, woo me, woo me!'"

Lucy realized in a tidal swell how perfectly Scott had chosen. She dared to have some fun. "*Woo* you? *Here*?"

"Watch it, Luce. That's your *quote* talking. But look. We have it." Shelley's on-the-spot retrieval had confirmed the match. "It's 'As You Like it'. Read it with Gav' last month. Girl, in trouble, runs to the forest—"

"Forest Park?"

"Shh. No. The Forest of *Arden*. In *England*."

Lucy bobbed her head.

"She pretends to be a guy so the man she meets can practice his wooing—see, 'woo me'?—on 'him.' Neat thing, 'him' is actually *her*—the woman he loves."

"But why doesn't she just—?"

"Shh." Shelley's turn to raise a finger. "'Don't, 'Coops insists, 'question a dramatic convention'." She caught his lilt and accent perfectly. "Point is, it all works. Mr. W. S. is..." Her finger started to take flight but returned to poke Lucy's chin. "The ... *Guy. Who. Wrote. Your. quote.*" With the next three syllables, she knuckled Lucy's noggin. "*Will. Shake. Speare.* We match."

Lucy was so thrilled that she almost "spilled" her threesome's devious plan. She resisted that, but what she couldn't resist was seizing Shelley's hand.

Shell withdrew it, but the gentle squeeze she gave as she did was just enough encouragement for Lucy. "Shelley, I have to confess. I *have* seen you. (You, not the sigh.) Round campus. I've been wanting to meet you."

"Well, you have." She squeezed Lucy's shoulder, then removed her hand and put it behind her to clasp the other, like a philosopher strolling with a disciple. "Well, what say we join this rotating set of bodies. Make a circuit and get acquainted."

They edged into the wider clearing. "And say—blame it on Gavin—I feel like being an instructor. So then, in this play of ours. We have a boy actor playing a girl who plays a boy in the woods..." her voice trailing off as they arced to into the clearing, "pretending to be a girl to help…" They became a compact binary molecule in the revolving mass.

* * * * *

By the time their leisurely promenade brought them back into earshot, Lucy had acquired two brimming cups of red wine and was examining Shell. (She preferred chardonnay but thought it tactical to match her new match.)

"But seriously? You never gorge? On *your* recipes?"

"Gorge, no. Test 'em? Sure. I can tell from an atom or three." She recalled that nursery of blue ones on Astrid's lips. (By now that colorful sight had earned permanent status. She'd even include it when narrating her romantic history for Scott.)

Then she let her hair down for Lucy. "What I really like is tending to people. Food's just a way," and shook her real hair into a lavish curtain.

Lucy's ears gave her tongue the perfect segue. "Hey, Shell. Listen! Over there—*our* food. Sizzling! And Scott did promise us a feast. And right there: An empty table…" She took a defining breath. "Would you–I'd love it if you'd eat with me."

Still flattered, always convivial, Shell agreed. "A delight."

Lucy stooped to a convenient subterfuge to mask her reigniting desire. "And on the way you can actually *meet* Scott." (A sweet offer but a move that time's tick-tock would frustrate.)

* * * * *

"Scott. This is Shelley, my new friend. Shelley"—she giggled—"meet my perfesser, Scott. Dispenser of green, meet a real, live gold."

At last, and for the first time, Scott's hand traced that (by now all-too-familiar) diameter across the flaming grill to greet the svelte woman. Remarkable the way the brain can bring time to a whispering halt. Or perhaps by now *not* remarkable. For Scott— another of Gavin's miracles, the habit was becoming second nature—it was the second time in the last half hour. He, the guy, noticed the golden triangle of chest, the broad shoulders, that flowing cascade of honey-auburn hair and firm, lean arms—all of it, all of them, lit and warmed by the grill. The sight and the firm feel of her hand stirred a gentle current in him. Now if Gavin were a woman …"

She, the woman, caught and noted with real pleasure the hazel flecks in his eyes, the jovial smile, and the smooth, floury feel of his hand. He must have sensed it, for his first words were, "A pleasure. Sorry for my palm, though. Lousy first impression." (Would she think that was his name?)

"Not at all. It's perfect for a feast." Five feet away Gavin noticed the conversation. Shell was saying, "You're just doing your job, chef. Why the flour?"

Scott could see the phalanx of outstretched paper plates forming a line before him. He heard (barely, vaguely) a few voices beginning to whine. "Hey, some of us *are* hungry." "Any time now, co-host."

Scott bowed his apology, resumed spearing a burger for each offered plate with one hand, without missing a beat with Shell, nor letting go of hers with his other. (It had never occurred to him to envy octopuses. Not once. Not until this special instant.)

"Flour?" he resumed instantly. "That's a trade secret. But for you, and your friend here—" (Lucy grinned.) "I'll confess." He stole a glance at Gavin. "Special recipe."

"Yours? Invented? Borrowed?" They smiled, as their two hands still tangled.

"Well, mine, but a recent book purchase helped. Egg yolks, flour, and" (he abandoned her palm and put his freed one to his mouth, pretending to hide the secret from Lucy. The gesture reminded Shell of Ben with Astrid) "... nameless spices that work wonders."

Lucy harrumphed. "Now don't you two guys get started."

Shelley darted an amused eye to Scott, observing, "Say, perfesser. *All* your students this pushy? Your influence?"

"I maintain a dignified silence." He winked at her. "But let me suggest…" (new wink to Lucy) "Do some further research on her. She's a remarkable young woman." (The advice brought a blush to Lucy's face that started edging down her neck.)

Shelley swiveled her head toward the girl with mock pain. "Well, since you insist." Lucy recovered and butted a playful head at Shell's upper arm.

"Okay, Scott, sir. My friend Lucy's asserting herself. Let's get our two plates loaded, shall we? A delight, Mr… Do you *have* a last name?"

"I do. 'Preston'." And you?"

Next on the cooking line, Gavin was making her plate sink with an especially heavy potato. As Lucy tugged her away, Shelley mouthed her two defining syllables "Jas-par," eyes twinkling. Scott deciphered them, first try, his lips miming her syllables as she backed away. She nodded. Then she handed her plate to her new match and retrieved a bright red Cardinal hat from her back pocket, to free her billowy hair from the heaped plate. (That cap would help him recall the moment; though, when he did, he'd require no such assistance.)

275

Then Lucy, at the end of the row, steered Shelley by the elbow. "Look over there. Table's still free." Her voice rose tentatively. "We've been good. We mingled."

Shelley, her plate nearly collapsing from its wealth of succulent fare, yielded. Lucy guided her, laying Shell's plate across from her own at the wooden table's far end.

From fifty feet away, Scott looked over from time to time. And was pleased to see Lucy wholly engrossed in her. (Shell, right? Yes. Shell. Shell Jaspar.) Occasionally tentative, Lucy's more confident self was flooding over the shy one, like a rising stream that smooths old landmarks, leaving a few barely visible in its depths.

Keeping the Feast

Over dinner, Shelley could not help revisiting her own landmarks. "God, I love this Park. Feel like I grew up here."

"So you've been here? On this very spot? Tell me, tell me."

"Well, not *this* spot. Not far, though." Her recent research and new teaching instincts wanted to educate Lucy on its history. Her brain, though, doing its miraculous two-time, was spooling a memory that was less historical and far more private and sensuous: the splash of a waterfall, a whiff of cabernet, a breast's gentle rise and fall. "And I wasn't standing."

Lucy, eager to unearth a moment in Shelley's life, didn't catch the sad smile. "But was food involved?"

"Partly, yes." A full smile returned. "Part of that elegant picture." Sadness and candor prompted her to add, "Lucy, I'll be honest. Sorry. I was with the perfect woman for the girl—no the *woman*—I was becoming."

Lucy had noted Shelley's kind but distant behavior, but now, discovering her former romantic leanings, she *had* to find out more while her own heart could stay tight on its leash.

"You *were*? That *is* romantic. Well, is there anyone *now*?"

"Today? No. Why?"

"Well. I told you I've seen you. There's a girl I've seen you with."

"Girl?"

"Woman. Student. Professor? I don't know. In Holmes, having coffee."

"Oh, probably La Shonda? No. She's my cool bud. She's," she fingered those few beaded strands, filling the air with soft clicks, "my 'coif' guru."

"Well, she gives good advice. I like your hair that way."

"Do you?"

"God, do I. Shell," (now *she* had to be honest) "I have to be honest."

"Always best, Luce. But thank you."

"Well, you make it so easy. Thank *you*. Now. I've seen you around campus. Damn. Already said that."

"Say it, Lucy." Shell wanted her to say it.

She took a deep breath and leaned toward Shelley, her eyes again directly into hers. "I think you are just so wonderful, so gorgeous. I've wanted to meet you forever. There, it's out."

Shell understood. She remembered circling the track, hoping to catch, eager to impress an older girl. The memory and her instincts tried to help: "Why so shy? You thought I'd be offended?"

"Well, maybe."

"Well, Lucy. Good news and bad news. Offended? No. I'm flattered. And I admire your cool."

Lucy, though basking in the kind words, detected the warning.

"I do try. I've come so far this year. And Scott's helped."

"Scott definitely seems cool." (She glanced down at the few grains of flour that clung to her hand, and briefly over at Scott as he "cheffed" with authority.)

"Oh, he is, he is. But don't hold back." (deep breath here) "What's the bad news?"

"Up front, dear Luce. The bad news is our timing. I really have gone off romance. Last year *was* wild. I think I was drowning that old sorrow. Had to explore. And boy, lady, did I."

"Boy *and* lady, I hope?"

"Oh yes. But even the seniors here were not weighty enough—I discovered in time that I wouldn't find another *her*. Not *that* way. But that didn't stop me trying."

"I can't believe I'm talking like this, but I think I'd love to hear."

"Well, Luce, I'm sorry. I'd just rather not. I went through it, but it's a phase I've passed."

Lucy felt comfortable enough to observe. "Damn. Just my luck, huh? Born a year too late?"

"Probably my loss too, you know. Don't sell yourself short."

"But Shell," Lucy's eyes nearly twinkled and a wry smile lurked just under her lips. "You don't *have* to give it up all at once, you know. You might explore a *little* more, seems to me. Think you were too hasty? Stop and reconsider?"

Shelley smiled. "Ah, my Luce. Tempting as it is, and cool as you are—and, say, gosh I love that blush." (The blush then blushed still more.) "But you can't keep up old habits if your heart and mind aren't in them. And mine aren't. I've moved on. Now it's nuns—or maybe monks—that suddenly appeal. I still love to cook, but, more and more, I'm craving books. Books and privacy. Your lucky match tonight is a novice nerd, not a real match."

When Scott happened to look over, he saw Shelley and Lucy in what looked like deep conversation. Shelley was sitting up straight, engaged but with her hands knitted in her lap; Lucy sat on her hands but with her eyes still glued to her "match." From time to time, he saw Shelley dig into her hamburger, her eyes (or so he hoped) rolling in pleasure.

* * * * *

Within the hour, most of the "double party" had wafted away, many partiers having first exchanged cell phone numbers. Some even called each other while they stood there, to confirm the digits, so the clearing soon chirped like an aviary. The phrase Scott jotted later was "a convention of harmonious crickets." (He, or, oh well, *I* liked it.) As several of these new friends headed off, some single, most in pairs, they bore appropriate containers for midnight munchies or morning snacks back in the dorm, plastic housing which Shelley had so thoughtfully dispensed from her bulging knapsack.

As Scott helped Gavin stash the slender remains in his trunk, he came across Esther joined with Anita to form, Scott thought, a fond Steve sandwich. The guy stood between them, doing some fancy juggling with four or five salt and pepper shakers. The women were transfixed by the arcs as each rose up, up, up, slowing, hanging, then sinking down, down faster, into the blur of the juggler's hands. White grains and gray grains kept seasoning the whirs.

Anita, sporting a brimming cup of cabernet in one hand, flung her other arm across Esther's shoulder; she watched spicy apogee after apogee, like a cat eyeing a hovering bird.

"Hey, Neets. What say we invite our juggler back to my room, eh?"

Their libidinous camaraderie amused Scott, though it shocked his old, if dissolving, Puritan side. As he approached, Esther said, "Well, Scottie. You finally found something the slut and I could agree on." She and Esther both raised two fingers to their foreheads in salute.

"Amazing," Scott laughed. "What an evening."

Steve looked over at Scott and at his two new friends and let his hands slow, catching each shaker adroitly as it swooned back to earth. Soon he stood at rest with the spicy cornucopia nestling in his arms.

"Yes! Thanks, Scott. Great introductions. Great party!"

"We T.A.'s live only to serve."

As Scott headed back to Gavin, he heard Lucy speaking earnestly to Shelley as they walked toward the lane. (She was reveling in her *own* instructional premiere as a teacher, inspired by Shell.) "But it *is* Jupiter, Shell. I know. People at the Science Center said. It's tonight. Live! Pictures from Io."

Lucy's words stirred Scott deeply. From Io? Really? If he could get Gavin into bed (easy enough), *and asleep* (a major hurdle) he'd slink out and dial it up. The dim ember deep in his brain began to pulse brighter, though its rays were still feeble.

"Come join me. I'll prove it to you."

The two women climbed aboard Shelley's bike.

"Sure it can carry me?"

"Sure! Just slide onto the handlebars. I'll pedal; you navigate."

* * * * *

(Only a small chunk of what Scott had predicted in his "young novel" came literally true that night. For one thing, it was *Gavin* who nuzzled *Scott*. And Scott was driving.)

Encounters: Some Distant ...

By the time they came through his door, Scott felt himself dividing into two, but each half harbored hope. He'd been in firm charge of the fiesta, so one of his halves felt he'd earned the right to celebrate the splendid evening. He felt proud of himself, grateful to Gavin and, no surprise, aroused. Yet, elbowing for equal attention, was that inchoate but earnest idea born on the hilltop.

The first thing the newer Scott did as they entered was to walk to the kitchen where, with a determined sigh, he tugged the month of April from the calendar, a day late. He hated to part from any physical vestige of those incomparable days. "Why couldn't April have 31? August could spare one excessive dog day. Frigid January could have lent a day." That afternoon, as he'd kneaded those spices into his "fiesta burgers," the old Scott's fingers had reached for April but made his other hand swat them away.

But the hill had lent him an insight: May would bring, was bringing, new wonders—different, even painful, but wonders nonetheless. He'd have to accept whatever time would harvest. Of

284

course, when he entered the bedroom a minute later and beheld those shoulders, that chest, elegant neck, cascade of hair (and the eyes)—he was his. Saying yes to every next request. Still, even in the throes of passion, he felt Lilliputian distractions like spiders' threads whispering across his soul—the densely wooded but loquacious hill; Lucy's methodical voice talking of Io to the culinary Shelley, Shelley listening attentively at their private table, Shelley's powdery hand.

By 3 a.m., his body sated for the moment, his ancient but newly awakened curiosity told him to go see. He pushed the covers to one side, revealing that (still) glistening and (for once) still body of Gavin's. Flipping on the set, he twined his legs and arms around the couch's comfortable cushions and grew instantly rapt. The set's ghostly flicker cast a shimmering nimbus on the walls.

He kept the volume low, so those soft JPL Californian whispers barely tickled his ears. He became entranced, though, with the transmission of the slow dancing of the two spheres. Jupiter's orange presence loomed like a curious giant over the camera's shoulder, heaving into view as the scout whipped around Io and trained its electronic eye backwards. The shots flowed like the slow riffle of a deck of photos.

But the next shot arrested him. A close-up focused on Io's surface more tightly. What was that? Stuff spewing? Yes. But what? Spray upon spray of …lunar lifeblood? Even the Laboratory folks were stunned. After several minutes, the in-house JPL cameras panned to their mission control head. She hazarded a remarkable first guess: volcanic eruptions. "This is incredible. We provincial earthlings have never before witnessed—live!—three-dimensional eruptions on *any* alien body—moon or planet." Io's very innards were being churned, radically churned into continual upheaval by the orange monster's irresistible force. Io, in thrall to the relentless tractor beam, could scarcely maintain her shape. (Scott was taking the cosmic dance personally.)

Scott started to revel too (a new old sensation) in the ruby lips of that mission manager. (She was a former astronomer who'd signed on as chief of this remarkable planetary initiative.) Her eyes and throat brought Scott to attention even as his scientific imagination soared with the cosmic implications of her ad lib hypothesis. Soared too (or, perhaps, simply took a side-trip) toward Lucy. Were they watching? Or was the girl simply using the planetary excuse to put some romantic moves on that—um, stunning woman? Shelley? Right, Shelley? ("Jas-par," his lips silently reshaped her syllables). He wouldn't blame Lucy if she was. *He'd* be, if he were she. And that devoted but endlessly nomadic Gavin would probably encourage him to pursue the rapture. Damn him.

Whether due to the wonderfully fetching *and* articulate Dr. Lewis on the screen, or to a voyeur's appreciation of a romance between two undergraduate women, or maybe to all three, Scott

286

found himself drawn to alluring images he'd been ignoring lately. From day one, Gavin had been all he desired. But at this moment he was so stirred by both these cosmic and amatory mysteries that he scarcely noticed that Gavin had slipped in and was stretched alongside him on the couch.

"So, mate. What are we seeing?"

"We are seeing Io and Jupiter. Marvelous. The god is stirring her depths. Now. Well, thirty some minutes ago. Time takes time in space, hon."

Gav nodded the same kind of nod he'd nodded at the Science Center's star show—an understanding nod: knowing wonder, subdued surprise.

"And, my man, comfy and alluring as you are, you are at the moment distracting me. That moon is spewing its magma, seeding that vast neighborhood with gas, rock, lava and, who knows, uranium? Some might spew our way, think? Into *our* skies. Purple our majestic mountains, dust our amber waves?"

"Poetic hypothesis, sir, but I have other business in mind. May I dear sir, be your giant? Stir *you*?" He was insatiable.

"Is your fountain never still. Oh, fine, whatever. Your call. Just hush."

"Nothing more?"

"I can offer you but my divided attention. Tonight, I am but half yours."

Before long, sure enough, Scott was scarcely aware of him, piqued and entranced as he was by that lunar upheaval. Sure, Gavin's whispered endearments and challenges engendered the usual tingles and shivers and fed as usual Scott's usual lust. But the objects of his desire kept phasing in and out. First, that brunette on the screen. But soon, on her heels, a flickering, alluring parade: Lucy's pale and delicate features; brilliant black curls and tan neck. Steve? Yep, Steve. And (last minute addition) Lucy's friend: Shell Jaspar—firm arms, broad shoulders, laden plate. And then again Dr. Lewis. (For Shell, much later, he edited the list severely but suavely.) Gavin was turning him on, but it was they he was successively sampling.

Moments later he kissed Gavin's subsiding eyelids. "Get some rest. You've done enough."

Then he swiveled his head to command a new angle on that planetary dance. With a final caress, Gavin undocked. Scott could not deny himself one last languid gaze before the man disappeared.

... And Some Local

Not more than a couple of miles away, in Lucy's dorm room, Shell and Lucy were having a pleasant late evening together—companionable, but not, in spite of Lucy's hopes, romantic. Never mind, her heart was still hooked. It was enough that the gorgeous, bright and friendly woman was, oh yes *sitting* there. *Next* to her. In her *room*.

They were sitting on her university-issue couch, transfixed by that same "live feed" from Io. Shell was admiring its fluxing colors and changing perspectives, her aesthetic delight enhanced by Lucy's scientific expertise. She was providing animated detail about the space probe's history: its launch, the various gravitational slingshots ("Astrid's Cassini," Shell silently sighed) that got it there; how long it would stay in Jupiter's neighborhood. She was estimating, eons hence, its fate.

"You are such the expert, Lucy." Shell was sitting up straight on the couch, still in awe of the screen's cosmic dance. But from time to time she turned to Lucy, eager to sip from what seemed her bottomless fund of information, giving Luce her rapt but occasional attention.

And as she sat there, a May evening two years before was surfacing. A fresh old perspective requesting her attention (though far briefer than usual) ...

She was dozing in a more horizontal position. Astrid was shaking her, "Hey, sweet girl. From your Starshine: a special treat."

"Treat? Where?" Shelley's opened her sleepy eyes onto Astrid's loving, hazel ones.

Astrid rotated Shelley's head on the pillow and aimed it out her western window, "Look, babe. It's the evening star. Venus. Our guardian." ...

Lucy continued to bubble with enthusiasm. "Yeah, it's what I was checking at the Science Center. Day I saw Gavin and Scott. On the escalator." (Shell grinned at the report of that more terrestrial sighting.) "Jupiter, its moons, the asteroid belt. Gosh, I've loved that whole business since I was, I forget, ten or eleven? Some girls rode bikes and had slumber parties. Me? Stars and planets. Or fiddling with my chemistry set."

"It made me feel ..." she wanted to add "... like such an outsider." But she didn't. The verve and candor she brought to cosmic matters dissipated when the topic was Lucy. She longed to open up to this stunning and sympathetic woman, but her throat began to feel thick, to ache—a sob, suppressed but rising. She tried to take refuge in predictable matters—trajectories, gravitational suspense, the lumpy couch. But she sputtered to a halt.

"Oh, God, Shelley. I'm sorry." Her throat caught. "I am *such* a jerk."

Shelley turned to her in concerned amazement. "Luce? Luce. What is it?"

Lucy shook. "Oh, Shell. I'd *so* looked forward to tonight. Hoped we'd meet. And now, having you here, it's wonderful."

Shell put an arm around Lucy as her words began to cascade. "I've always been so shy, and on top of that, always ashamed of the attractions I felt, you know. I did find a group online. I could talk."

Shell pivoted to hold Lucy's hands. "Go on. Tell me. And—listen to me, lady— *never* apologize."

"Yeah, I'm trying. But here's something I didn't even tell *them*. You're the first I'm telling. Last year, there was this junior at my school. Took Chemistry together. I loved the way her nose scrunched when we poured out chlorine. And she seemed to enjoy my company. Often came to sit with me for experiments. And what did blind dense me do? Nothing. Never said anything. Got extra diligent recording our data."

"But Luce! You *should* have. What if *she* hoped you'd try?"

"Right. Right. But I didn't. What if she was *hoping* but didn't know it? But I didn't. Didn't say a thing. And then I thought, well, college. Fresh start. Meet someone who gets me. And, sure enough, who swings into view? Shell. Too good to be true, and I made myself try for you. Do you know, I even talked Scott into my plan."

Shell ran her hands through Lucy's hair and cupped her neck with her palm, trying to calm her. "You *knew* what you wanted. You *went* for it." (Shell remembered her words to dad and Averill about Astrid.) "And, well, a little devious too, sure." She smiled at her effort to tease Luce and tugged the girl's nearest earlobe.

"Tonight, Shelly. It was a dream come true. But I *should* have known better. Who am I to meet, much less impress someone like you? Someone beautiful, and someone who enjoys my company. And I blow it."

Shell released her neck and looked firmly into her eyes.

"Lucy, stop it. Listen to yourself. We're sitting with each other; you're educating dense me with all your marvelous knowledge. How'd *that* happen? Well, *you. You* got your Scott and my Gav to buy your plan. And then, at the party, you opened up to me. I *am* impressed. So strong, man."

Lucy began to dry her eyes and wiped her nose. "You think?"

"I do."

"God. I am feeling so dam' silly. You're right. I should be enjoying the moment. Instead, a big baby."

"Not at all. You say you got yourself psyched up for it. I know all about that too."

"*You* were psyched up for tonight?"

"Oops, no. For that woman two years ago. Stunning. Took her months before she noticed me." (Shell exaggerated a bit trying to reassure Lucy.) "And when we did meet, had our first incredible date, she warned me off. But I wouldn't listen, not during our glorious spring and summer."

Lucy's eyes shimmered. "That waiting. Did it seem to take forever?"

"Really did. Took all of March and some of April before she even noticed me." (Some more considerate exaggeration.) "Seemed forever."

"I can't imagine you holding back. *You? Shy?*"

"It's true. Finally took some steps. Just like you, hon'."

"The things I am learning tonight!"

"It's called college, girl. Now, listen, Luce. Shell's advice: When you get home, *call* that girl. No, better yet, don't wait. Do something from here. *Write* her. She'll be impressed, hearing from the new, dynamic college woman. Us girls who're drawn to girls, we just have to trust our instincts. Act on 'em."

"I know. I'm starting to anyway." Lucy nearly smiled. "But. But still, what if *she's* not interested either? Never was?"

"Then you're no worse off, are you? Plus you'll know. You've spent all this time not knowing about me, right? Could've used the time to look for someone else. So she isn't into you. You cross her name off. Your candor will impress her, and it'll give *you* real confidence, can't lose!"

"You're so wise, Shell. I think I'll start listening to you."

"Heck yes. In fact, listen to *this.*" Shell's enthusiasm was catching. "I'm thinking, as your new friend. Say, an idea: get you out more. That Science Center? It was a good start. You found out about my Gav' and your Scott. But, sorry Luce, have to say, it's a tad nerdy. No, let's start watering you. We can form a two-woman squad."

294

Lucy was thrilled at the invitation but couldn't subdue her old self. "But I leave in a week. What's the point?"

Time for Shell's irony, the habit Astrid helped tweak. "Now that's just *great*, woman. Right. Don't even try. Find an excuse"— before reverting instantly to the caring Shell. "No, let's *make* time. How about tomorrow? Screw my report. We'll walk to the Loop, grab a sidewalk café seat. Shall we meet the world, eh Lucille?"

"Ha. 'Lucille'. That's what Scott calls me."

"Well, there you are. Me and your t.a. guy agree. Scott's clearly sharp! And see, everyone wants to help."

"Well, then. It *is* my wish. Let's!"

"Good answer. We'll help you meet someone. Maybe some bright cool woman."

"*Another* one, you mean." She actually ran her fingers through Shelley's hair.

Shell caged the hand in hers, squeezed it and returned it to Lucy's lap. "*See* how cool you are?" She poked her arm with an affectionate knuckle: "Devious ho!"

Lucy's giggle arose from her heart.

* * * * *

After all the stresses of that hectic day and the tensions of the week—planning for Shell; meeting her; the bike ride; dinner; Io; and now all these confessions, these tears—Lucy was drooping. Her head slumped onto Shelley's shoulder, but she revived long enough for a caring thought of her own.

"Well, what about you? Can we find you a woman? One you *would* go for?" (She actually smiled at the thought.) "Or, heck, what about something new? Maybe a guy? An older guy? More mature than these seniors? Hey, like Scott. He's great. He's not for me, but I love him. Yeah," her eyes creased with amusement, "you could steal him from 'your Gavin'."

"From my Gav? Never. I wouldn't." (Shelley in due course reported this chat to Scott: "Did you know it was Lucy who planted the idea? For us?" His answer: "That Lucille. I *knew* she was a woman of uncommon brilliance.")

* * * * *

Shelley hadn't realized how exhausted Lucy was until she saw her eyelids fluttering.

"Guess I wore her out," she whispered to herself. She pulled Lucy to her sleepy feet, and walked her to her bed.

As Shelley pulled the sheets up to her chin, Lucy was just awake enough to say, "Selfish I know, but would you stick around? I'll fix us breakfast. You can sack out on that couch. Here. My pillow."

As Shelley switched off the light. Lucy revived one last time. "Know what, Shell?"

"Luce?"

"Someday, I'll brag about this. This incredible woman."

Shell caressed her cheek. (Astrid had seen to it that affectionate gestures came even more naturally to the naturally affectionate Ashella.) She then retreated to the couch, where she watched the last few transmissions of the cosmic dance. She hefted her bulging book-bag, rooted around in it, and retrieved her journal. (Gavin assigned them to his students to write their reactions to their literature. Every two weeks he'd collect them, read each closely and comment. His last one was "Ashella! Wonderful insights. Do I see an English major in the making?") She thumbed her nose at him next day, but decided to continue hers, as a personal diary. The moment on Lucy's couch cried out for reflection.

She swung her feet up from the floor and rested her back against the couch's arm. "What a night, old Shell! Lucy. A sweet girl. Nice that she likes me. Cool for you, Shell. Hope I didn't hurt her. And I *did* enjoy chatting with her. Loved it when she started speaking up. And those burgers. Wonder, is his recipe online?

"Oh, well; a new day. Better find more books. Will they let me borrow for the summer? Why wouldn't they? I love this place! And who knew? Right here, good old St. Louis!"

Then, she stopped writing and simply thought out loud: "Lucy says hang around. Fine. I'm not tired at all. I'll do some reading. Doze if I have to." She laid the journal aside and slipped out a book from her bulging backpack, an anthology of 19th century St. Louis authors. She read for a good hour, totally engrossed, then did in fact doze calmly on the couch.

* * * * *

The St. Louis sun had reached a point on the ecliptic just halfway from the vernal equinox to summer solstice. It arose on May 2 just after 5. So did Scott. He'd slept on his couch for maybe two hours. When he awoke, his widening mind turned to… "That Shelley. No, I mean Lucy. Now which …?"

He sidestepped the question and sent an email message to the entire class, hoping they'd liked "our Fiesta." To Lucy's, he added a private p.s. "First priority is study for our final. But, Monday, please: an update. You guys seemed to hit it off."

His curiosity wakened him still further so, instead of retreating to Gavin, he slipped a kimono on and raided the fridge. It now fairly bulged with foodstuffs, the result of Gavin's carnal bequests (and catholic requests). A host of Asian spices lined up in the new rack Scott had hung on his wall. In the fridge, carrots and kohlrabi (recently replenished); in a basket to the side, acorn squash, sweet potatoes.

"But no hummus." He laughed. "Should have asked her for some."

He settled for a slather of cream cheese and strawberry preserves—one more spur-of-the-moment invention. As he nibbled, the computer's resonant C major chord (Gavin's perfect pitch had informed him) announced a message. From Lucy? Or Shelley? Nah. Could it be Steve? "Don't be ridiculous." Or that Ron? He was intrigued enough to wake the machine from stand-by. Just a University message—the usual start of the month "Calendar of Events." In a bright red box on the screen he noticed an alert, "Next Stop Mars." That night at Sagan Hall.

Scott stuck a left-over gold post-it on the screen. "Mars tonight. Time?"

* * * * *

Shelley and Lucy shared her hummus at sunrise on a bagel Lucy managed to toast on her (illegal) hotplate. They laid plans for the evening's scouting expedition—Shelley insisted. Then she biked home and slept soundly for a few hours. When she arose, she checked her computer before turning to the pile of books on her desk but the message reservoir was low: her recent embrace of the monastic life was thinning her ranks of correspondents. (Some guys *could* take no for an answer. Women too. Stopped asking, after just two no's.) Then purely on a whim she lectured herself: "What the heck. Don't be coy. Thank him."

She dialed the university's electronic site and found Scott's email address, courtesy of the English department. She wrote him: "Hi, burger man. I want to thank you (and oh yes my Gavin) for your fiesta and the great food. And I guess I have you to thank for my new friend, your Lucy. We got to talking and I never got back to you. But those burgers. Man! If professing doesn't work out…

"Listen to me talk. I hardly know you. Acj"

These were Shell's first documented words that were sent Scott's way. When he purged his files in late August and came across them, he paused, then hit "save".

Martian Dreams

Shell's message swam (out of the blue, appropriately) onto his turquoise screen—his chosen May color. (His choices began to welcome and display a widening rainbow of shades. Even peacock.) The text was the last thing he'd expected. Well, nearly the last. "Look, Gav'." He signaled him to come peer over his shoulder. "Your Shelley isn't just stunning. She has discriminating taste in food. And Chefs!"

Gavin leaned on his shoulder to examine the message. "Ah, words from the Shell! Very nice. But what about our plan? She calls Lucy her 'New friend'. Just *friend*? That all?"

"Nah, think she's just being nice. 'Quite the diplomat,' I'd say."

Gavin smiled. "Not so sure. Always nice. To everyone. She's a wonder." Considering he had spent at most fifteen seconds with her—one floury handshake, a few exchanged words, plus two mouthed syllables—Scott was surprised at the twinge of jealousy Gavin's comment stirred.

But that gold note on his screen helped him refocus. Mars: that was the day's real business. And from nowhere a curious thought: "A place for Gavin? Now why on earth ...? Crazy." He kept the thing in his heart, though. And that trembling image from the hill? He felt it growing into a steady pulsar.

A rare Friday department meeting—professors only (Assistant, Associate, Full, and Visiting); wine and *hors d'oeuvre* to follow—meant Gavin had abandoned him. "Our first Friday dinner apart, hey mate? Our fifth (?) week-i-versary. But I'll make it up." Yet even that deprivation felt fore-ordained. Yes, something was rising from the shadows which, he sensed, the evening might bring into sharper focus. "What's this? Male intuition? What *is* this?"

* * * * *

The cerebral and cloistered Scott Preston had never realized what an articulate and engaged community of folks lurked, just out of sight, beyond the department and university. "Dark matter?" he wondered as he sat in Sagan Hall, an early arrival. The auditors that night were diverse. One man in a yarmulke sat in the row ahead of him; another two or three, similarly "hatted", were scattered nearby. (Were God's chosen contemplating yet another holy land? Scott gave a genial shudder at the theological implications.)

Something else struck him: many in that eager audience would be in their graves, or their bodies donated to Science—out of circulation either way—before any Mars landings would take place. "And yet here they are, heads and hearts stirred by a vision of a future they'll never see—travel thru space, colonize planets, tour and survey the entire solar system." The insight made a career-long impression.

High above and well behind the speaker's lectern burned a massive projection of the red planet, far more detailed than the disk at which he used to aim his telescope; far ampler than the one that had nested among Gavin's magenta flowers. Each time his eyes returned to it, an excited curiosity took firmer hold.

Scott turned to gaze around the room's wide semi-circle and up to its spacious balcony. A face or two seemed vaguely familiar. Maybe from MoHist? From campus? Could this be another lurking band of fellow spirits, minds, adventurers?[2]

What about that striking older woman halfway across the lecture hall? Brilliantly coiffed hair, and a tortoiseshell lorgnette dangling from her neck? And there were crew-cut men (also one or

---

[2] Those five or ten minutes proved, when he would recall them for Shell much later, the first blush of a dynamic future. By then, they'd both become active participants on the internet, a "site" where a continually changing set of global voices can meet from minute to minute and generate scintillating discussions of countless matters. On history, Shell took the lead; on literature, Scott. On music, a lively engagement. (It was the historian Shelley who insisted Scott write and insert this information. "Your novel is permitted footnotes.")

303

two women ditto)—slovenly, bearded (one of the men), two with beads clicking (one man, one woman); and yet another, of indeterminate sex, with an equally indeterminate but vivid tattoo on her or his neck.

An impish white-haired grandmother led in what might have been her granddaughter—zaftig, grumpy, impatient. Scott's new sharp vision tried with depressing success to picture the woman the girl would grow into here on the planetary surface as the evening's proposed space colony assembled itself thirty-some million miles away. These were new and rather cosmic sights, but they could make neither Shelley nor Lucy materialize. Their absence depressed him. Why? And where'd that day's insistent craving to talk recipes come from? He could do that any day (or night) with Gavin.

And what about those whiffs of sage and jasmine jouncing his imagination all day?

No time to reflect further. The speaker began, and the evening exploded—with diagrams and graphs, with history and predictions. That shimmering screen loomed like a call to action. So was the sight of hand mics being deployed throughout the audience to encourage a truly communal consideration, to form a fellowship.

Especially during the q and a session. That was when a wiry woman raised her hand to ask about "what might seem an unrelated matter; or too recherche? But I've always wondered."

"I shall do my best, madam," replied the speaker (a doctor Priyangeli Ashok) draped in an imperial purple kaftan. "Please share your wonder! We want to hear."

"Thank you. Well, then: we know about g's and stresses and orbital insertion. Your descriptions were brilliant. Vivid! But what I've never heard anyone explain or even describe are the *sounds* up there. Not at lift off and not later at Mars. But before, up there in silent orbit. What do they hear? Static? Fragmented transmissions? Anything? Or does deep space, like some poet said, 'moan round with many voices'?"

Scott sat up: "Someone else knows *Tennyson*! Not just me and Dad." Wonderful. So many kindred minds jostling in a world he'd opted out of for so long.

His widening eyes helped a new insight blossom. "What *about* space? Room out *there* for poets?" The notion born twenty-four hours before on that Park hill began to assemble bones. "And won't they need folks to teach it? Would *I*—? No, no. But what about—?" A panoply of brilliant globes against the rich deep black space unfurled for him. "Would *Gavin*—?"

Wrapped in his meditation, he missed the lecturer's answer. But he tuned back just in time to hear a voice he thought he recognized: Rich? Rob? Yeah, Rob! The fellow he'd neglected to email about the picnic. His dark hair was netted now in a paisley bandana. "Sure enough. The kid has a life!"

And the "silent" kid was speaking. "Hey, man. Or lady, I guess." The room snickered at his correction. Dr. Ashok joined in: "Lady will do. Fire away, sir."

"Another lit question for you. Those first folks who go up there? That first space colony, when they assemble and they, say, 'light out' for Mars? Would they kind of be like Huck Finn? Is that the sort of thing he'd do today, place he'd go, place he'd, uh, 'hang' if he were still around?"

Scott was delighted. "What we *discussed*!" Well, not Rob. He'd sat there distracted, as usual. Now it dawned on Scott: *Not* distracted. The fellow simply processed ideas at a different pace, his own pace, like a coral reef accreting its various firm grains, deep under-water. Scott was astonished again by the way that seemingly miraculous ideas can propagate. *Not* miraculous. Actually merely pedestrian. It can happen *anytime*. "No wonder Gavin loves teaching. And"— it was the first time he'd articulated it—"I do too." (Then the recurring confession …) "He's what I want to be."

The speaker threw out a teacherly compliment. "The young gentleman, like the lady, asks a brilliant and literary question. And they, quite conveniently, steer our discussion away from Mars and back to the actual heavens—that space platform. I love their focus on literature, and it's vitally relevant. I have a confession. The title of my talk—'Next Stop Mars'—is a bit of a bait and switch. For the next decade, maybe more, the real focus, less sexy or mind-blowing I guess, is preparation. Training and education. As I hope I made clear, our first mission is the way station. It will be the vital means toward our much farther, considerably redder goal.

"Indeed, we shall be using that silver sphere of a platform for decades. It's up there waiting, even now; and soon it'll be expanding, like a medieval cathedral: labs, work-out bays, classrooms. We have positioned it a million miles out, at a triple gravitational balance between sun, earth and moon. Well, for all you English types, I better say 'balanced *among*'."

More chuckles.

"And we won't just train colonists. That unique facility will allow us to conduct extensive experiments. Some of them, more particularly, on people—on us so-called *'homo sapiens'*. Here's why." Her distinctive Indian lilt lent the venture even more intrigue. "The effects on colonists' off-spring of a prolonged low-g environment? Of recycled oxygen? In twenty years—imagine this—we may literally breed a new generation of folks shaped first for space and then, in real and deliberate time, ideal transplants for that new, red world. A 'brave' one, eh lad and lady? All of you? All of *us*.

"And, speaking of literature. Consider our future infants? Fostered in incubation cabins, with their brain cases expanded, as Professor Hawking predicts, unconfined by pelvises or wombs: what sort of new readers (dare I call them 'novel readers'?) will this procreative manipulation shape? Scary, no? Exciting, yes?"

As she'd begun spinning the future, seemingly *ad lib,* the room as one grew rapt; as she continued, it murmured amazement. "So what this brave heavenly world will need is, yessir, above all, worldly teachers." Scott felt her words and vision pulsing inside his head. "For technical guidance and practical enlightenment, sure, for the crews from earth. But also (imagine *this*) to acquaint, first, our colonists, but then soon, maybe, these new creatures, this modified species, with *our* species' past. Our *heritage.* Our books, music, science. Tutors for that new modified generation. So yes, young sir! We need some of your independent-minded Hucks to salt the pot as we breed new minds."

She halted, a twinkle in her eye. "Any volunteers?" She laughed amiably. "Show of hands?" She raised her head and stared into the balcony. "What about it, bandana-sir?"   •

Rob stood up. "Sure. I'm in. But give me three years, will you? Got books to read. Classes. Some thinking to do. I want to let my teachers do their mind-numbers on me." Scott swiveled around for a better look. Rob saw him and, as he sat down, saluted.

A few amused hands waved like slender stalks. Scott's was genuine and insistent (though he wasn't raising it for himself). He felt like he was in a warm, dry, watery bubble, ascending. He felt the gray vapor around him radiating, heard a thousand petals whispering. If ever there were a place for his man to "hang" for good, in perpetual motion …

* * * * *

He hardly recalled his walk home and barely noticed that he had clambered into an empty bed. He plunged into a dream—a series of them, it turned out. By now that new, fat, blue journal sat beside him. It was proving the perfect nursery for his fevered imaginings each time he awoke.

He had not dreamed in quite a while. (Gavin provided more than enough fantasy, day *and* night.) And, good male that he was, he rarely dreamed in color. Tonight was different. In the first dream, he sees himself rise up from Gavin, as from a second self, a yolk abandoning its shell. He *makes* his body turn away. He looks up to see the flat white ceiling dissolve to dusk blue, then cosmic black. Pinpoints of light appear, then grow into a full planetary system, inner spheres zipping, and a bulging, gassy, Jupiter lumbering jovially.

In a split-second the collection of globes shrank into a mobile, then to a pinpoint. It withdrew, withdrew, withdrew into a galactic arm that spun faster and faster. The camera retreats, takes its place in a shower of spinning galaxies that are soon sucked into a black vortex. Awaking, he tried to net the full vision within those blue covers.

Later, like a modern Scrooge (but different: *Scott's* three spirits were of his *own* invention) he plunged into a second slumber. He found himself jogging. The sun traced an arc from east to west; so, too, the moon, half a lap behind, like at Dr. Priya's star-show. When the two slid into alignment, he felt himself arise and hang suspended above the world's blue surface, dancing and weaving among the flotsam and jetsam of satellites and deep-space telescopes.

Then, from below, the brilliant arc of a rocket, spewing a billion diamonds in its wake, and bending his gaze toward some vast, silver—what? Terrarium? Nursery? Far below, the creamy earth; the sun, a distant sterling pendant; the moon, a vibrant but muddy brown. All in an arrested dance moving to a sweet but unheard melody.

The curtain fell; he awoke; he scribbled. When he slept again, the fable resumed; through the crystal of the hovering alabaster station and piercing its cloudy precipitation, he spied fronds, willows, slow creeks. Among them men and women pace in shifting pairs. He shivers as the pale fronds scatter more diamond glitters. They fall and germinate. They blossom into amber clusters.

At the third waking, it was with the blind zeal of a confused convert. Awoke to see Gavin gazing at him fondly, his finger on that open journal.

"Your eyes, man. Rolling in what looked like ecstasy."

"No, not ecstasy. Vision maybe. For you."

"For *me?* Wonderful past all whooping!"

"It *will* be, all in good time. Tomorrow. Come with me."

Gavin as always deferred when his follower led him.

A Calling

Spring on that bumptious day in May felt poised on the cusp between the chill of March zephyrs and July's hot gusts. Those two seasons' branes were fondly rubbing, wooing and reconciling. Scott drove Gavin fifty miles north and west of the city to a winery, Boone's Mount. It nestled in a quaint small town perched above a bend in the Missouri River. It's near the spot where, two centuries previous, Lewis and Clark, those two "voyageurs," had initiated their continent-defining adventure. Knowing that gave Scott some further proprietary confidence, twice in three days.

From their secure and comfortable height on the flagstone patio, sculpted onto a primordial basalt extrusion, Scott and Gavin surveyed the verdant world below, shimmering fields of infant corn. Around them, another throbbing hive. A few tables boasted teal pennants and golden sombreros, in early homage to the newly-popular celebration, *Cinco de Mayo*. That festive setting echoed the vibrant array of visitors, in full color, and newly-hatched from their gray, late-winter mode. A slender but thrilling tongue of cool air slid itself into the warm breeze that ruffled the young leaves, puffed napkins into golden blossoms and fanned the two men's hair.

Scott, with scarcely a tremor, curls public fingers around Gavin's wrist and lets his eyes glide over the panoply of folks. Two tables away, two women, clearly engrossed in each other; on one of them he feasts his eyes. Her tan, bare arms flow out of a sleeveless, low-cut rose-pink blouse. His eyes trace, and then retrace, the flow of the fabric across her breasts. With an effort, his eyes select another table where a slender, whitehaired gentleman, with thick veins across his hands, regards with calm anticipation a carafe of vibrant red and a single sparkling glass.

Farther along the terrace's lip sits a fit couple in spandex biking outfits. They'd climbed to the height from the bike-trail at the winery's foot, a trail that in fact ran the full width of the state. It was a converted rail-road line. (Shell, not knowing of it, hadn't yet researched it. She would in time. And in time she'd start reaping its benefits.)

In the patio's center, a young mother and father bounce a chattering two-year-old up and down between them, while an infant reclines—still, curious, engaged—in a small seat at the table's center. A far corner of the teeming terrace had been reserved for suited businessmen: a pair of vintage oaken tables pulled together and bristling with phalanxes of cell phones and fax transmission pads. The modern sea of technology was sending its first tentative tongues up this once safely rural escarpment.

Scott felt triply charged: renewed, first, by the fiesta; refreshed next by the lady scientist's "Mars," then rendered nearly visionary by those three dreams. The newly confident and gallant host strode off in search of the vineyard's prize cabernet. The small general store, a nineteenth century vestige of rural commerce that was now catering to a dynamic new community, yielded some fine English Stilton along with Japanese rice crackers. Scott grabbed a small plastic tub of what a recent experience made him hope was hummus. (It proved, though, to be a mere but perfectly adequate pate.)

The locale seconded the two men's natural inclinations for an educational moment. It offered Scott the perfect cue to instruct the always eager Gavin, this time, on flood plains, their nature, origins, and benefits. "Floods, repeated over Pleistocene eons since the last glacial advance, sculpt and shape valleys like this and help hone our Holocene era lives. They call the really big ones 500-year floods. We had one a few years back."

"Ah. So y'all're safe for a while? Maybe another half millennium?"

"'Y'all'?! Bravo: sir, you are gettin' more and more Missouruh every day." Gavin kissed fingers, touched chest, bowed.

"Well, and as to safe, so it would seem. And up here we are impregnable, flood or no."

"Ah, but still: 'oh earth, what changes hast thou seen'? Right? And down there —yeah, where they're paving that access road—that's where the 'The silence of the central sea' whispered?"

Gavin loved to push Scott's Tennyson buttons. (Who can account for a grad student's taste in poetry? And how could Gavin know he was echoing the woman's query at the Mars lecture? Sometimes coincidences do seem to breathe together: they "conspire".)

Scott turned from poetry to pedantry. "Actually, no, there *was* a huge silent expanse, but not here. We're north of it by a hundred-some miles. The edge of that sea lapped at what we provincial and merely human Missourians call 'old' Ste. Genevieve, our first French settlement. A Jurassic New Orleans."

"Where does your expertise end? Now, then: what about this winery?"

"This winery," Scott explained, not missing a beat, "connects Missouri to the world. Our earliest *German* settlements sprang up just upstream from here. A town named Hermann," (he pronounced it accurately—"hair mahn"—and Gavin instantly whispered it and committed it to his encyclopedic memory.) "Those early pioneers had fled to the heart of America after 1848,

315

voyaging mile after mile after their revolutions failed. The minute they saw it, they felt they were beholding a purified image of the misty, winding Rhine that dwelt in their minds. For them, it was a new Jerusalem."

"Our pioneer Daniel Boone portaged furniture across the wide Missouri not fifteen miles east of here. A generation later, these German folk brought not just their vintner skills, but their political ideals. Those ideals of theirs helped keep us in the Union a decade later. Their vision *shaped* us."

Gavin nodded appreciatively but did his usual hand-spin to move Scott along.

"So you see, Gav'. Folks *can* take their spirit and their ideals with them. What are space and Time? Mere 'rags' says John Donne. But like those good Germans or Milton's bad Satan, people can and do take themselves wherever they go. And so, my own sweet voyageur, can you." Gavin looked at him, eyes narrowed. "And your point, liebe historian?"

"Ah. My point? Suspense, my fellow ... um, 'pimp'— That's the word I could tell Shell was too polite to say two nights ago. She restrained herself at 'kinky.' *Attend*, sir!"

* * * * *

He turned to the brilliant shimmer far below their feet in that fertile flood plain. The emerald stalks' shimmering shoulders bowed toward the river bend. Among the waving fields, workers snaked, examining a young stalk here, spraying a weed there. A man and a woman, weaving among the tasseled rows in that sea of green, seemed a pair of porpoises sporting playfully in green foam. Scott, in high fictional gear, began to compose a story about them. "How about this? Um. *Each day they made love in a freshly seeded row. They married in an apple grove. Their kids migrate first to Idaho, where their corn skills—*"

"And their ideals too? Don't forget their ideals."

"Yes. Yes. Their nourished ideals help them raise chickpeas, and their business skills help them open—what?—a web site for novelists? Sure. Hasn't happened, but it could."

Gavin trilled his sip of wine from cheek to cheek. (Hard to do while smiling, but he did.)

The vision Scott's imagination had been trying to birth since Thursday re-awoke.

"See that baby corn, man? Reminds me of what my Mars woman was saying."

"Mars woman?" Gavin winked. "I abandon you for one evening and see what miracles spill forth."

He turned to the table behind them and aimed a gossipy thumb at Scott. "My friend here says he met an alien."

"I did not." Scott pulled Gavin around to face him, waving an apologetic dismissal to the amused foursome behind them. "I met a NASA *project* manager. Name of Priya. She *talked* about Mars. About...now *listen*, love: Hydroponics. Low gravity in space, even tree trunks would—will—grow slender. They might even float."

"Ah." Gavin nodded. Then his mind moved in: "And all this relates to me how?"

"You are going to have to absent yourself from felicity a tad longer. I'm strewing some crumbs here."

(Scott was treating Gavin with the same loving suspense "his" novel is treating "his" readers at, yes, this very instant.)

Gavin was happy to trust this latest of the many new phases of his new Scott. Watching each one arise and displace its predecessor gave him the same pleasure Scott got from watching Lucy reforming herself. (Same pleasure Shell got observing that same work-in-progress.)

"Thanks, Hansel."

"De nada, Gretel."

Gavin sank into a watery reverie

* * * * *

As the sunny terrace grew shadows, their four eyes turned—Scott's eager, Gavin's patient—toward a yazoo bend of the Missouri on the far horizon. Between that distant, glittering, and yet to them motionless "s" and the part of the river that was flowing past their terrace, other bends wove in and out of sunny fields, groves of trees, gleaming bridges. Scott thought it the perfect moment to unhamper a collapsible telescope (prescient lad, he), extend its short legs and (careful lad, he) uncap its lens.

He tightened its high-resolution focus, to let Gavin observe the life gushing past in the nearest reach: a speckled trout; the twisty fins of a blue gill; the sleek slithering of an innocent water snake. A leaping fish here, a crawdad there, would pop a head out of its watery universe, sniffing perhaps for some airy wormhole to a farther bend, longing perhaps to shuck its creatural nature, but settling for the sunny shafts of the here and now.

As the purpling twilight began to ease in from the east, a party of jovial voyageurs slid into view. Dancers. Two of them danced a jig on a wide silvery platform that tied a pair of canoes into a catamaran. A soft, distant fiddler—a woman in the bow—strummed the travelers into harmonious airy motion down the wide river. The woman swayed to her music that was not yet audible. In time the strumming came through, a bit thin of course, and two seconds out of sync with the two men's view (just as, less musically, lightning predicts thunder). The beat set their fingers tapping to the dancers' gyrations and it kept the air echoing long after boat and dancers passed from sight, swallowed by a green turn.

Gavin raised his full globe of fresh red, "A toast, man. To this gorgeous moment with you. And to more Missouri than I ever knew, much less suspected, lay in wait. A perfect climax to three splendid days, Scottie."

Scott bowed in reply. The man was right: The fiesta. Mars (a place of whose planetary influence Gavin was still unaware.) And now this. All this. It was indeed a *diem* to *carpe*.

So, he launched himself. "Now you listen. Ready?"

Gavin signaled an encouragement that Scott no longer required. "This third day of ours could be the start of something even more glorious. For you. A new life, in fact. Cosmic, in fact. Recall our first evening on your balcony? Mars?"

"Yes, yes. Our first night. 'Sigh,' as my—your—our—fair lady Shelley mutters from time to time."

"She does? Hmm. Big on self-pity, is she? You and your Shelley. Bet you'd stick around here for *her?* Bastard."

Gavin shook his head firmly and gave him the "hurry" twirl. Gavin spoke out of his own interest, but he's also providing our readers a special favor.

"Well, that first glorious night. Even then, you made it all too evident that no 'here' could ever lasso you—not even me, whom you insist on calling the 'incredible' Scott. Nope. I think you're a fool and a numbskull, but those are your conditions." Gavin made Scott's hand concave and deposited a kiss. Scott didn't even bat an eye at the table behind.

"So you agree? Well, then. What better spot for you than— don't you dare laugh—-dangling like Milton's God above those spinning globes of his Creation, above the earth and moon at least, tethered for safety to brother sun?"

Gavin looked puzzled.

Scott felt his way less and less tentatively, as those three nocturnal visions exploded like a single diamond.

"Listen, listen, listen. I have it. Those dreams? My dream."

In his growing enthusiasm, he knelt beside the professional voyageur's chair on the emptying terrace and looked into his eyes. "You know those stationary satellites? What's the word? They never move?"

Gavin began to massage Scott's neck. "Well fact is they *do* move but they do so in sync with us. There's a term for it. 'Geo-synchronous'."

Scott stayed the hand, calmly unwound each finger, and molded it to the foaming cup of red. "Yes. That's the one. Now hear this. That Mars woman explained. There's a spot still farther out, a spot where the gravity of earth, moon and sun all perfectly balance. Well, that's where they've assembled a station. A perfect, dynamic stasis."

"They've *done* it?" Gavin's eyes blazed.

"Yes,' she *said* it and my dream *confirmed* it. It'd be like living in a crystalline terrarium."

"Ah" Gavin's humor and literary knowledge surfaced for a moment. "One could breed cucumbers. Like your Mr. Gulliver."

"Not any one. *You* one. Aye, you. For, now get this: They're looking for a few good men. Yeah, I thought *that* would grab you. But, yes, women, too—so a tempting double dip. They want to start training right away. You could actually leave this summer, like you were planning your whole life. A place for the eternal nomad to go to."

"Truly?"

"Truly. Do you have to ask? No, here's the point dear man: *that* could be where you'll live. And, one hopes, breathe."

"And have my being?"

"Yes, have your being. Perfectly! Until now, *you've* been in motion. *You've* traveled the globe. Up there, though, raft upon raft of folks from down here will come to *you*. You'll teach, guide and help train that new happy breed, those 'pilots of the purple twilight', setting out on stellar missions. Every six months, you'll welcome an entire new generation, men and women. You'll turn those dry engineers, calloused mineralogists, yahoo space buccaneers into readers and philosophers. And equip them with their past. *Ours.* You'll do for hundreds of *them* what you've done for little me. My one pain? My single loss? It's nothing compared to the hundreds you'll liberate, set free into the cosmos. You'll be a permanently visiting professor."

At that instant on the emptying terrace, they gazed into one another's eyes. Gavin trying to absorb Scott's daring notion, Scott, still kneeling, instilling (regretfully but instilling anyway) that passionate vision.

Gavin's eyes sparkled, as he caught the healthful infection. "Anything more?"

"More? Hell, yes. You'll always be moving—that's clearly your life's mission—and yet you'll be at rest, racing in place with the moon. You said you have no home. Well, then: a permanently nomadic place beckons."

Gavin grasped the point and raised a deliberate palm, but Scott was unstoppable. "And that *view*. Lord, love! You'll see the dancing equipoise of the globes. I glimpsed it in my waking dream. From nearly any window, the blue-and-cream earth, the sun a distant huge diamond, the moon a vibrant but light-tan brown. And farther off, the planets in their stately orbits, Jupiter's vast epicycles, its Io eternally reforming."

As dark now fully descended, their hands swirled red liquid, their heads lolled backwards and their eyes gazed upwards. Far to the east in the purplish black they beheld the slow hover and slide of a bright satellite, its surface gleaming in eternal sunshine.

Tears clogged his voice, but Scott made himself speak the morose but ebullient and liberating words. 'I may not *be* your future, but—*dammit, damn it*—I can at least *shape* it."

STAGE THREE:

On the Verge of Sublimation

Final Game

Those three days, nights and journeys that straddled the May 1 crossing day—that communal fiesta, "his" Mars, "their" winery—filled Scott with an invigorating despair. He felt—excuse me, no: he *knew*—that the best six weeks of his life had peaked. They peaked on that windy terrace above that darkening stand of infant corn as he voiced his first lover's destiny. He never did discover how or where he'd found that voice, found the courage, in that place and at that moment, to hint, to suggest—no, to urge— Gavin to float free into that imminent eternal hover. Even now, he could foretell the stomach-dropping whoosh that would hurl the man into what Gavin was already delighting to call "perpetual pedagogical equipoise." (Damn his enthusiasm. And, oh yeah: damn his highfalutin' lingo).

They could both anticipate the pain, but Scott failed to foresee any rewards it might yield. He was deeply divided. He knew the end of their time was looming, and the sole, slender consolation was that it was *his* inspiration that would bring it to a close. Driving home from Boone country at dusk, they had never felt so close nor been so affectionate.

"And you're *sure* you want me to go?"

"No."

"But. You just ... *You're* the one who..."

"True."

"So, then, you don't?"

"No. But I do."

One of Scott's hands massaged Gavin's neck, and two lips kissed his nearest cheek (briefly, in the interests of safety). That suspended the debate for a time.

The memory of their three-day rapport—its ebullient restraint; its resigned commitment—would last. It would still be whispering, soft but audible, to Scott and to Shelley when they started their springtime walks to "her" waterfall. Scott felt *his* loss the more intensely, of course. Still, Shell's pain, though far slighter, was a "two-fer." Losing her inspirational (and hot) lit professor Gavin was sad enough, but that loss brought back Astrid all over again: Her mind. Her heart and smile. Her lips.

Scott and Shell would pause at that spot in the Park for her to snap the shimmering young cascade, a caught glimpse that she later fed into her bulging "album-for-all-seasons". No matter where they roved, after an afternoon there, or a languid but alert stroll through the Science Museum, or, yes, even back home tangled in sheets—the sad memory still rustled. But time in good time does deliver blessings, no matter how effective their initial disguise. Shell, the wiser because the more experienced in loss, would reassure him as needed.

On the rooftop terrace Scott which later set up in his new "digs" (another Gavin term he adopted; Shell got hers from Ingrid), the couple would sit. Perched near a folder of maps or stack of diaries, she'd nurse a glass of cranberry juice. Or, wineglass in hand, she'd nest eagerly near Scott; he'd be reviewing, typing, often concocting his journal—some of it the words that survived the edits and which you are now seeing, live. (I—well Scott anyway—assure(s) you.)

At twilight, on appointed evenings and at calculated hours, they'd pause and scan the sky. The first one to see Gavin's beacon sliding away would seize the other's hand and point, palm guiding palm, or finger finger. When "Gavin's hogan," (her metaphor), finally eased away, she'd blow it a brief kiss, then pivot to Scott for a much longer, a much more tactile exchange. But those coming attractions were still tightly-wrapped buds.

At dusk, at the winery, Gavin's eyes had blazed at Scott's kind, cruel suggestion. They blazed higher still on Monday, when he used Scott's land-line to call Scott's Mars lady in Houston. Deep down (well, not *too* deep), Scott hoped they'd reject him, sight unseen. He knew better, of course. And, sure enough, it was a delighted Gavin who replaced the receiver. In a heartbeat or ten, he'd flown to Houston, met the mission chief, impressed her. (Impressed all the NASA folks, *mightily*. And why not, given his effect on Scott? On Shell?)

Yes, Gavin proved a perfect fit for a planetary venture ("'course he would, bitch"). He handled the high-g chambers as if born to them, his heart thumping like a long-distance runner's: 57 beats per minute, even under a 5 g force. He brought both fortitude and aplomb to the nearly six hours of weightlessness (simulated but no less real) that each new band of "settlers" would face on every first journey to the station. Within ten days, he'd outshone his astronaut colleagues, though many of them had been training there half a year. Nor, five years later, would his semi-annual check-up reveal any of the degradation of eyesight that was sparing none of his fellows. Gavin was judged—and he quickly proved— uniquely fashioned for "elsewhere."

Yes physically, a perfect fit. But what fanned the interviewers' fervor was the commitment he brought to the mission, an articulate dedication that was more one of a citizen-activist than of a merely useful adjunct and instructor. His professorial credentials were of course impeccable, but what confounded the mission authorities was his visionary imagination. It gazed far beyond even the huge, daring undertaking. His deepest commitment, he insisted to quizzical eyebrows, was to "your species."

He reminded them of Dr. Priya's vision for the space station, which her new apostle Scott had duly transmitted to him. Gavin reminded them that the station would house a successive series of assemblies—of miners and pioneers, sure, but also hydrologists, astrobiologists, botanists, as well as a professor or two. "Well, then: why not philosophers?" He advised them to gather, in his words, "a select but growing house of tellurian delegates." And to accommodate that expanding body, "make the place a working laboratory, a functioning microcosm of your kind." Once aloft, he'd repeat and refine that vision to each new raft of earthling arrivals, and, in good time, to those *future* species which the visionary Dr. Ashok had predicted the station may breed. "Your achievements, inspired by your vision, will spread in half-a-parsec leaps across the universe, to speak for our tiny vast corner of space."

And he kept going, contemplating more than space: Anticipating time. "What will earth's culture prize in a thousand years? What will folks spinning on a star-homing comet or dangling in space above spinning globes, like Milton's God, want to read? What will they prize? Ever adrift, will they be 'up' for tales of alienation. Or of love?

"Yeah, imagine the folks who'll flip the pages (or tap the holographic screens) of some novel, sitting on an Alpha Centauri B evening balcony, awaiting the muezzin's call; anticipate workers hammering sheds together in the Martian outback, snuggling under the covers with tired muscles using forefingers to page through an electronic version of it; and of course technicians or managers or dieticians toiling in space stations hanging suspended like brilliant diamonds between any of a thousand planet-moon-star gravitational trinities."

That sort of cosmic free-thinking blew the interviewing committee away. It made his appointment enthusiastic and unanimous. (In a ten-page essay he wrote for the mission's public journal, "Stellar Stirrings," he went further still. Shell and Scott jotted down some rich nuggets, and committed them, snippets anyway, to memory: "Our task is our heritage," "emissaries to new species, on new worlds" "resonate in the farther heavens" "Be at home *ad astra* and on *terra firma.*")

So, no: those program chiefs were no help to Scott. They left him a sole option: to grieve over what was now the inevitable post-partum. Gavin's life had always been the living definition of picaresque, but at least, during their first months together, he'd returned for those weekly honeymoons, brief intense reunions that would stoke and stoke Scott's affection. Now, though, his training excursions lasted not two or three days but a full week. Two weeks once. (We saw the effect a five-day separation had on Astrid and Shell. Multiply that by nearly three and try to imagine.)

* * * * *

The last weekend in July was "our last weekend." Scott was determined to provide a memorable final forty-eight hours. He'd see to it that Gavin would soar aloft savoring a quintessential St. Louis (*and* uniquely American) experience: baseball. Saturday's game promised a stellar pitching match-up—the "pick game of a 'pick' series"—for Gavin to carry up there, a feature-length hologram for perpetual imaginative feasting.

As they awaited the game in their terrace-level loge boxes (the grad student's one final splurge), Scott noted the progress of the rosy, sunset glow cast by the stadium's miniature arches, tiny refractions of the city's defining landmark that lay just to their northeast. Those sunny half-circles were spangling the near outfield when Scott and Gavin arrived, but their pace soon accelerated and in no time they were nibbling at the lower left-field wall. Scott watched them slide, climb, then flee, their shapes more and more distended, across the far stands and up. And gone. Before the lights came up, deep purple shadows engulfed it all—players, fans, pennants.

There was everything to say, and nothing. Both tried to be jovial. That was easier for Gavin, of course, "all before" whom lay not "the world," but the ever-rolling vastness of space. They chatted, sipped beer, gazed around. Scott, the genial pedant, had purchased two scorecards, one to teach Gavin the sport's rudiments. "And here. A blank one. Take it with you. Tune us in. Jot a down-to-earth record in the heavens." Above, below, all around their box, shimmered a veritable sea of Cardinal red, patched here and there with vivid pockets of Cub-blue. The scintillant tapestry proclaimed a century's loving rivalry. Scott's sad mind could still spew metaphors: azure flecks in an incarnadine sea; a Monet cathedral at mid-morning.

Gavin, with the novice's usual vital eagerness, would interrupt their contemplation of the game's flow to ask, "Now. Bloke in black? Arm up means the runner-guy is what you call 'out', yes?" or "If the pitcher's supposed to throw to the batsman..." ("batter" Scott reminded him) "... well then, why did he turn and hurl it to the fellow on that white square?" ("first baseman; the bag. He's holding the runner close."—"What?"). Nine innings were scarcely time enough: the vast slice of American jargon that Scott served up kept them distracted. Blessedly so for Scott, who treasured every such distraction.

Eternally considerate, Gavin was concealing his minimal worries *about* his next life, as well as his vast enthusiasm *for* it. Instead he was trying to paint rosy pictures of what "your new year" would hold. (He was still calculating by university time, not solar, much less interstellar—yet.) "Think of the world that awaits *you*, man. Preston, the emergent chrysalis."

333

"Well, sweet. What's emerging is *your* doing. Your midwifing."

"No, no, love. Lucky timing. You were on the *cusp* of sublimation. I just showed up, held your hand, dialed up the flame."

"You held more than *that*, sir." Shared smirks. "But the results will last. The 'me' you helped shape will last."

"Yes, yes. But time, my sweet, ticks and beckons. So who knows what green explosions lie in wait? Some stud in the Loop? Some lady on some winery terrace? Perhaps some stunning, wise undergrad of advanced tastes? My fine student Steve, maybe? Some female Gavin-babe wandering into our Holmes? (My Shell, maybe?) Endless opportunities!"

Scott's eyes widened at each proffered prophecy, but he resisted. "What? Another someone, with your charm, wit, knowledge? *And* your moves? *And* willing to stick around? Futile hope."

"Ah, but … Recall the lady in the rose blouse?"

"Sure. Fine! But one delectable moment can't compete with the hours and days and days of my Gavin memories. They'll chime endlessly.*"*

"No, dear sir, no. You above all should know—and in *time* you will: There's never an 'always.' And no 'never' is permanent. No, my babe, hon', young sir, sweet love: it's *flux* that rules."

* * * * *

Before Gavin's next query about baseball arcana, a ball flew up and backwards. The umpire wheeled out of the catcher's path, the catcher—mask flung, tumbling in an arc behind him—sped toward the screen. Gavin and Scott gazed in silent awe at the ball's blazing white "ampersand" (Gavin's instant metaphor) etched against that vibrant red and blue background. Ten thousand faces joined them, heated in frozen anticipation. Within seconds, the glowing ball peaked. All eyes zeroed in on its descent, first slow, then accelerating more. And more. Hundreds rise from their seats as it rushes to the expectant mitt. A cheer, flecked with groans, rises and rises, grows, grows … and … subsides.

The park breathed again. And then, as Scott's eyes bubbled up the third base line, a sudden sight: a scarlet beret, luxurious strands cascading.

He peered closer. "Gav! Look. Look there! It's —"

Scott had to lean over and perform his frequent service of, man to man, pulling aside Gavin's flowing strands.

"It's … um, damn"—his mind's eye saw those lips forming an "ahh"—"The Saint? Cecelia? Your—oh of course: *Our*. Shell!"

335

It was. Eyes fixated on the action before her, knees folded against the seat in front of her, Ms. Jaspar was assiduously marking her scorecard. Around her neck a camera; at her feet, a bulging knapsack. Gavin nodded, beamed.

Every few minutes thereafter, Scott would aim his binoculars her way, to stock his memory with a further riffle of sights. Shell marking her score card intently; Shell cocking her camera at a dynamic third baseman retrieving an errant throw; Shell, between innings, dipping into her bulging sack, extracting a volume. One time, Shell bobbing her head and beating out a tattoo on her knee. Gavin watched him swivel to capture those sights, and he suspended his questions. He preferred to beam—paternally at Shell, maternally at Scott.

* * * * *

Another ball flew back three innings later and the spinning small globe once again focused gazes, halted time. But this time momentum and gravity had other fish to fry: the sphere arced toward the two men. It did. Scott's eyes grew magical lenses that caught its seams turning ever more slowly and then even rotating backwards, like car wheels on film. He stood, reached, stretched and lassoed the ball in its last parabolic gasp. ("Like snagging drifting cargo into the space shuttle's bay" would be Gavin's retrospective simile.)

The eyes of the stadium swung their way; the stadium's multiple cameras swung, to telecast it in real-time. The ball, Scott's glove, the two men's faces—all of them blossomed, 100 feet high and wide, on all the stadium's screens. Those videos were educating that vital but fluctuant community which our wondrous technology now captures and can instantly display.

It was on the right-field screen that Shelley saw them. Eyes wide, she stood and pivoted instantly—from their pixelated images to their living selves. Scott's gaze was drawn to her. When she fired a thumbs-up and licked a celebratory finger, Scott found he longed to chat with her. But the logistics were in "baffle mode." He shrugged his shoulders, wiggled a weak thumb, and, as an old memory took charge, mouthed an extravagant "sigh." Shelley read the shape, echoed the shrug, then, lips rounded like his, blew an extravagant kiss his way as she sat down. (Then a second one, she signaled him, for Gavin.)

As the Cards took the field in the top of the ninth and the fans stood to cheer each final out, Scott's eyes skittered downward again. Shell, fully sated on baseball, and now in search of new sensations, was already heading up the aisle. She stopped right below them, hefted her camera with its telescopic attachment, pointed it, clicked. When she disappeared under the overhang with a warm wave and bow, her camera bowed with her.

* * * * *

Late that night, Scott lay in Gavin's arms. After an intense while or two, sex was out of the question. Gavin switched on the lamp and reached into *his* substantial bag beside the bed. From it he drew forth a slender green package swathed in bright, lemony ribbons.

"I meant to leave this on your pillow in the morning. A last silent bequest. But no. Now's best."

"Where?" Scott's head by now was buried in the pillow, eyes shut tight.

"In my hand."

"What is it?" He sat up and faced Gavin.

"For you. A small memento. It's for, well, everything. For you, city-history, Missouri talk, you, the winery. And tonight … baseball. And you."

Scott, his throat aching, set his pillow aside and began to bring the precious relic into the light. Inside the green wrapping nested a crystal box. Within it, a swatch of something gold in a smaller crystal, with a length of silver chain attached to it. "Gorgeous case, glowing contents, love. So thoughtful... but, er: what is it?'

"It's a locket, man. Of my hair. You know I'm not vain, but you say that hair's what you first noticed. So in honor of what you call your parents' quaint Victorian customs: a bit of me to keep. On a dainty chain."

Scott leaned over and grabbed a thick tangle of the far more abundant real thing and let its silken strands caress his lips. When he slipped the chain over his head, the crystal and lock came to rest on his chest.

He took Gavin's hand and placed it under the pendant. "Feel me thumping? Every time I do you, you'll have me in a continual vibration."

Sex, turns out, was back in the question.

Ghosts

Gavin's *almost* final St. Louis departure (and his last terrestrial exit before the starry launch) came next morning.

As the hot Midwest summer haze swallowed that silver jet, despair flooded Scott. He had a short-term worry: would the launch go safely? But his long-term worry was far more devastating: would he see him again? Ever? On earth? His brain knew better, but his heart allowed him one further self-deception.

The road blurred as he drove home. "*Make* him go? Hard. *Let* him go, impossible."

For a week he did nothing but wallow in their aromatic sheets. Curl his arms around, bury his face in, a damp pillow. His inner ear spooled sad operas—the lonely, descending plaints from "Dido and Aeneas" or "Acis and Galatea," a pair of old, old but remarkably poignant tales of tragic love to which Gavin had introduced him. The loving, wise mentor, in training for his cosmic voyage, used them to reacquaint Scott with his past. Those baroque melodies jostled side-by-side with songs of, well, *comparatively* recent vintage—"September Song" or "Yesterday." (The musical tastes they had come to share were—depending on one's view, life, or tastes—either eccentric or catholic.) But, for that first week as a widowed bachelor, those sad operatic tales only made his brain ache; their seductive melodies left him unmoved.

Same, sadly, with a series of gorgeous piano colloquies with flute, clarinet and *cor Anglais* in the more contemporary Ravel concerto; same too for Purcell's tenor and counter-tenor hymn of praise to the "amorous flute," in honor of their favorite (no, their only) saint, Cecelia. Each and all only confirmed what he'd soon be missing—and, it seemed clear, for good. Each provided just one more painful memory of evenings of sensuous delight—delight first from the music, and, soon, from what its melodies, harmonies and rhythms had invariably led to.

Yes, their shared saint failed him. And, what was worse, at night *all* the tunes dried up. In those all-too-recent good old days, several centuries of music would whisper through him as Gavin lay breathing (or recovering) beside him (also recovering). They'd lifted him, in spite of their sad and sober lyrics, into immoderate rapture. *Now* when he awoke, nightly at the dead of night, that was all he saw, heard or felt: the dead of night.

One time he reached for and opened that hand-worn, blue, journal-cum-confessional where he'd been revisiting his old life and revising his new one. Its pages looked alien. Inky creepings. Indecipherable squiggles.

Yes, the inescapable fact was:

"Gavin? …*Gone*."

But still, but still. One thing was certain. No matter his grief and despair, there'd be no going back to that dead, orderly world of the pre-Kuiper Scott. He was adamant. *He'd* sent his guy aloft, so … it was up to *him* to accept responsibility for that good painful deed.

* * * * *

One Monday, he awoke to feel some sweet static pulsing; he wondered if this might be *the* day, the lift-off, that (sigh) ultimate separation? A proprietary sliver of hope sent some vague excitement into his despair. It urged him toward campus; convinced him in fact (or was it just sentimental masochism?) to revisit Holmes.

The impulsive decision proved unwise.

Well, nearly.

He wended his way through the shimmering but enervating August heat. The deserted, unlit hall, dank with plaster, fit his mood perfectly. A paint-spattered tarp covered the hall's back half. And what about those old, reliable tables in the far back? Pushed in random array to the center for the do-over. Those handsome walls on either side of the hearth? Those walnut mummies now slumped to the side. Holes drilled ten feet up, all around the room's circumference, had left powdery residue on the tarp. From several of the holes hung wires, tangled like Gorgons' hair.

No croissants, no inviting bowls of jellies, no toasters. Microwave unplugged. Scott punched *pro forma* the buttons on the lone coffee machine—no special blend today: decaf, lukewarm. He settled for it, shuffled to one unmoored table, and began sipping the bland, plaster-infused liquid.

Then a sound, over there. Pacing through the curtained doors from the outer atrium was … what? A silhouette against the Quadrangle's burnt background. "Gavin's back?" He poured sarcasm on the fond hope. "Yeah, right. Sure." But still the shape approached. And as it did, it grew familiar. A woman. (He saw and he *heard* a cascade of memories old and recent: her jolly mouth shaping "Jas-par," her mimicked "sigh," her bowing camera.) The fiesta, that game. Shelley!

She'd biked over in that debilitating August heat. Damp strands of hair lay on her neck like limp snakes. On her feet, tattered and tennis shoes, their blue long-since scuffed into gray. (Two years of daily use had had their effect; but, like Scott with his calendar sheets, she hated to part with them). No socks, her laces clicking; around her neck, for a change, no camera. Ah, but over her left shoulder one vital sign: a bulging book-bag.

She looked his way, squinted, then gave a weak waggle of fingers. She frowned at the coffee urn, shrugged her shoulders, replaced the cup she'd selected, and plodded his way. Her eyebrows offered a tentative lift; he nodded, smiled. Then his eyes resumed their languid stroll around the room settling finally on his cup, around which his hands were folded.

"You mind?" She waved a thumb at an empty chair.

Scott allowed another weak smile. "Please." She sat down, a matching ghost, she at 10 p.m., he at five.

"Hey. Is it really you? Miss Jaspar?" (He recalled the shapes her mouth had formed.) "Shelley."

"Right. 'Tis" She stowed the book bag with a firm thud onto the chair beside her. "Man, am I bushed," she explained before he could go on. "And the day's barely half done."

"Nothing personal, but the way you look is the way I feel." He lowered his eyes to study his hands around the cup.

"Well, Scott." He continued his examination but offered a faint smile.

"I feel just about the way I feel." She hefted her bag and rummaged in it.

"Well at least you're ready for *something*. Books. *Used* to be my life-blood."

"Hell, sir. If books don't do it for an English T. A., I guess you're sunk. As for me, today I didn't even pack my camera. Park waterfall under repair. This place dark too."

"Damn. *Not* your day."

"Damn. *Not*."

They resembled two figures of stone in the deserted, unlit hall.

Then, ten seconds later, the silence was punctuated by a returning workman climbing the scaffolding at the east end, giving his drill a few preliminary whirs. She revived. "Hey, I'm sorry. Being damned selfish. Sorry, Scott." She peered into his eyes. "'Scottie' too familiar? Lucy called you that. Her special nickname."

Scott looked up, smiling at his student's name and revisiting his and Gavin's noble deed. "No, no. I like it. 'Specially if Lucy said it." Shell nodded and ran her fingers through her hair, to pull aside its two damp tent-flaps.

"But 'selfish'? You? No. Not a word *I'd* use. No. Not from what I've seen."

"Kind of you. But I still *would.* I'm slighting you. You're down?"

"I am." He paused: "Gavin."

"Our Gav'? No way. You had a fight?"

"No. No." His eyes sought hers, then tumbled. "Gone."

"Gone? But just one of his 'jaunts,' right?"

"You didn't know?"

Shelley shook her head. "I just *saw* you two. That game!"

"True. But nope. No longer." He lacked the energy to explain. "Take my word. I pushed him from our nest. On the very next day. He's prob'ly a million miles away."

"Oh, come on. Bet it just *feels* that way."

"No, no, no, ma'am. He is—well, he *may* be—literally that far." He pointed toward the ceiling. "*Gone*-gone."

Her face sank back into the depths. "I won't pry. But, fuck. Wow. My dear Coops gone? Today really *does* suck."

He scanned the high windows to the south. "Only today? A week for me. No sight, no word."

"Really?"

"Put him on a plane ten day ago and I'm *still* recovering. Will I ever?"

"I know *that* feeling. When *my* sweetheart left town? Devastated. Cried every hour, some nights. And *I'd* known it was coming. Knew it all that summer. Astrid *warned* me. Warned me- on our first date, would you believe? But when you love, if you adore someone ... knowing doesn't help."

He gave a limp wink. "Same here. *I* knew he'd leave. Even warned *me* the day we met." 'No home for me.' 'Your world, not mine.' 'Always entirely *en route.*'" His eyes rose to greet hers. "So. Partners in grief."

"Wow, he was pretty blunt. So, yes: pards." Then she mouthed the syllable "sigh."

"But Shell.... I'm sorry. Is 'Shell' too informal? That wonderful smile says no."

"Call me 'Shell?'" That smile widened. "Oh, yes *please*."

"Anyway, I've seen you really happy, glowing in fact. At the fiesta. And teamed with Lucy. And at that game: week ago? You were a live-wire. *You've* clearly recovered."

Her smile gave a reserved confirmation. "Okay, fine, Scott. Better? Some days. A little."

She then sighed and examined her fingers, tapping her index finger with her left thumb. "So, new pard': listen to this two-years-plus veteran of grief lecturing the two-week newbie. It'll hurt. But..." she nodded as she repeated each word. "It. *Will. Pass.*" Then that faint smile: "Mostly" She crossed her arms firmly: "It. Will. *Modify.*"

Scott almost smiled and allowed some gentle sarcasm. "Nice, eh? The lowly junior-to-be consoles the once-confident t.a."

Shell answered with the smile that kept growing on Scott. He nodded, lips also flickering. They sat in silence for another minute. Then she pushed herself up from the table hefting her bag with determination.

"Going? Must you?"

"Better. Got to renew these."

"Boy, lady. Wish *I* could get stamped. Get renewed."

"Say, not bad. From a guy in the dumps, Scottie. Well, if you *do* hear from our guy, tell him, well, tell him his Shell misses him."

"*When* I do, *if* I do, I will. He was an admirer."

Her smile blossomed. "Thanks, Scott. It means a lot. Super teacher. Turned me on to books. And, not to mention, one cool babe. Turned *me* on too."

"Right twice. And here's something more: the man had perfect taste, and astute judgment. Which makes *me* an admirer too. (But. Have to be honest, ma'am. I came to that all on my own.)"

"My, my. Two compliments. The day's getting better." She beamed as she edged away from the table. "Bye, Scottie. Cheers."

He loved hearing Gavin's old salutation sharp on the heels of Lucy's nickname. He smiled as she withdrew. The exchange (possibly abetted by some male chemistry) prompted him to let his eyes linger on her disappearing figure—unkempt? Sure, but, hey: he'd never suspected bare ankles could be a turn-on. Nor clicking laces.

He kept his eyes on her until the door closed behind her.

Shell turned west and strode toward the library, hand tapping on her wrist in syncopation, bag beginning to jounce, laces continuing to announce her progress.

Seasonal Hibernation

When the last wisps of her dissolved, the hot, close hall felt chillier and more bleak, even with that purposeful whine keening more intensely at the far end. He gazed toward the ceiling, where aimless dust motes sank and rose in the pale summer rays.

He levered himself up, pitched the cup's stale residue and walked himself out of what now felt like one of Robert Frost's "desert places." (One of the usual pleasures of teaching lit was discovering when a work he taught as a work of art, of word-choice, of technique, also proved its painful accuracy. That fine New England craftsman also *knew* things. He *felt* things. He *lived life*.)

He took one slow turn around the campus. As if *that* would help, revisiting "their" spots. More accurate now to call them spots where *he* would walk solo—walk, think about Gavin, sigh; walk, walk; think, think; and sigh. The one new prop, however frail, was Shelley's consoling words. *She'd* lost, *she'd* recovered. "Ah, well. I'm happy for her, and it was sweet of her."

But his loneliness resurfaced. "Well, Shelley, words are cheap. She lives her life, me mine." (Yep, even his grammar failed him.)

* * * * *

Still, on that day and for a good many weeks thereafter ("*bad* many" is more apt), the empty campus didn't just express his life; it forecast it. He descended into the dull but reliable underworld of teaching, of reading, of grading, while striving to conceal his grief from all eyes, whether indifferent, prying or sympathetic. That spring he'd had the foresight, sharpened by the always considerate Gavin, to request a couple of summer classes. Might help distract him. But by now there was one place he could not bring himself to revisit. The radiant memory of Gavin's late-winter arrival, seconded by that listless encounter with Shelley, conspired to make Holmes Lounge fully *non grata*. It *was* the emptiest place imaginable, even when late August made it one of the busiest.

Any occasional spurts of relieving energy, any upbeat moments, were transient. And rare. An electronic epistle from the heart of space might help, though both men knew that too frequent contact would mean too frequent pain. (That's what Shell had learned from her first Niagara of needy emails. It took that formal letter on her mother's stationery to teach her.) Still, neither man could deny that Gavin's extra-planetary adventure was *sui generis*. Yes, it *was* exciting to imagine him a million miles out there, nested in that heavenly way-station where the planet's future pulsed. He could see the guy, spinning tales (some known) and visions (yet-to-be-baked) to each fresh batch of explorers destined for future planets and their undiscovered moons.

Gavin's description of the take-off was unforgettable, though the account didn't arrive for two weeks (bureaucratic and security demands). Turned out it *had* occurred on the very day Shelley'd drifted near him in Holmes. (In recalling that day, he regretted his subdued conviviality.) "The flames below us were radiant. The heavens deepened from azure to black, but somehow they still glowed. Our diamond flames kept spewing in fistfuls. Arriving at the station felt like easing into a silvery terrarium. Our weightlessness *en route*—our training made it second nature—disappeared upon arrival. (The station's controlled spin.)" Gavin's delight was palpable: Scott saw it shimmer on his screen. And the feeling helped shunt his melancholy aside. It filled him with both delight and pride: selfless delight at Gavin's stellar delight; and (the new old stand-by) renewed pride in helping him achieve it. He felt he'd earned at least a glancing back-pat.

But all such fixes were fleeting. All autumn long and half the winter, trees shadowed his loss. The delicate locust trees went first, shedding their tiny, yellow, early September apostrophes. Elms in turn made their generous October contributions, while oaks and maples saved their nobler offerings for November. When chilly gusts would sweep those throw-offs into vortices, Scott saw

Gavin's face forming and disintegrating in billows of yellow and red, all scurrying wildly to the southeast. All fall long, gumball trees squandered their cruel and spiky asterisks. Come January, and the deliberate creep of a new semester, the shivering pin oaks' shriveled remainders seemed even more dispiriting than the bare limbs they shivered among.

The department's required end-of-term student conferences in December did unleash new if slender freshets. Face to face with a thoughtful boy or vibrant girl, he recaptured, for a half-minute maybe, some of that smiling, ironic or even jovially sarcastic manner Gavin had helped instill. He'd pin a student with a show of unsmiling rebuke—"And I suppose you think this—*this*?!" (waving a sheaf of marked-up sheets) "… is your best work, Mr. Grimes?" The fellow (or woman, Ms. Townsend, say) would freeze, caught in the T. A.'s glare. Then after a beat or two, he'd melt with a laugh. "Yeah, well, you're right. It's splendid!" The fellow or woman would exit with a new and earned spring in his or her step. One such conference yielded the memory of a tall woman's emerald green eyes and wide smile; another, of a young fellow's hearty and invigorating laugh, followed by a "phew," and the pretended wiping of a brow.

On Friday, the final day of conferences, two infectiously bubbly students dialed him early. (A decade later they'd've "texted" him. Technology's ever-rolling stream keeps serious novelists who strive for accuracy on their toes.) A special request.

("Actually, sir, can the two of us come in together? We sort of have plans for the afternoon.") They insisted he let them bring him something from Holmes. So as he reviewed with them their highly successful semester's work, his tongue swirled its first sip of a new latte. It was, *they* educated *him*, a recent gourmet addition from that place he was avoiding.

"Mr. P! You don't *go* there? Cool place, newly fixed up. You know their motto? 'Come Holmes'?"

"Well, then. I'll put it on my list" (he mimed pulling out an electronic pocket planner and tapping it "done").

"List, Sir?"

"My *list*. See here?—" he mimed pointing to an imaginary screen, "quote, 'things my students tell me I have to do'."

"Yes. Do it, Scott." They laughed and headed out. "Get *out* more!" Their hoots echoed down the hallway. They were a walking, breathing proof of young love's promise. Scott enjoyed the display but was not yet ready to absorb the message.

Rodentine Renewal

The short days between January tenth and twenty-fifth bring to the northern hemisphere winter's two coldest weeks. (For the dark solstice's icy grasp to register takes time, just as July's heat peaks well after June's sun-halt.) That year the weather redoubled the trees' message. It was doing its reliable best to stymie any freshening of Scott's new year's spirits. He'd unwrap himself from his tight sheets each morning, fresh from some comforting dream—Gavin's silvery smile, say, against a starry backdrop. Or, accompanied by a fading whiff of cinnamon, fresh from an erection. When, swung from his cozy cocoon, his feet would touch the cold, hardwood floor they, like it, would shrivel. Some days, he'd glance out at "their" special balcony, on whose bare stone, all too frequently, iron gray fog would huddle or sleet patter.

His sadness somehow gave birth to its own pitiful vanity: he felt, he *insisted*, that he was the most forlorn man who'd ever lived. The truth, though, was that he was not unique: a fortnight of raw and icy gloom had scotched everyone's mood. So the English department chair, a jovial but, like many literary types, mercurial fellow, sent out an email first thing Friday. "Our gloomy tribe needs a party. Our gray world needs life. Angie and I need it too. Stir-crazy. Now! We'll host. Any ideas? And when?"

Scott read the pre-dawn message seconds after he'd un-swaddled himself. The words on the screen, for a welcome change, warmed him. He sat and wrote, nearly without reflection: "How about this? We could do it tomorrow or even Sunday. But *I* say compromise: Friday! Commandeer the ground hog's feast. Our former colleague Gavin" (not a few lips smiled at the neutral epithet) "and I had quite a feast last May Day for my comp and his lit gangs. Our joint gala. We celebrated Spring's crossing day." (More nods; they'd heard.) "Well, now. A magical nine months to the day, it's the *winter* crossing day. It's the day of that Ground Hog, colleagues!"

He wasn't finished. As his hands hovered above the fetal keyboard, the memories of that festive hot May night rolled across him in waves. (Twin waves—the real one and the fictional prophecy he'd read to Gavin.) As he wrote, he heard, saw and smelled again that chirping hive of students, who'd come laden with offerings, and swathed in festive aromas. "And wait. Wait! Another thing. February's when our sophs consider their majors. True? So, sir and colleagues, why don't we invite any interested ones? Start a new tradition. And if each of us brings a dish" (his mind's eye caught Shelley spooning hummus)—"Twill be a bash. Banish our blahs. How about it, sir? Colleagues?"

Scott tapped the "reply all" key to let his notion flood out, a gurgling decanter, to adjuncts, to fellow grad students, and to the full spectrum of professors. Several colleagues were up and had replied with delight by the time he'd shaved and showered.

So had chairman Ross. "Inspired, Scott! Now, everyone. Spread the word. And your sophomore idea? I love it. Any of you who teach 'em, invite 'em! Our place at 8. And oh yeah, my Ang' has a great punch recipe from a colleague in Antigua. Wants to try it out on us."

* * * * *

For the first time since summer, he felt a stirring, like the one Gavin had ignited the spring before, to get lungs and legs back in shape. He let his car sit idle and he'd walk to campus. As he strolled, he felt—he *swore* he could feel it—the warm glow of the sun on his back. The sensation was all the more remarkable considering that clouds shrouded the sun all morning and the campus was wrapped in a chilling fog.

That solar lapse had posed a worse dilemma for the day's most celebrated meteorologist, the Zoo's ground hog. At sunrise, the clouds hovered thick; but through them, as it climbed above the southeastern horizon's limb, a thin red disk began to pulse oh so

357

dimly through the roiling vapor. A shadow? Yes? No? Zoo visitors squinted. The rest of St. Louis debated.

"Yes, there it is."

"No, it isn't."

"Look now! There?"

"Nope, can't see it."

(The woodchuck, characteristically, could not care less; no one bothered to tell *him* of the day's rodentine honor. Awoken from his hibernal tunnel by the day's warmth, the creature feasted on a pail of clover and grasses.) St. Louisans would just have to exercise six weeks of patience—keeping exact sky and temperature records—and then deduce the woodchuck's prediction retrospectively.

An hour later, however, there was no denying the season's first bumptious puff of southwestern air. (Gavin from his special vantage place could decipher the signs and anticipate the effects with one earthward glance.) The frolicking mild currents, lifted north- and east-ward by a howling, snowy storm center in southeast Idaho, were licking warmly at the snow-caked prairies of South Dakota and nosing along Nebraska's panhandle. The thousand-mile front of clouds shimmered southeastward the length of Nebraska, dipped through northern Missouri, then ran diagonally across Illinois, Kentucky, Tennessee, the length of

North Carolina, and finally drifting out to sea across that state's (and America's) eastern-most point, Cape Hatteras. By nine a.m., the warm and windy dome had migrated another fifty miles northeastward, tendering St. Louisans a prophetic whiff.

Whatever its effect on the grumpy marmot (he retired with sleepy if well-fed relief to his shadowy lair) it inspired Scott. He surprised his ten o'clock class with out-of-the-blue witty retorts; he even teased his first-years about being excluded from that evening's festivities. "Too bad *you* guys have to wait a year. Ha." When a few flipped him off in response, he chortled and extended a tongue.

He decided, when he dismissed the bubbling group, to take the advice of those two lovebirds and "come Holmes". He zipped up his lap top computer and slid some unmarked papers into his dad's battered brief-case. Once through the portal, he patted the shoulders of three students he found hovering near the coffee and then he strode toward the side table that was groaning with a newly resplendent array.

Famished for the first time in six months, he loaded a tray with a pair of rollicking apples, added a sizable blueberry compote, and asked out loud for one of those novel lattes.

A leisurely arc down the hall, tray in one hand, briefcase in the other, aimed him toward his old spot by the hearth. It was now handsomely restored. *En route*, he nodded at several salutes and

359

bowed to several friendly gestures, trying to connect a name with the guy who waved or names with the group of ladies who saluted, one with a shrill, two-fingered whistle.

"Ah. Planning that essay in your heads, eh, ladies? Three pages, don't forget. Nine a.m. Tomorrow. Oh, and say: personal favor? This time print it out for all of us, will you? You made it hard for us last time."

"Oh yes, Senor Scott. We will. *We* won't forget. Just not today. Today we *party*." Bobbing heads, gesturing hands.

Those sights and sounds confirmed those two summer students' report: Holmes *was* a new universe. Bright silvery computer ports were sprouting around the perimeter's restored mahogany. There, in what had been that cold, disused hearth, blazed a real fire enclosed behind a pair of new bright crystal panes, guarded by an intricate golden grate. His mind's eye considered but quickly vetoed his old barricade. Instead, he placed a couple of inviting chairs at the table he selected several yards out from the back.

He flipped the papers onto it and began to read and absorb. A new impulse of vitality had him commenting at length on each, the loaded tray just within reach, yielding new pleasures as time ticked. He worked for a while (his pen of choice that morning was dispensing green ink), but then inhaled deeply, paused, and glanced up. The south wall's high windows were glowing bluer and bluer. Fifteen yards away, one of the Holmes workers clambered up and threw open a sash. Spring's breezes began dancing, as if to make Holmes *their* home too. And just at that leisurely instant—remarkable!—those two amorous students traipsed up to his table, arm still in arm. They proffered a chilled cup of some sweet icy treat, beads of water forming and flowing down its side. "We thought you'd like. A Groundhog treat, Dr. S." They scurried off before he could reply but he wafted a maternal smile in their wake.

These real things were enough to delight his heart, but on the scintillant walls some buoyant holograms began shimmering some bonuses. The one over *there*? Oh, that was Gavin smiling across the table at him, his tray a jumble of jellies, his blond bronzed hair, face, neck, shoulders blotting all behind them. The handsome torso faded and a second hologram became the face of—_who_? The radiant face (his own? Gavin's?... no) was aureoled by sibilant cornrows (he fancied he could hear what he was seeing) woven into … oh, ah: *her* auburn hair. It caressed her smooth bare neck and curtained her firm, broad shoulders. Shell? Oh, yes. Next her hand, floury and warm, across a flaming grill. Then vivid Shell aiming a camera their way. And over *there, c*urtains of heat turning to vapor and, through them, two ankles gleamed.

361

Scott abandoned his green ink and his hand leapt to the keyboard.

The visions fled.

Shelley Bikes and Reviews

Shelley wasn't there to hear her computer offer its musical ping. (She could hum or sing it, perfect pitch, unprompted. "Nice C sharp," Scott later informed her.) She was out biking—her thrice a week regimen, pursued with monastic devotion even in these bleak winter weeks. A half-hour circuit: east from her Southwood digs to Skinker, north past the Archives building and then east again into the Park from its western entrance. Southeast then to the Waterfall, up the hill to the Art Museum and southwest down to the Zoo, then—northwest from that sacred picnic site—home.

Even after thirty months, the healthful jaunt always produced smiling sighs.

She always loved revisiting her rich, mixed past. But she admitted it also helped firm her calves, and to tighten (in moderate fashion) her thighs' supple flesh on which she loved to slather lemony lotion. (In brief, her monastic impulses did not go soul-deep; her radiant vanity still glowed. For that, Scott will in due course be grateful.)

But, yes, as Lucy had learned to her chagrin, Shelley *was* growing both more sedate and more disciplined, and her old spontaneity was subsiding tad by tad. Her flat-mate's last-minute year-abroad opportunity had left her on her own, a single woman in a roomy and comfy apartment south of campus. (Ben and Averill covered the higher rent. She used her treasured MoHist grant for the security deposit.)

The week she moved in, she asked Ben to bring over two stools from the kitchen nook, and also scored, with her usual successful persistence, his comfy computer chair. She made a further request, the framed 10 by 20 inch family tree, the result of a suggestion Astrid had planted in an email from an internet café in Kuala Lumpur. On the swinging door into her kitchen Shell hung that labor of global love. She liked to gaze at it, tracing its branches, as she sat happily ensconced on one particular stool. (Some days she'd perch on the other one and pretend she was "her Astrid" interviewing "her Shell.")

Her social life was bubbling at a gentle minimum as she sank more and more (and more blissfully) into a college junior's sober way of life. She insisted upon seeing the steps one evening every two weeks; at the start of each month, she'd draw their joined faces onto the 1st and 3rd Thursday squares on her calendar—another kitchen feature. For the first, she'd bike to their house, borrow the family car and chauffeur the pair to a new place and novel cuisine—Persian in the Loop; Italian on "The Hill";

Indian overlooking the airport. (There she, Ashley and Ang' would offer guesses as to the destination of each roaring take-off.)

On the third Thursday, they'd stay over and practice a new dish which the steps would take home the next day to Ben and Ave. They'd add the hand-copied recipe to their bulging repertoire. At bedtime, having once more exhausted the entire Narnian chronicles, she read them extracts from the Lewis and Clark diaries to lull them to sleep, two innocent Corps initiates, eyes wide.

So (as Scott, a gracious poor sport, would concede in time) she *was* a full-fledged History major. And, healthfully parochial, she was finding St. Louis and Missouri history particularly fascinating. A sophomore course had hooked her: it traced and examined the region's natural and geological history from the Jurassic Era right down to that recent "five-hundred-year flood".

Last fall, the novice major went to the department chair to request an independent study of the region's hydrology, a notion that flood had inspired. Averill even drove her up to the confluence of the Missouri and Mississippi in West Alton, the wide juncture which Scott and Gavin had scanned from the winery. The spot was not far from where Lewis and Clark had set out. No undergraduate had ever inquired about such a course, but the department scrambled to find her an adviser. (When she and Scott celebrated her 21st birthday at "their" winery—yes, it had been his and Gav's, but he gladly welcomed her as co-owner—they learned to their mutual delight that they shared even more: millions of years of intimate regional familiarity.) She'd also selected herself into a bi-weekly seminar at the city's Central Library about the city's park system's origins and its new extensive system of biking trails. She would spend a March weekend exploring them.

Now, in her Spring term, she'd just embarked on another seminar on that Lewis and Clark expedition. She mentioned it in an email to Astrid. (She was doing graduate work in Urban Planning, having sling-shotted herself far beyond Ohio, Cassini-like, then far past Kuala Lampur and well into a Master's program in Aberdeen.) "Well, of course, what else would I expect from you? Boy, girl, I wish we could paddle up-stream together. (Tim winks and says better not. Says 'hi.')

"Oh and hey," she added later that day, "and this is for your private ear, sweet. I've seen him sneak an admiring peek at this local bloke, Jocko. Gotta admit, Jocko's hot. But the sex with Tim? Out of this world. And you'll be pleased that Tim *loves* that tongue and thumbs move of yours. Your version of Mark's move? Yeah, but every few weeks or so I see him consulting with himself about popping the question. But babe I'm just not ready. Gosh he is wonderful. Thoughtful. Generous. There is so much living to do, for him *and* me. We're like you. I'll keep you abreast.)"

On fall afternoons she'd bike to Olin Library (Scott was right; it had become her home away from home) then slip into

Holmes for a late-afternoon shot of caffeine. Sometimes, when she entered, across her mind's eye fluttered rich images—of Gavin (a lot) or Astrid (dimmer, but still frequent, and exuding teasing whiffs), and even Scott (once, maybe twice—but only his image). Some days, she'd return to Olin, feeling more aroused than usual. She'd admit with a shallow sigh that she missed those old wild nights. A little anyway. So she'd reach for a new set of documents on the shelf and sigh, "Damn it, guess I'm starting to mother all these facts and drawings. Or is it 'father'?"

She did look forward to her monthly chats over tea with Ingrid at MoHist's Merriwether Café. She was developing a fondness for scones and cream, one pleasant result of her belated unearthing of Annie's British heritage, a genealogy Ben found he was eager to share. (On one visit he added several post-its onto that family tree on her door. New discoveries he proffered about her mother let *him* revisit Annie too.) It turned out further that Ingrid had done graduate work in Library Science at the University of Sussex, well before Shell was even a gleam in Ben's eye. So yet another British bond. Shelley caught the archivist's (and a woman's) bug right away for the story of Sacajawea, the Corps of Discovery's indispensable guide. Some days, in a delayed outbreak of sophomoric pride, she named herself an honorary "Corps member."

On the seminar's first bleak January days, hooked anew, she just *had* to learn about Sioux, Ozark, and Mandan culture.

367

(When she mentioned that newest effort over tea, her enthusiasm recaptured Ingrid's heart.) Shell dropped by the university's Music department to investigate. Would they have any documents or recordings of tribal chants? They weren't sure; they'd check.

They did and they did.

She tried to read those primitive scores. (Anthropologists treasure the written fragments that are so rare in oral cultures). But until she'd mastered the skill, she charmed a professor into laying aside his cane and playing an extract on his piano. Some nights she'd wake and feel the insistent rhythms flow through her, and her feet would begin to pulse. When she came in a week later, he showed her a new chant he'd unearthed. Turned out she could sing it at sight once he'd anchored her to the first note. She astonished him.

All these novel interests coursing through her kept her brain in an eager geyser. Learning was trumping lust. So, that cherished video of Astrid now sat at rest on a higher shelf in Angie's room. On the rare occasions when her mind re-ran it, she simply felt a calm daze which became a cozy sleep. Her pile of books, notes and maps towered on her bedside table, guardian angels.

* * * * *

Today, those warming winds of the Crossing Day riffled through her hair and helped cool her pistoning legs. The same first whiffs of spring that had spurred Scott at dawn now urged *her* farther a-field. She stopped at the waterfall and turned off the flow of music in her earphones (another Astrid "mix"—Broadway tunes, French chansons, Scottish airs). Recently, she'd been biking past the fall, but on this day she dismounted and, on old impulse, jogged up the path beside the barren waterway. She halted for a full half minute at the old magic spot. Though the place was brown with crinkled grass, her memory saw green, and her nostrils sniffed Cabernet.

She strode down the slope, pushing aside branches on which bare buds were erupting with microscopic determination. She remounted and cycled up Art Hill. King Louis' inverted sword at the Museum's front was at once a sword and cross (war and peace—another flash of *sfumato),* and pointed to that ever bluer, ever milkier sky. The sun had finished burning through the earlier layer of scudding, nimbus clouds.

"Keep going, 'ma belle'!"

Heeding herself, she circled back to the Historical Society's home on the Park's north edge ("I do love those scones. And oh, my, just think: real berries in four weeks!"). She sped west along Lindell Boulevard, the World's Fair's "Pike" (as Scott had taught Gavin, and she'd unearthed on her own.) The last living St. Louisan who had walked that festive boulevard, age five, had died the year before. So any accounts of that astounding civic, national and global celebration were now under the auspices of MoHist—as well of course of any dedicated amateurs who frequented it. Shell was feeling a new proprietary interest.

Right on Skinker to Delmar, then left into the Loop, where she and Lucy had "hung out" the morning after May Day.

"Oh there's Café Natasha. Damn, I wish Ang' and Ash had liked that cashew broccoli. I do like Ashley's new earrings, though. She'll be wowing all the Hosmer lads any day now. And those eyes. *Her* next stage!"

Her shoulders sank out of their swaying motion and her legs stopped pumping. She dismounted to walk her bike through the Loop's busy heart. She imagined Lucy's thin alto voice speaking under the actual, lively dance music that was Astrid's next selection. As it reached a sweet g-major cadence, she clicked it off the better to recall Lucy's voice and that sleepy inspiration she'd murmured. "What about someone older? A guy?'"

"We were sitting right over there. Blueberry. Was she right? I wonder. Scott. Does he still miss Gavin? Poor guy. But man, lady, can he cook! Shell, face it: all you do is cuddle with diaries and yellow documents. Funny, we both called her 'Lucille'."

Brandt's Café was shimmering on her right along the sidewalk where tables would blossom before long. "Cinco di

Mayo's on its way, Shell! Mark your calendar. Well, yes," she answered her earlier question. "Guess he never goes to Holmes. Did I scare him off? Bore him?" She chuckled. "Oh, well. *His* problem."

Those thoughts reminded her of Gavin's witty fervor and how he and it had turned her on to literature. He'd nearly sold her on his particular love, Philip Larkin, with his eloquent celebration of modern despair. She rejected the gloom but Gavin helped her embrace his craft. "No. History's the real me. Of course, there's sweet old Professor Tompkins. His wild white hair. Love it! Take a music course next fall? What about a Lit minor? Might look good for grad school. Scott might know. Do T.A.'s teach seniors?

"Sweet Astrid. I hope Tim works out. Or if Jocko'll steal him. Or *her?* God, I wish, I bet, they can have it all as long as they want. Their own paradise! But time: will it tick for them? Say, I wonder if her Mark guy's still around. *He's* an older guy. I still remember those moves of his she pulled on me. Wonder, would I still enjoy those moves now? Time ticking."

She hopped on the bike, re-engaged the gears and climbed the gentle incline through the University City gates. She admired the stone lions that guarded that entryway to the west. She still recalled that Freshman writing unit that had them explore that suburb's founding. And the Fair. "Would all that interest him? Literary dude? Shh. Enjoy the ride."

She'd been on the road an hour—twice her recent regimen, and her legs could feel it. "Better head home. But think. A life of history? I do love all that research. But ten years, could I end up like Ingrid? I do like our chats. Nah. Wonder why she's never...?"

She turned her music back on, to the third dance in that orchestral suite by de Falla Astrid had included. "Hey, I *like* this. That beat. And all that brass. Are those castanets? Wild. My Astrid still *gets* me. *Shapes* me. But I wonder, hmm. Do I shape her at all? Maybe in bed, anyway. Heh heh."

Her legs pumped now in rhythmic determination, as she aimed to complete the day's extra-healthful loop. Thighs aching, calves starting to quiver. But the heart and mind were all a-stir. "Scott...?"

Their Final Hours Apart

Shelley did complete her circuit, stow her bike, and jog up (more slowly than usual) three flights to her place. There she reheated the other one-third of yesterday's batch of muhhamara she and the steps had created. Then, as she savored her first spoonful, she dialed up the BBC Third Programme's mix of music and news, then decamped, bowl in hand, to her computer. Soon the screen glowed and, before the tiny trumpet could announce the new message, she anticipated it and sang the ping. It announced a message from an unfamiliar source: "gsburgerman".

Intrigued. Her eyelids scrunched and her forehead creased; her mouth paused in mid-chew. "'gs'? S? What S? Stan? Ooh, maybe Sara? Wild Sara. Nah, been a year. Can't be Scott—or ... wait. *That'd* be too much of a coincidence. But I *have* been thinking about ..." Her hand felt all floury. "Burger, eh?"

So she clicked on it and read the invite, where he'd signed at the bottom "Great Scott?" Her eyes lit up. "Ta da! Old Scott. He read my mind. But you're a year late, my man: I'm a junior. Hey, Lucille's bet. Put it to the test? Yeah."

So: "Kind of you to suggest I cook; but I recall your burgers. Say, I tried to email you last May. Your fiesta. Ever get it? Well, I challenge *you*. Let's compete: see whose dish gets licked the cleanest by, when? Pick a time. Midnight?"

She concluded with a firm announcement. "I'll aim for nine. If you're there, I'll see you."

* * * * *

Some force had inspired a geyser of other emails to Scott that day. One came from Lucy. She thanked him for the invitation. (He'd sent one to the previous spring's superb Comp class, now sophomores; to hers he added a private p.s. Four others responded with "hi's" and two with "thanks, but we're on a retreat".)

Back home last May, Lucy still thought of Shelley now and again, and sighed. Couldn't help it. But she did find the initiative to follow her "new friend's" advice: she gave Heather a call. Heather was delighted. They talked for half an hour, recalling Chemistry adventures, Lucy giving her advice about her coming first year at college. They spent a terrific summer. Heather alas had chosen an Ohio college (not Astrid's but in the same region), so they too went through a sad withdrawal in August, Luce returning to campus. Shell was delighted at Lucy's new gumption. (She even felt a twinge of pride in inspiring it.) Upon her fall return, Shell pitched in to raise Lucy's fluctuating spirits—coffees in Holmes and a dinner in the Loop.

Lucy's "regret" to Scott read: "Well, I've chosen Astrogeology. Wouldn't be right to steal English hospitality. But but but... Hey, what about Shelley? You could *try* to talk her out of History. (Fat chance!) Too late but so what? Imagine and dare (like you made us do about Huck, you crazy man?). Think of what you guys share—recipes; your hometown; those damned Cardinals? Well, the last thing you need is me playing Cupid. But, dear Scott, your and Gav's plan. So sweet. And I made a *new friend*. So, dammit, invite her." (Not that he needed any further urging by then.) She signed it "Lucille."

Gavin's email was longer, what with the huge swath of slow time on his hands and deep space hovering in perpetual prospect. Far above these merely earthbound preparations, he was enjoying his daily—and by now (ironically) pedestrian—round of cosmic wonders.

"I can see from here that you're having a major terrestrial day. An ever more verdant green (deeper than two days ago) is edging farther up in Mexico, and Greece, and Myanmar. Your sun is dancing north. Out here" (he prefers it to "up") "we miss out on Spring. But as for me, I feel I'm 'walking on sunshine' as that song of your dad's you played for me says. This morning on my way to the *bolshoi* terrarium (our biggest, in case your Russian's rusty), I dropped in on the agriculture 'pod." (They're experimenting with pulverized lava: it's the closest we can come to the basalty soil of Mars. See what we can grow.)

"And in my favorite garden they're cultivating hydroponic trees. You had it right about those glades of Mr. Handel. Our gravity's so low, it's like they can dance on their roots. And our gently circulating air moves enough to provide, well, if not his 'cool gales,' some fine room-temp currents. If you ever get here, we'll stroll. Sorry, shouldn't tempt you, hon'. But love dies hard, you know? (I know, I know. *I* skedaddled. But you, sweet, did help push.)

"Wait. Some in-house humor. Our main group here are the Mars colonists, in training, plus a few 'space-lifers' like me. But last week a new crew arrived. Mum on the details, but I can hint (psst): the Webb Telescope. These guys and women, well they all stick to themselves. Probably security orders. (Or they're snobs. Who can tell?) Well, guess our nickname for 'em? 'The Spiders.' Get it?

"I'm tickled to see you reviving. Now, my babe. This gathering tonight! It was *your* idea. So go. Who knows what golden lad or, hell, lass might cross your path? Which're you into this week, love? Well whichever. As our favorite chorus in *Dido* commands, it's time to 'Banish sorrow, banish care!' Yeah, I know: things didn't work out well for the Queen, but *you* can make it work—for you, and for my—I mean your and our Shell. (And, sweet, what I love about her, and what *you'll* find is that she's *her* Shell.) I feel things coming together for all three of us: me in my

376

heavens, you two on your earth. Please confirm tomorrow. Or, well, (ha) next time you're free..."

The loving message came as Scott was getting himself together for his first almost "date" in what seemed forever. The word inspired a childhood memory: his "granny's" scrumptious dates recipe. Stuffed with walnuts! Dredged in powdered sugar! His mouth watered in retrospect even as he put the finishing touches on his newest experiment, *chana palak*— chickpeas and spinach. "Food of love? A fancy dish for a fancy dish?" He blushed. Really, he did.

His hands stirred the paste as his eyes scanned Gavin's words and his imagination revisited those childhood sweets. And as he shaved, he listened to an Australian hookup on the BBC. After playing the American Samuel Barber's gorgeous piece, "Knoxville, Summer of 1915," the host introduced a (typically probing) panel discussion (two Aussies, a Brit, and a New Zealand English professor, first name Med) on two artistic matters. They explore the way great music can capture the spirit of a text, not just convey its words. And, more profound: Can one small text capture the spirit *of an entire era*? Small-town America. A microcosm: the country of the eve of the Great War. It slowed down his getting dressed, but it gave him a spur: "Maybe a conversation starter for the historian? And, oh yeah, does she like music? Makes two topics."

He buttoned the new teal shirt he'd bought. "And of course our food competition. A trinity of interests?"

At long last, he was ready. He draped the locket around his neck (something new) and (something old) hooked Gavin's knife through his belt loop. He was about to pass over his threshold when the recently disregarded nursery of life and art (something blue) swam into view. He pulled it down, flipped through it, slowing to read a sentence here, a page there, eyes growing wider. "Not bad, Scott man. But Lord does it need revising." (A reader might well nod if he or she knew how many words in this paragraph weren't there at that skim. They didn't make it until the fourth re-write.)

He snapped it shut, "First things first."

* * * * *

Shelley was ready by 8, an hour early. In her recent comfy isolation, she might spend Friday evening in the darkroom she'd contrived in her spare bedroom. (She had researched—and found she liked—the old techniques.) And a new discovery (one that Lucy had mentioned: the chemical smells.) From time to time she might hum one of those Mandan chants. (Did it one time and then enlivened a reprise with some reggae syncopation.) Some days she'd use her journal to brainstorm and jot down ideas for her Seminar. This time, though, as she cast her eyes toward it, she resisted. "You can get to it when you get home or, what the fuck, tomorrow." She giggled. "Oh, belle. Bad girl!"

So efficient, so well-prepared, she decided to rest her eyes, trusting her brain's jostling molecules to wake her in time. So she sat in that big computer console chair (the one she would move to Scott's place—*theirs*) and her past resumed its visit. She stretched out her tight hams from the day's long jaunt. She really did. But then…

She was sitting with Astrid near some swimming hole. They were alone. "Let's drown our sorrow. Come play!" Astrid raised a silent hand for Shelley to kiss. Shelley seized it, but instead of kissing it, wrote numbers on it in blue ink with her creamy finger. Then she dragged her to the water's edge, and they leaped in perfect sync, hands clasped, sinking toward the cool, gray bottom.

Shelley pivoted her companion and whispered (the water no impediment), "Close your eyes. Try this." They began to swing in a waltz. Their lips fused and they rose, their legs a tight cocoon. Shelley found her hair twined with her companion's in a shared golden curtain.

It slid apart like tent flaps opening, and through it peered—a face.

Scott?

Scott. He smiled a smile, as flour spangled his cheeks, and his hands exhaled dill and caraway. As she and Astrid burst the surface, he dissolved. Their dizzy motion spun their watery laughter into an airy and aromatic cascade.

Final Party

The day's festive avalanche of emails, then that beautiful radio concert (and the discussion that followed) meant that Scott entered the party later than he'd intended: 9:15. He cut a swath toward the kitchen through which sweet acrid wreathes of cigarette and pot smoke rotated, and involved in happy cahoots a wisp of mild February fog. He positioned his *chana* upon the stove's warming pad.

By it was a pot where some creamy compote was murmuring toward perfection, its lid lighter than air. "*Is* he back?" Habit and hope were ineradicable.

He hefted his bag and extracted a second offering. (Yes, he's cheating.) It was a shallow bowl of cucumbers bathed in yogurt and dill. He knelt to lay it among the gleaming platters that were nestling around the buffet—a laden table that bristled with red lobster claws, pale white herring, bright green pea pods. At the front of the array a china plate flaunted a gold stack of pancakes bulging with fresh blueberries. "She cheated *too*. Bastard!"

That's when he glimpsed her. She was peering from the living room, gold and blue flames flickering around her on the raised hearth. She glanced for a beat at her watch, then started her eyes pirouetting around the room. Her red tongue slid in regular laps across her lips, back and forth, back and forth. On its tip, less after each slide, some creamy blue dip. On her trim, athletic fingers, a delicately balanced saucer.

His competitive impulse dissolved as his eyes glommed onto her emerald sweater, its generous "v" introducing him (and a growing few others) to her firm white shoulders. His gaze remained anchored and noted a handsome jade pendant which complemented the sweater and lay just above what experience assured him would be her breasts. Unprompted, his eyes lingered and slid, slid more. And lingered.

And it was then—a bare instant for them but nearly a lifetime for curious, engaged or merely impatient readers—that, yes, their eyes docked.

* * * * *

Shell swung her clasped knees to the floor, stood and walked his way. She folded his hand into both of hers, warm from the fire. "This is strange. Me welcoming *you*?" She tapped his nose

382

with her cool but authoritative index finger. "Politely late to your own party."

"Guilty as charged, ma'am."

"Well, in any event, thank you."

"For?"

"Why, for this." That dainty authoritative hand waved at the room, the hearth, the milling guests. "Throwing it." A smile he'd seen before crept, like the sun, up her face. "Inviting me."

"Here's a secret: it wasn't just for *you*." The smile flowered further. "And, oh yes, before we go on, an instant confession. I love it when you do that."

"Do what?" Several wisps of memory deepened and modified the smile.

"Nothing major. Just that smile. Pardon the liberty, but . . . well, it's perfect."

"Sweet of you. But, here's the funny, boring thing. Smile? I do it when I'm happy."

"Then I'll take it as a profound compliment." She reciprocated his bow.

"But now," he continued, "I have to be coolly professional. I must deny myself."

That smile made room for a quizzical look.

"I mean it. I'm here on a sacred trust: your academic future. So. Over there. Our department chair, Dr. Ross. Not too late to rescue you from those dusty historians."

"You're always free to hope, book nerd." She stuck out her tongue. "Fat chance." (Lucy's prophetic words.) "But, come. *I* have a *higher* priority: our real business here. Our food fight—um, competition." Her hearty and melodious laugh was irresistible.

"Ah, yes. Can't neglect *that.* But still, first, please. Let me play the host and beg you to mingle."

"Mingle, eh? Like at your fiesta?"

"No. At *ours. Yours,* actually. Gav confessed. He gave you full credit."

"I plead guilty. But *your* devious plan was part of it? So sweet of you. And it got me a new friend. But tonight, a promise, please. Can we skip the post-its?"

"Promise. I swear. Yes, I *did* send out some invites, but relax, you're safe. She regretted. Cupid's off-duty."

Shell leaned a jovial elbow on his shoulder. "Well, maybe once *was* enough. But still, but still," she tugged on his nearest ear. "I'm a young woman who likes to have things both ways. Let's not banish Cupid entirely. You follah?"

Scott gave the elbow that rested on his shoulder a gentle tap. "I do."

"And here's something more for you, Scott. A personal story. We had a teacher in high school. Name of Violet. She'd always lecture us: 'Ladies! Be assertive. If you're wondering something, *declare it*. Don't ask.' Still, for you, I'll disregard her advice and inquire: *Do* you think I'm being too forward?"

"And I answer: 'Forward? Not a bit. *I'd* say just forward enough. In fact, since you ask, my vote is for *fast* forward!"

She smiled with pleasure. "Yes, Cupid does have his uses."

He raised his eyebrows, she *winked*. They saw eye to eye.

* * * * *

"But wait, wait. Listen, Shell."

"Ah, more orders, I see." She began tapping her foot, dislodged her arm and put one ostentatious hand on a hip. All with that smile though.

"No, ma'am. No. Patience, please."

He'd meant to pivot her but, when he placed two cool hands on her two warm shoulders, his mind went blank.

He made himself recover. "First ma'am, please ma'am: some orientation. Over there's the kitchen." Now he did pivot her. "You know. Where you brought, ahem, *both* your offerings?"

"True, sir. But, say: could be there's someone I'd like to impress."

Scott made an ecstatic feint to grab his heart, but hewed to his plan. A second quarter rotation. "Now next, splendid Shell: over there's the hearth. Where I just now laid eyes on you."

"*That* I noticed."

"And I *noticed* you noticing." He urged another quarter turn toward the western dining room: "But third: no more distractions. There's Dr. Sam. And just to his right, if—I mean *when*—you get that far, is Professor Durgin. 'Estella,' if you care (or dare) to be forward with *her*. Her specialty? Diaries—women's diaries. As literature."

"Tempting! I'm *way* into diaries."

"You'll take charge, I am confident. But, word of warning, she *can* be a bit abrupt. So, if you would you rather have *me* introdu ... ?"

"No, young sir. You soon-to-be-Dr. Scott." She rejected the offer. "Dear sir: *I'd* rather."

"Then she's yours. Before too long, though, I'll catch up with you on—what say, our second?..."

"No. We should try some self-discipline. Let's say our *third*..."

"*Exactly.* I beg pardon: our *third* circuit. Mingle first ..."

"'First. Then we shall have each other to look forward to. *And,* if all else fails (I know it won't), we'll have our food."

She seized his hand, made it a cup, and deposited a cool kiss. Then *she* rotated *him.* "Go treat yourself to a pancake. See why you're going to lose."

She and her gale of laughter disappeared into the swirl of smoke and chat.

* * * * *

He paid his respects to colleagues, trying to crawl himself out of the shell into which they'd all noticed he'd withdrawn. He talked shop, he chatted Dickens and Fielding, Larkin and

Dickinson with full professors (his higher opinion of Larkin's world-view than Shell's would provide ample food for roof-top debates); he consulted with fellow teaching assistants about summer teaching opportunities. (They called themselves, both the men and the women, "T and A's," a vulgar inside joke). But yes, from time to time he caught (okay, fine: more than once he *sought*) a glimpse of her circulating in each room, usually at the center of some group or other—undergrads, departmental authorities, and not a few of his attentive fellow T.A's.

* * * * *

During his second circuit (of *course* he was counting), he happened to glance out of the solarium's window. And saw four black-clad musicians—two men, two women—braiding in varying patterns up the brick walkway. One woman balanced a cello on her shoulder and moved arm-in-arm with a man caressing a violin. The other two hovered behind them, one nursing a viola, the other sweet-talking a bass fiddle as tall as she.

Scott let them in. Their leader (well, the first among equals), the willowy cellist with bare strong arms under a bright red stole, smiled at him.

"Are you the host, young sir?"

"Nope, sorry: just the guy nearest the door."

"Well, we thank you. Now to business: do you know a Scott?"

"I do." For some reason he indulged his coy side. "Quite well, in fact."

"Would you take us to him?"

"Can't." Scott's monosyllable prompted a quizzical look. "I'm sorry. Can't why? Cuz' you got him." He shook her firm cool hand. "Now, come on. Admit it: you *knew*."

"We didn't. Honestly. We're from Gavin."

"Oh, really? His transporter's back up? Sent you down here from the heart of space? Remarkable!"

"No, no, no. Just a message. From *him* in space; to *us* down here. And now to *you*, ditto."

"He's a marvel. And the message?"

"—Is that we are to serenade—"

"Serenade me? The man truly *is* out of this world!"

"—serenade," she persisted, "*two* of you. You and someone named Ashella. Goes by Shelley? A girl, I imagine." She allowed herself a smile.

"Forgive me, but 'a girl' does not do her justice."

389

Scott was beginning to solve the mystery but wanted her to confirm his hopes, "But why?"

"Gavin might know. We don't. His words were, 'Find Scott, find Shelley. Play for them.'"

At that precise and lucky instant, Shelley was completing *her* second circuit. She shimmered into the entry hall from the swirling haze. "I be here, Scott. One loop left. What gives?"

She'd just ladled a fresh supply of her blueberry crème into its boat. The warm kitchen had prompted her to shed that already-revelatory sweater, though perhaps a practiced instinct had also played a role. At her sleeveless blue-green top, with its delicate spaghetti straps, the five observers, in company with some fortunate by-standers, stared.

She passed the boat like a chalice around the circle. "Please, everyone. Dip some fingertips!"

Scott's eyes, their will their own, began a delighted if irregular ascent: hands, boat, top, straps, neck, top again … and at last those blue eyes. His tongue took over. "Get this, Shell. These four folks are from Gavin. My, your, *our* Gavin. No, don't ask. He sent them to, and I quote, 'serenade us' unquote. You and me. Don't ask."

Before Shelley could register more than surprise, the cellist added—"And, beautiful lady, we do have other gigs tonight. Can you find a spot for us? And are there any requests?"

Out of the blue, without consultation, Scott and Shell said, "How about de Falla?" Both sought, same instant, to specify, "A dance."

Boy and girl turned to one another, amazed at first, then simply amused.

The grad student's "How did you—?" chimed with the junior's "Now where...?"

"Enough," Shell took charge. "We can compare notes during our 'later.' For our 'now,' let's hear them."

"Let's."

The svelte cellist, after a brief exchange of nods about the ad lib (they sussed that this was a crucial moment) again asked where.

Shelley knew. "Listen. I saw a spot, my first pass. Just off your Rosses' glorious kitchen."

"Lead the way, as that observant lady says, dear 'beautiful lady'."

She ran a hand along his shoulder and gave his neck a firm, soft pinch. Then she pressed ahead, running interference through the bubbling swarms of professional English folk and eager student folk. Scott turned to the quartet. "Let's follow our Shell. She's a woman with a plan."

She was. "Look. Look here. A quiet alcove—ideal for listening, and we won't distract folks." They set up in a quiet corner.

On the way, Scott snagged a plastic plate, unhooked Gavin's handy knife, and carved a good-sized square of his delicacy. He scurried to catch up. She waved him to a chair beside her, curled two firm fingers around the wrist on the hand that sported the plate. He dipped a finger into her boat and smeared the cream on his *chana*. "So great to *relax*. No fancy airs."

Shell was anticipating the rhythm, tapping her other palm at first on her own thigh and then reaching over to tap Scott's arm.

In no time at all, the music flowed, music which both caressed and enlivened them. It matched (magic? expertise?) the rhythms Shell had been tapping. The final dance was in ¾ time and further joint (and wide and catholic) exposure would make it their favorite meter, at once lively and lyrical. "Norwegian Wood," Strauss waltzes. Endless Handel gems: "Love in her eyes sits playing." "Love sounds th'alarm." "The king shall have pleasure in her beauty." *And* the Welsh hymn tune "Hyfrydol." Also, Scott informed her, the sweet opening of "Knoxville."

As they nodded their heads and absorbed the dance's flow, a freshet of charmed observers drew near the nook. When they noticed the young couple, however, they edged along. They could recognize a private moment when they saw one, even if admittedly a private moment for six.

Now and again, Scott would offer her, on the tips of his fingers, a corner of his Indian delicacy, bathed in her rich cream. "Dare you?" he whispered the first time. At the first taste, her eyes grew wide.

After that first dance, as the four paused to tune, she whispered, "And thanks for pushing me toward Estella—'Stella,' she insisted. I suggested a study of our Wash U and the cultural role played then by St. Louis women writers—turn-of-our-last-century business. Fannie Hurst, Marianne Moore, Martha Gellhorn."

"Splendid! And?"

"And she didn't say no. In fact," that radiant smile, "she was intrigued. She thought it brilliant." Shell pursed her mouth into a prune and observed, "'You propose to correlate those writers' fiction and private diary reflections, with the spirit of the city of that day?'"

Scott saluted the dead-on imitation. "Seems now I'm in the company of a history major who's actively considering a lit minor? 'Be still my beating heart'—quoting my Victorian grandmother. See? Some family history for you."

"So kind of you to share. But do I also detect you taking credit for Stella?" She stuck out a tongue.

But she withdrew it the minute he began moistening her lips with the two food offerings. In good delicious time, the plate was empty. Before long, the music ceased. The four players acknowledged the two friends' quiet applause (and that of a charmed, intrusive by-stander or two) and beat an efficient, smiling retreat.

* * * * *

Shelley sat silent, then arose and gave her hair an intense shake. She stood over him, parted it and looked into his eyes. "It is now officially 'later'. I declare. We made our rounds. We've had a serenade. Time, sweet sir, for *our* mingle."

As he lifted her chin, he saw one remaining smidgen of that *palak* and cream near that quaint scar at the moist corner of her mouth. The tip of his finger rescued the inviting dab, and his tongue licked it off.

"Forgive me again, Violet. But one final question, dear sir. Are you sure got it all?" She tilted her mouth toward him. When they kissed, he knew exactly where the hands should go.

"Still not sure. Permission to keep trying?"

* * * * *

About thirty seconds later:

"Would you care to take your giving mood for a walk on the professor's balcony? We can talk. Talk and, well, explore? What say, Shell-bell?"

"Shell-bell! What made you say that?"

"I dunno. Maybe cuz it rhymes? Music to my ears? Why do you ask?"

"It's what my first love, my sweet Astrid called me. Wow."

"Bet she was wonderful. Hope I can meet her?"

"Alas, the sweet woman is worlds away. But yeah, you'd adore her. And say: speaking of adorable people, wouldn't this splendid evening be perfect if we could catch sight of our Gavin."

"It would indeed, but alas, no. By now he's out of range." He directed her eyes to his watch. "I know. I still try to time him now and again."

She rubbed soft fingers on his watch, attracting his hands to cadge them.

"But wait. But wait—"

"Ha. More orders?" Both hands moved to *his* hips. "Hmm?"

"No. No Gavin, but there's still Mars! Would you care to meet? And *this* time, I *do* insist, let *me* introduce?"

* * * * *

They climbed up not to a balcony but, as Dr. and Dr. Ross had been eager to explain, to a genuine widow's walk, a rare Midwestern rendition of a common New England feature. As they purposefully walked toward the planet, their fingers wove into a double-helix. To reach the place they had to climb a flight of stairs that hovered above them, concealed in the upstairs hall's glowing white ceiling.

Shell unwove their hands and took a determined stand. Eyeing that lofty ceiling, she asked Scott to lift her. "Raise me, please," so she could seize the pull-rope—to open, as they later teased each other with loving hyperbole, "our stairway to heaven."

As they ascended, Scott's mind was racing with calm assurance. Back to his shelves. Ahead to his pillow. On the former already lurked that blue Diary; on the latter, he predicted with growing but modified confidence, a cascade of auburn hair.

"I see how to start it," he exulted, but did so *sotto voce*. "Something simple. Something like 'There she was. She *said* she'd make it'?" He didn't know if those words would last, or last unmodified. How could he know?

But it *was* a start. Minimal, true, but a start. Could he, even then, imagine how vast a universe might spring from that one atomic moment?

Not yet. But give them time.

www.ingramcontent.com/pod-product-compliance
Lightning Source LLC
Chambersburg PA
CBHW060220030726
47499CB00004B/1128